It Happened One Homecoming

A Collection of Short Stories

It Happened One Homecoming

A collection of short stories, Volume 1

Cheris Hodges

Published by Cheris Hodges, 2024.

This is a work of fiction. Similarities to real people, places, or events are entirely coincidental.

IT HAPPENED ONE HOMECOMING

First edition. September 20, 2024.

ISBN: 979-8227749321

Written by Cheris Hodges.

Author's note:

Love takes time and when two people are destined to be together, it only takes a little spark to make that happen. Welcome to homecoming at Johnson C. Smith University where love begins, lasts and makes for some great stories. Let me be clear, these stories are works of fiction. But if you think you recognize someone in these stories, you don't. I made them up.

I hope these stories take your back to your carefree and happy days and make you smile.

Thank you for reading and I hope you enjoy.

Cheris

IT'S TIME FOR US
Story One

Chapter One

Shauna Carter wasn't a fan of weddings, but when her college friend Clinton Harrington invited her to his second shot at matrimony, she had to go. For one, she knew it was going to be an epic party and a chance to reconnect with other classmates who she hadn't seen since their last reunion five years ago. The class of 1999 was a historic bunch and though they didn't keep in constant contact. But when it came to big milestones, they showed up and showed out. And since Shauna was launching a line of haute couture fashion, going to a wedding gave her the chance to be the billboard for her brand. Cameras would be everywhere and her gold halter dress with a high low hem and hand sewn bead work around the bodice and neckline made a huge statement. She didn't just look good, she was stunning. All she could hope for was that the right people with good taste would love her outfit and want her to take their money.

Pulling into the Crystal Room's parking lot, Shauna smiled when she spotted her classmate, Gregory Hoffman walking toward the entrance.

"Greg," she called out after getting out of the car.

He turned around and smiled at her. They had been friends since they met in the introduction to computer science class during their sophomore year. Greg had sat beside her and proceeded to copy her notes. She crossed over to him. "Where's your much better half?"

"Our little girl was feeling under the weather today, so she had to stay home. But I couldn't miss my boy's big day."

"Right," she said. "I can't believe Clinton is doing it again."

Greg nodded. "Once is enough for me. If something ever happens with me and Kayla, I'm returning to my college ways."

"You know you don't have the same knees you had back then. You might want to make your marriage work. Because it's hard out here in these streets."

"That's the plan," he said then gave her a questioning look. "But you're still single? How, Shaun?"

"We're not going there. Don't be that married guy," she said.

"What do you mean?"

"Thinking the whole world needs to be married to find happiness and joy. Granted, you and Kayla make it look easy and y'all are couples' goals. But I have other things going on. Look at me, you know who made this dress?"

Greg tilted his head to the side and nodded. "You did this? All right now."

She spun around. "Sure did. And I'm having a real woman fashion show, so tell Kayla to call me. She has to be in the show."

"Oh yeah," he said. "She was saying that she followed you on Instagram and you had some really nice clothes over there."

"This is my year to make my mark on couture fashion," she said. "It would've been nice if Clinton's future wife had allowed me to design her wedding dress, but she wasn't feeling it. I don't think she likes me," Shauna said as they walked into the venue.

"Why, because you used to mess with her man or something."

"Umm, no. Big Boy and I have always been friends. And for the record, he's never been my type. Y'all football dudes were mean."

"I resent that. Our team wasn't that good and y'all didn't have any sympathy or empathy for us." Greg snapped his fingers. "Especially that damned Lily."

Shauna started laughing. Their friend, Lily Graham, had been the sports editor of the student newspaper and she didn't hesitate to call out the football team after every loss. And they lost a lot. Shauna had been surprised that Greg and Lily became friends, then she found out the Lily had been helping some of the football players with their research papers to make up for her columns. But when the quarterback—who was known for his interceptions—needed help, Lily took his whole work study check to rewrite his paper.

"Where's her mean ass anyway?" Greg asked with a laugh.

"Last week she in Lagos. This week, who knows. After her divorce, she sold her house and started traveling the world to write. It's worked out for her because she stays on the *New York Times* bestseller's list."

Greg shook his head. "That sounds like something she would do. Can't say that I was surprised she cut old boy loose."

Shauna laughed sardonically. He had no idea how desperately Lily wanted her marriage to work but there was only so much she could take. It all came crashing down when her ex told her that she needed to get a real job. He could've said anything else but that. Writing was Lily's calling. When she'd gotten a seven-figure deal to write a mystery series, it came at the right time, the moment she'd signed those divorce papers. That loser wouldn't get a dime from her.

Shauna always thought Dominic Thomas and Lily didn't fit, but she hated how hurt her friend had been over him. Not that anyone else knew. And Lily would kill her if she shared that story.

"You know the best love stories were made on our campus," Greg said with a smile.

"Yeah, if you were lucky. We all can't be you and Kayla."

"Homecoming is coming up, you never know what could happen on the hallowed grounds of JCSU," he said.

"I hope I get some orders for my new line other than that, I have no expectations," Shauna said as she patted her thick auburn hair.

Greg shrugged as they made their way inside. The ushers handed them purple and white programs then pointed them toward a pair of empty seats.

Shauna sat down and studied the names on the program. One stood out, Michael Broussard.

She nudged Greg and showed him his former teammate's name. "Michael Broussard is in the wedding and you're not?"

"Damn, I have seen Mike B in years. I think he moved to Raleigh and got into cybersecurity after he left IBM."

Shauna nodded, thinking back to junior year of college when Lily and Asia King, swore Michael had a crush on her. But he was so quiet, and she never paid it any attention.

So, why was she thinking about it now? *Damn you, Greg for talking all that love story shit.*

* * *

Michael Broussard waited for his moment to walk down the aisle and wondered why he'd agreed to this groomsman shit in the first place. Because Clint asked. So, what he'd broken up with the woman he'd thought was going to be Mrs. Broussard two weeks ago and she was supposed to be his plus one for the wedding. He was fine. Today was about Clint's second chance at love. Mike smiled and fell in line with the other groomsmen. Leave it to Clint to have the brothers of Omega stroll in as if they were still stomping the yard at Johnson C. Smith University, the historically Black college where he met his brothers and some other lifelong friends.

But unlike his parents, who had attended JCSU in the 1970s, he graduated without a wife or even a steady girlfriend. Things were different in the 1990s, people were focused on careers and futures that didn't include marriages, at least in his experience. When he told that to his parents, his mother called bullshit. Truth was, he never had the guts to go after the one who got away. And –was that Shauna Carter? Michael almost tripped but he corrected his step and smiled a little brighter. Who knew she would be here looking like a whole damn snack wrapped in gold?

As the groomsmen made it to the alter and then the bridesmaids, representing the pretty girls with twenty pearls made their way down the aisle. When he'd arrived in Charlotte for practice and met the bridesmaids he'd been open to a little wedding fling. Mike knew how weddings affected women and he wasn't going to turn down wedding booty. Glancing at the woman he would be escorting down the aisle, he realized that she was pretty, but she was no Shauna Carter. And they hadn't connected enough for him to even think she'd give him a dance, let alone a blowjob.

Moments later, Destiny Samuels walked down the aisle in her ivory gown, glowing as a bride should. Mike was happy for his friend, for putting his heart on the line for a second time and finding love again. That was Mike's fatal flaw, allowing . . .No, he wasn't going to think about that today. He wanted to send good vibes to his friend and his new wife. He wanted nothing but happiness for Clint and Destiny—for the rest of their lives.

The ceremony was quicker than he'd expected. It took fifteen minutes for Clint and Destiny to be pronounced husband and wife.

He and the bridesmaids danced down the aisle to the tune of *Candy Rain* by Soul For Real. How ironic, that was the song playing the night he'd seen Shauna at the pool party.

JCSU had just lost homecoming. And it was an embarrassing lost, 55-7 against Shaw University. The last place Mike wanted to be was at a party. The defense and the offense let the Bulls down, but a loss wasn't going to stop the homecoming celebration. Alumni had returned to the campus with top shelf liquor, food that tasted better than anything the cafeteria had to offer. That energy lit the campus like a Roman candle. Most of the offensive line had headed off campus to a party, but Mike let Clint talk him into going to the school's pool party.

"I know you saw School Daze, *bitches going to be in here half naked with low self-esteem who want to make us feel better with our dick in their mouth," he said before they headed for the pool.*

"And you wonder why you can't find a woman," he chastised.

"I'm looking for a good time, not a lifetime. You should follow my lead."

Mike shook his head. "You're going to be seventy and single, I'm good with that." Checking himself out in the mirror, his bruise from the violent hit he'd laid on the opposing quarterback didn't look that bad. Still, he grabbed a white tank top to hide the purple mark. "Let's go," he said.

The girls taking the entry fee waved them in. And Mike was glad. His blue speedos didn't leave room for a wallet. As soon as they approached the pool, Candy Rain started blasting and every girl in the room jumped up and started dancing as if those brothers were singing just to them. And there she was. Shauna Carter in a black and white bathing suit. The way her suit clung to her curves as she moved to the beat of the song entranced him. He wanted to take her in his arms and sing off key in her ear. He'd wanted her since the day she walked into the computer lab chewing gum and dancing to whatever she was listening to on her Sony Discman. Her moves tonight were even more impressive.

Wait, her friend, the girl from New York was pointing at him. Now the whole trio was looking at him. Mike glanced down at his swim trunks and yep, he was giving her an erect salute. Mike headed for the door, feeling as if he was a middle school kid just learning that this stuff was natural.

Mike didn't have a lot of regrets, but never exploring things with Shauna ranked up there with not buying Apple stock in the 1990s. Was today his chance to correct that mistake? It looked as if she was hanging with Greg, which was a good sign, that brother was so committed to his wife that a naked woman could hop on his lap, and he'd push her away. Mike wanted to make that kind of commitment to the right woman, and he'd thought he'd met her twice. However, he'd been wrong and decided that he had missed his opportunity in college. *But look at opportunity knocking again.*

* * *

Shauna yawned as she walked over to the bar with Greg. This was the part of weddings that she hated the most, the photos.

Yes, the couple want to put their memories in pictures and record the best moments of their lives, but damn it, she was hungry.

"What are you drinking, Shaun?" Greg asked.

"Something fruity. I'm not you and Lily, I don't do that hard stuff."

Greg laughed as he got a double scotch on the rocks and a pineapple vodka spritzer for Shauna.

"Where did you say Lily is?"

Shauna shrugged as she took a tentative sip of her drink. Oh, it was good. "She's hard to keep up with. Out here living like she's Carmen Sandiego."

Greg drained his drink. "We should call her," he said as he dug his phone out of his pocket and then ordered another drink.

"Don't be surprised if she doesn't answer," Shauna said in between sips of her drink.

"Graham," she heard Greg say. "Where are you? Me and Shauna at Clint's wedding on our fifth drink. Let me put you on speaker."

"I really hope y'all aren't calling for help because I'm in Brazil," Lily said. "Hey Shauna."

"Hey girl. You don't sit still at all do you?"

"Catch flights not feelings and I know you haven't had five drinks," Lily laughed. "Your lightweight ass would be on the floor."

"She's weak like that?" Greg questioned.

"Yes I am when it comes to five drinks," Shauna said.

"Hey, I'm about to get on a boat, y'all have fun and I'll see you guys at homecoming!"

And with that she was gone. Shauna laughed, wondering where in the hell Lily was going on a boat in Brazil. Shauna glanced at her gold watch and realized it had been an hour since the wedding ended. "How many pictures are they taking?" she whispered to Greg.

He shrugged. "Guess that means it's time for another drink."

"What the hell," she said as they ordered another round. Two drinks later, which meant three for Shauna and five for Greg, it was time for the reception to start.

"I'm going to make sure you're right up front to catch the bouquet," Greg said, his words a little slurred. "Tonight, you're going to find your husband."

"Okay, Greg, you're doing the most," Shauna replied with a laugh.

They headed into the dining area and found their names on their assigned table. Shauna was happy that she would be sitting with someone she knew. Then their other table mates joined them. Two older couples and a pastor.

Shauna set her drink down as everyone started talking about how beautiful the wedding was and how lovely the bride was. She fought the urge to stand up and low key show off her dress because this wasn't her party and the women at her table probably wouldn't like her new line.

"Excuse me, where did you get that dress?" one of the women asked.

Shauna smiled. "I designed it."

"You remind me of Diahann Carroll in that gold. Do you have a shop in the city?"

She shook her head, but reached into her purse and handed her new favorite person a business card. "This is my online boutique and I have all of my latest designs listed and you can join my mailing list for exclusive pop up shops."

The woman took the card and smiled. "I don't do a lot of online shopping, but I'm going to give this to my granddaughter."

"Well, thank you."

The woman turned to the other lady at the table. "Elizabeth, look at her dress. Now you could wear something like this to the gold and blue ball for homecoming."

Greg smiled. "You all went to Smith?"

"Sure did," the women said.

"We did too," Greg said.

"Aww," Elizabeth said. "All of us found love at JCSU."

"Eh, no we didn't," Shauna said. "This is just my classmate."

Elizabeth turned to the other woman. "Shirley, these young girls don't know how to multitask anymore. You have to get the degree and the man. Two things can be true at the same time, you know."

"Miss Elizabeth, they don't make Smith men like they used to," Shauna said.

Elizabeth laughed. "That's why you must kiss a few frogs until you find your prince. Ain't that right, Albert?"

He snorted then stroked Elizabeth's hand. "You just weren't paying attention. And I don't want to hear about no damn frogs today."

The preacher cleared his throat. "God's time is always right on time. Look at Clinton, he finally got it right with my niece."

"And didn't they meet at JCSU as well?" Shirley said. "That place is so romantic."

Shauna was about to roll her eyes when Greg hopped on the love train telling the older alumni how he met his wife at an intramural football game. Shauna needed another drink. Slowly rising from her seat, she felt good and not tipsy. Lightweight, ha! As she turned to head to the bar, she ran – literally—into Michael Broussard's chest.

"Shauna? Shauna Carter?"

She looked into his chocolate brown eyes and smiled. "That's me, Michael."

Chapter Two

Mike knew he probably had a goofy grin on his face, but he didn't care. If the one who got away was a person, he was looking at her. Well, that was rather redundant, but seeing her looking like this with her hand on his chest short circuited his brain.

"You look beautiful," he said once his heart returned to its normal beat. "I'm surprised to see you here."

"Same. How are you?"

"Good. Man, it's been forever. Do you mind if I get a hug?"

"Not at all," she said then extended her arms.

Mike wrapped his arms around her and inhaled her womanly scent. Was this what sunshine smelled like?

She pushed back from him and smiled. Just sexy. And that red lipstick set off her mahogany brown skin and those pretty brown eyes.

"Okay, Michael, I'm .."

"Mike!" Greg exclaimed from beside them. When did that joker show up?

"G, what's up?" He dapped his former teammate and good friend.

"Man, it's been a minute. You're still single right?"

Mike nodded.

"So is Shauna."

Okay, his boy was slightly inebriated. But Mike appreciated the information. *One less question to ask.*

"I'm going to get a drink," Shauna said. "Greg, find some coffee."

"Mind if I join you?" Mike asked Shauna.

She shrugged. "Works for me."

"Yeah, let's all get a drink," Greg said reminding them that he was still there.

"You sure you need another one?" Shauna asked.

"I'm good, besides, we all need to catch up."

Mike wanted to tell Greg to go sit down because the only person he wanted to talk to was Shauna. But that would be rude.

"Let's go," she said then started walking. She moved like a gentle breeze, hips swaying like palm trees. Greg elbowed him in the side.

"I see you looking. Hey, you better make your move this time," Greg said.

"Man, stop."

Greg shook his head. "Didn't you have a silent crush on her back in the day?"

"Whatever."

"Maybe you should speak up now."

"Greg, chill. We're good."

"And you're done with that chick from Miami, right?"

Mike sucked his teeth. "So, you're almost drunk, right?"

He held his fingers a few inches apart. "Just call me *the love doctor*, I'm going to make this thing happen. Finally."

"Stop it," Mike said. "You have no idea what that woman wants."

"What all women want, a chance to catch the bouquet when they play *Single Ladies*." Greg laughed. But Mike was still intrigued by the fact that Shauna Carter was single.

* * *

Michael Broussard had the nerve to still be fine. Finer than he was in college. Tall, lean and muscular arms that felt way too good when he'd wrapped them around her. Was this the same quiet dude she'd known from their work study assignment in the JCSU computer lab?

Shauna walked over to the iMac computer that someone said wasn't working. She hated this part of being in this lab because nine times out of ten, the user had messed something up. Looking at the screen, she saw there was a problem.

"Damn," she muttered. Part of her wanted to just put the out of order sign on the computer, but she had been challenged by her professor to do more problem solving with the computers. The only problem she needed to solve was telling her parents that she didn't want this degree anymore. A career in computer science wasn't in her future, but she was happy she'd be able to put some of the coding she learned to use as a designer. She'd just created a program that allowed her to produce designs on her computer. So far, she made three outfits for her friends to

wear during homecoming and to toot her own horn she did a damned good job. She was able to save money by not having to buy extra sketch pads and boxes of colored pencils. But she did keep a budget for charcoal pencils because those were her favorite design tools.

"You good over here?" Michael asked, seemingly appearing out of nowhere. He did that all the time, despite being a bigger dude. It was as if he was Batman or something. She turned and looked up at him. Did she sigh? Yes. She sighed. What was wrong with her?

"Yeah, just trying to figure out this issue here with the Mac."

"Need some help? This one always displays an error message. I think it's the hardware."

She started to say something smart, but Michael smiled at her, and she felt a tingle. What was that all about? This man didn't like her, he was just nice and smiled at everybody. Lily had laid out a whole list of things that Michael had done to drop hints of his undying love for Shauna. He was only quiet around her because he didn't want to say the wrong thing. She'd seen him looking at her when they had been doing community service at the church on Beatties Ford Road and the look on his face had been anything but holy. Shauna told her friend she was wrong, because Michael rarely said three words to her that didn't have to do with the computer lab or class. She gave him a slow once over and drank in everything about him – low swung sweatpants, white tee shirt and those rippling muscles.

The football team may have been trash, but they worked out a lot. And it showed.

"Shauna?" he said breaking into her thoughts. "Did you do it?"

"What?"

"Turn the computer off?"

"No, I hadn't gotten around to it." Michael pressed the button and shut the computer down. His fingers were long and thick, there she was thinking about how they would feel deep inside. . . She needed to walk away. But her feet wouldn't move. She just stood there watching him go through the motions of restarting the computer. Shoulders, chest, pants, damn he had big feet.

"Look at that," he said forcing her to look into his eyes. Brown eyes with gold flecks. Okay, he was fine. . .Or was she horny?

"Oh, it's fixed. Good, I'm going to – uh – go check the sign in sheet." She dashed toward the front desk and told herself that Michael Broussard wasn't interested in her at all. And she was going to hide Lily's coffee for getting into her head the way she had. "What are you drinking?" Michael asked bringing her back to the present.

"Umm. I'm going with a lemon drop martini," she said, her voice breathless. Why was he taking her breath away? He still didn't like her. Hell, he could be married. These days not seeing a ring didn't mean a thing.

"You know the drinks are free, right," Greg said. Shauna smiled and silently thanked the Most High that Greg hadn't finished his drink and was still there with them. Shauna turned to Michael and took an appreciative look at the way his tux accented his body. This was certainly not a rental, because that jacket hugged his arms as if it had been made for him. There she was looking at his arms again. *Stop it,* she chided.

"Shauna, what have you been doing with yourself?" Michael asked.

"Just running my business and dressing people," she replied with a smile. The bartender handed Shauna her drink and she took a nervous sip as Michael peered at her. Why was she acting like this? It's just Michael.

"As good as you were in computer science, I can't believe you're not running a technology department at a major corporation."

"Is that what you do?" she asked.

Mike cleared his throat. "I own a computer security company. If you were still in the business you could work for me."

"I don't think so, I've been doing my own thing for so long, I couldn't imagine listening to someone who thought he was my boss."

"So, that's why you're still single?" Greg asked with a snarky laugh.

"Shut up," she snapped. "I don't see how me not wanting to work to make someone else rich has anything to do with marriage."

"Or maybe," Greg said in between sips of his drink, "You've been waiting for MB to come back and look what God did for y'all today."

Shauna wanted the floor to open and swallow Greg like a hungry whale. Was he insane? Or did he know something she didn't? After all, Greg played football with Michael, had he said something years ago? *Nope, not doing this.*

"Ignore him, Shauna," Michael said. "You know when folks get married, they think it's their job to pair up the whole world."

"Right." She rolled her eyes at Greg and took another sip of her drink. Michael had just proved it, he wasn't interested. Game over.

"But," Michael continued. "Someone has been slacking to leave you out here without a ring on it."

"If you say so," she said. "Ever think that I made the decision not to get married because I don't plan on settling? My life goal isn't being some dude's plus one at events."

"Ouch," Michael said. "I guess I'll put my shot away."

She arched her right eyebrow. "And what does that mean?"

"Hello," Greg said. "This man was trying to shoot his shot and you blocked it before he even had a chance. Like damn Dikembe Mutombo."

Shauna drained her drink. Were these two serious? Now she wished the floor would swallow her.

Chapter Three

Mike wished he didn't have to sit with the bridal party for dinner. He wanted to explain himself to Shauna and punch Greg in the damn throat. Now, he hadn't been carrying a twenty-year torch for the woman. Two years ago, he thought he was about to join the land of matrimony. Darla Washington was supposed to be his forever love. Too bad she'd made three other dudes in Miami feel the same way. She was beautiful but being faithful wasn't in her wheelhouse. Maybe that had been his karma for how poorly he'd treated Jocelyn Edwards, the woman he'd been dating when he'd met Darla. Being someone who didn't like conflict, when the relationship started going to the left, he didn't talk about the issues they were having and started hanging out more. But a business trip to Miami changed everything and he'd cheated on Jocelyn. He couldn't keep that a secret because the guilt ate at him like a hungry dog.

She'd been hurt, but she told him that what goes around comes around. He learned a hard lesson. And after taking time to heal, figure out conflict resolution and one more love TKO, here was Shauna. Like, did he make all those mistakes in order to have a chance with her? Life wasn't this easy. Especially since she'd just made it clear that settling down wasn't in her future. *Or maybe it's you. She just doesn't want you to get the wrong idea about anything happening between the two of us. Maybe we're just destined to be friends.* He focused on his dinner plate for a second then he realized, he wasn't going to sit here and eat his food. He was going to shoot his shot again. All she could do was say no, right? They were adults and it wasn't as if what he was about to say to her would travel across campus and become the latest gossip. They weren't students anymore.

* * *

"I can't stand you," Shauna whispered to Greg after their meals had been placed in front of them. "Why are you so extra?"

"What are you talking about?" Greg asked as he cut into his steak.

Shauna glanced at their other table mates and decided that this wasn't a conversation they needed to have right now. "When Lily comes back to town, it's on."

"You know that man was flirting with you and has been waiting on this day for years," Greg said, a little too loud for Shauna's taste. The older couples at the table were tuned in as if they were watching a *Matlock* episode they hadn't seen in years. Shauna smiled and dug her fork into her shrimp alfredo.

"You know," Greg began. "MB used to like you in college, but you didn't hear that from me."

"Eat your food before I choke you," she gritted.

"What? You're telling me that all that time y'all spent in the computer lab, you didn't know? And nothing ever happened between you two? Not even during the blackout?"

Shauna stretched her eyes and wondered if Michael had opened his mouth about the night they said they'd never talk about.

"What are you getting at?" she asked in a near whisper.

Shirley snorted, not even trying to hide the fact that she was listening to them. "Sounds like something did happen. Girl, you might as well spill it."

"Stop it, Shirley," Elizabeth said. "Let them folk keep their business between themselves."

Shauna glared at Greg because she couldn't focus the death stare on the old women she wanted to become her new customers.

"I'm going to get another drink," Greg said.

"You sure you want to do that, son?" Albert asked. "You might need some water."

"Facts," Shauna muttered. "But since you've stressed me out, I'm getting my last one."

She and Greg rose to their feet and headed to the bar. Shauna glanced back at the wedding party table and saw Michael laughing with a bridesmaid. Guess he was shooting his shot everywhere today. And here she was thinking . . .What had she been thinking anyway? Twenty years is a long time to be sitting on feelings for someone. And a tad bit creepy, right? Or it's the stuff that beautiful love stories are made of – at least that's what all the Hallmark movies made folk believe.

* * *

Mike noticed Greg and Shauna left their table and he was about to follow them when the photographer showed up. "How many pictures are we taking today?" Nora asked, causing Mike to laugh. He normally hated pictures. That had been one of the reasons why he didn't have social media and the security issues of all those platforms gave him pause. How many companies had he saved because one of their employees had clicked a fraudulent link from Facebook, Instagram, or Twitter—X or whatever? Mike had a code to release companies from ransomware software and that made his Raleigh based company one of the most sought after businesses in the country and gave him more than enough capital for expansion. Mike knew he wanted to open offices in Charlotte and possibly Atlanta, but he'd keep his headquarters in the Research Triangle since it gave him access to some of the best and brightest brains in the country. But an office in Charlotte would allow him to work with some of the major banks to upgrade their security and the state's largest healthcare system. Being in Charlotte would allow him to mentor students from Johnson C. Smith, something he'd always wanted to do.

And in the back of his mind, he realized he'd be much closer to Shauna. But would that matter to her? She said she wasn't trying to be *some dude's plus one*. He just needed to show her that he wasn't just some dude.

Where in the hell did she and Greg go? He was sure they hadn't left. Or had they? The photographer finished snapping her pictures and now he could get up and find Shauna. He headed for the bar, since he was sure if Greg hadn't gone home that would be his next stop. Bingo. Mike spotted them at the bar having a hushed conversation that seemed a bit off putting. He walked over to them.

"Y'all good over here?" he asked.

"Everything is fine," Greg said. "Shauna just cut me off because the old man at our table said I was tipsy."

"And you are," she said, despite holding her own drink.

"But you're not?" Mike nodded at her glass.

"I'm good, because I know my limits, unlike your boy here." She pointed her thumb at Greg and laughed. She had such a sexy laugh, like the perfect saxophone solo in the middle of a slow dance. Did she laugh when she got an unexpected kiss? Would he ever know?

"Michael, get your boy. He's out here making up stories for the old people at our table."

"Stories?"

Greg waved his hand. "Y'all know what happened during the blackout, stop acting like. . ."

"Nothing happened," Mike and Shauna exclaimed in concert.

Greg drained his scotch. "Didn't know it back then, but now I know. Y'all have been lying for years. Ain't that some shit."

"What are you talking about?" Mike asked, hoping the sweat above his lip wasn't visible. Greg saw something, his wily smile gave it away.

"I'm going to leave y'all to it so you can get your story together." He winked at the two of them then headed back to the table. Once Greg was out of ear shot, Shauna speared Mike with a cold glance.

"You didn't?"

"We made a promise to each other, and I kept up my end of it," he said, throwing his hands up.

"Then what is he talking about?"

"It doesn't matter because the lights came on before things went too far and I'll always regret that," he said in a quiet voice. "Maybe we need to make up for lost time?"

"What do you mean? It doesn't seem as if anything was lost, you forgot about that night so easily."

"Shauna, sometimes I wish I had a Time Machine, because we need a do over." He wanted to stroke her smooth cheek and draw her close enough for a real kiss, but he didn't. Couldn't cause a scene, didn't want to violate her space, or make her feel uncomfortable.

"Michael, you—you're sweet. I always thought you were, but..."

"Neither one of us are the same people we were in college. It's time for our grown-up selves to meet."

"Well, I'm too old for long distance anything, so maybe. . ."

He smiled. "I'll let you in on a secret. I'm moving to Charlotte soon, so distance won't be an issue. If you're willing to see what could be, it's not going to be hard."

She smirked. She actually smirked at him. What did that mean?

* * *

Shauna didn't know what she was supposed to say to Michael. Was he for real? Did he really mean what he said? About college, about now? "You know what," she said. "This is a lot. You sure you're not having wedding FOMO vibes?"

"We can take it slow, if that's what you need to do," he said. "I'm glad to follow your lead."

"What if I want you to lead? Show me that you're worth it," Shauna said.

"Say less, I can show you much better than I can tell you."

She gave him a slow once over. Had she missed the hints in college or was she too busy trying to prove Lily wrong? Damn it, she hated it when that girl was right, she'd never hear the end of it.

"Have you finished your rubber chicken?"

She nodded. "I've had enough of the wedding food."

"What do you say we grab a real meal after they cut the cake?"

Shauna smiled. "Sure. Because I could go for some sushi."

"I was hoping to have my fish fried, but sushi works for me if that's what you want."

"You know, a Mr. C's fish plate does sound good. Do we really need to stay for the cake?" Shauna asked.

"It's your call. I'm down for whatever you want to do. Who knows if this will be my last chance to break bread with you."

"Then I guess you're going to have to play your cards right, huh? Let me get my purse," she said. When Shauna returned to the table, she noticed everyone had been concentrating on the bride and the groom sharing their first dance, so she'd thought she would be able to sneak away without being noticed. Of course, Greg saw her.

"Where are you going?"

"Home."

"With Mike? I guess that means you don't need to catch the bouquet after all."

"Oh, shut up," Shauna said then turned to leave. Michael stood in the doorway with a smile on his face. She wasn't sure if the smile was meant for her or the bride and groom. She glanced over her shoulder and watched the newlyweds as they swayed to the sound of John Coltrane's *A Love Supreme*. Clint and Des were vibrating love and happiness. Shauna wondered if she'd find that. It had been a long time since she'd thought about her so-called happily ever. Because her point of view on marriage had soured the day her married high school sweetheart sent an inappropriate picture of his Vienna sausage to her inbox on Instagram, on his anniversary that he was celebrating on Facebook. And speaking of Facebook, when an old church deacon told her in a private message that he couldn't believe her thighs were so thick and he wanted to feel them wrapped around his waist while he was deep inside her, she was done with the notion of love. What was the point of being married your husband had no intentions of being faithful? When she turned back to the doorway, she saw Michael was walking toward her.

"You want to stick around? You're moving kind of slowly there," he said.

"No, we can go. I was just looking at the happy couple. I hope this works out for them."

He tilted his head to the side and shot her a questioning look. "What does that mean?"

"Let's get out of here and talk about it," she said and held her hand out to him. What in the hell was she doing?

Chapter Four

Mike took her hand in his and fought the urge to kiss it. Maybe weddings did touch everyone in the heart but holding hands with Shauna made him think of saying "I do." He'd finally earned it because he wasn't the man who played with a woman's feelings anymore. Sure, it had taken his own heartbreak for it to happen. He could be the man Shauna deserved, not some arrogant playboy.

"Are we taking separate cars?" she asked. "Because I don't live on this side of town and gas is expensive."

"I'll follow you," he said with a smile. "You probably drive like a bat out of hell anyway. I hope I can keep up."

Shauna laughed. "Trust me, you can keep up."

Mike was hopeful that he could. He watched her as they headed for the exit. Damn, she moved like a sweet drumbeat, hips moving from left to right. His mind jumped to a late night scene with her legs wrapped around him while they made love.

He had to stop thinking about sex every time he looked at her. While he was extremely attracted to Shauna, he wanted much more than a physical connection.

"Oh, this you?" Mike asked when he spotted her F-Type Jaguar convertible. "And I'm supposed to keep up?"

"If you want to eat good you will," she said with a saucy smile as she unlocked the car.

Why did she have to say it like that? He was sure what he wanted to eat tasted like a slice of paradise with heavenly frosting. *Get your mind from between her thighs,* he thought. *Because when you had a chance to go there, you blew it.*

Mike sighed and thought about the night of the blackout.

The wind had been howling like angry dogs for the last two hours and an alert came from the university for everyone to shelter in place. Mike glanced around the computer lab and was happy that they were located in the basement of Biddle Hall. Most of the students who had been working when the thunder started booming ran out of the lab as if it had been set on fire. Unfortunately, he couldn't leave, and neither could Shauna – since they wanted to get their full work study check payment.

"You think we should shut the computers down in case the power goes out?" she asked from behind him.

"I hope they have generators to protect the servers," he said then walked over to the breaker box. "But you're right, we should shut everything down."

Shauna shivered as she walked over to the IBM computers and started the process of powering the PCs down. "Why do we have to stay here in the middle of a freaking tornado?"

Mike shrugged. "We're probably in the safest place on campus right now. Would you rather be in Brayboy?"

"You got a point there, champ," she said. Thunder boomed and the lights flickered. He watched as Shauna shivered. Was she afraid of storms? Without a second thought, he crossed over to her and drew her into his arms.

"You good?" he breathed against her ear.

"I'm sorry," she said then took a step back. "Storms just bring out the punk in me."

"I got you until everything passes," he said, pulling her back into his arms. Shauna looked into his eyes and Mike was undone. He kissed her, slow and deep. She moaned and it took every ounce of self-control he had not to peel her clothes off and do the one thing he'd wanted to do. Mike willed his body not to respond to her hips pressed against his, her breasts against his chest and the intoxicating smell of her perfume.

Too late. He was rock hard and breathless. She pressed her hand against his chest and broke the kiss. "What are we doing?" she asked.

"Something I wanted to do for a long time."

"Michael, you have a whole girlfriend, and I don't play second fiddle to anyone," she said, her lips hovering against his. And though he'd heard every word she said, he needed to kiss her again. Obviously, she did too, because Shauna leaned in and pressed her mouth to his first. Or at the same time. All he knew was this time, it was hotter, wetter and better than any fantasy he'd ever had about kissing her and he'd had many.

Girlfriend. You do have a girlfriend, he chided and tried to pull back. *He failed as his lips traveled down her neck and he pulled at her shirt. Did she want him to stop? She reached for the waistband of his pants as he massaged her breast.*

"No," he said as she gripped his dick. "We can't do this. Not this way. You're right."

She dropped her hand and took five steps back from him. "Wha-what do you mean?"

"I want you, Shauna, and I know I can't have you in a meaningful way. It's not fair to you and I can't be that guy with you."

"What do you mean? Whatever happens here, no one will ever know."

"I don't. . .Shauna, you deserve more than I can offer, and I can't..."

She turned her back to him and adjusted her clothes. Then lights flicked off. She gripped Mike's arm and gasped.

"You're not afraid of the dark are you?" he asked as he felt her tremble.

"Maybe," she said then let his arm go. "You know what, you're right, we were about to make a huge mistake and we should never speak of this again."

He wanted to say something, open up to her about his true feelings for her. He'd be willing to break up with Rayne if he knew Shauna would be his. But if she wanted to make sure they forgot about tonight, then he would. Stepping back into the present, Mike wondered if now was the time for them to be together. He hopped into his Chevy Tahoe and watched Shauna pull out of the parking lot. He was surprised that she didn't drive like a speed demon given that her car was built for speed. But why did he expect that she would? She did everything in her own way and time. He wanted some of that time to be for him and discovering what life would be like for them together. He watched her at the stoplight while she dropped the top on her vehicle. Mike smiled, thinking this was the perfect car for her, an attention grabber that made all the heads turn. She'd grabbed ahold of his attention all of those years ago and she clearly still had it.

But what did she think of him?

* * *

Shauna smiled as she pulled into the Mr. C's parking lot. How many fish plates had she and her college friends shared their sorrows over. Even Lily, who claimed she didn't like seafood, would show up and devour flounder, coleslaw and hush puppies while lamenting about the latest guy she claimed to love.

She emerged from the car and noticed Mike leaning against his SUV watching her.

"Why do you look at me like that?" Shauna asked when she crossed over to him.

"Like what?" he asked.

Shauna sighed and tried to put it into words, he looked at her as if she was a piece of art that many people didn't get to see. He looked at her as if she was important, as if she meant something to him, but how could she? And stuff like this only happened in sugary holiday movies.

"Never mind, let's get in here while we can still find some place to sit," she said with a grin.

"You know, I'm going to get you to tell me what you mean at some point."

"But you're not going to do that today. It's fish time," she said as he opened the door.

After eating their whiting, fried hard of course, hush puppies, fries and slaw, the duo decided to head to campus to and look at the place they used to call home.

"It's wild how everything around here has changed, but Smith is still the same," Mike said.

"That's comforting, though," she said as they walked over to Biddle Hall, the jewel of the campus and the highest point in Mecklenburg County. "I mean, coming here gave me a purpose in life and we have to make sure the next generation still has this place."

"You really believe in holding high the gold and blue, huh? What's the most exciting thing that happened to you here?"

Shauna laughed and pointed toward Myers Hall, her freshman dormitory. "Homecoming panty raid."

"Wait, how was that exciting?"

"Because me and my girls were ready. Lily, who always had a lighter, was like when that door opens, we're setting them on fire. She had a big can of oil sheen. Asia had the mop handle and was like we're going to trip them and then beat the hell out of them."

"Y'all were trying to go to jail," Mike said with a laugh. "What if I had been with the panty raiders?"

"If Lily had gotten to you first, you would've been charcoaled. She was not playing with them. But for all our preparation, no one showed up and we had an all-night party with popcorn, some cheap wine from Two-Way and prank called some boys over at Liston."

"Why did y'all do that?"

Shauna shrugged and grinned. "Because we wanted to see how many of them would come to the guard booth to meet Carmen Jones. Only one guy showed up."

Mike furrowed his eyebrows. "Who was Carmen Jones?"

"You know the classic movie?"

"Wow, you ladies were something else. I really don't remember Lily though. I know you and Asia King used to be together all the time when you weren't flirting with the football players."

Shauna held her hand up. "I did no such thing. They flirted with me. What did they tell you?"

"Oh, hold up, I'm snitching on my teammates, but there were a lot of guys who were crushing on Shauna Carter back in the day."

"That's a lie, because they never said a word to me," she said, with a shoulder shrug.

"Maybe they were just too shy to tell you how they felt," Mike said.

They or you?" she asked with her right eyebrow cocked. "I'm not going there," he replied with a terse laugh.

"But I am. You acted as if I killed your best friend after that night. And you couldn't say anything to me if we weren't in a group setting. I didn't change, but you did. So, the fact that I'm even entertaining you is Nobel Peace prize worthy. Why did you do that? I never even told Lily about those kisses and what almost happened in the computer lab that night.

I knew your girlfriend wouldn't have been happy and I've never been the type to start drama. I probably shouldn't even be standing here talking to you now, but this is growth."

"That was my mistake on everything. Dating Rayne seemed like the thing I was supposed to do. But my heart wasn't in it."

"So, the rumors were true, you cheated on her with those cheerleaders, the Blue Satin dancer and. . ."

"Everybody knew all that stuff?"

Shauna nodded. "Yeah and I'm glad I dodged that bullet. Maybe the best thing for us was to only be friends. I really would've hurt you if you played around on me like that."

"At that time, you're probably right," he said. "But things have changed, and people grow. Look at you, you've grown. Let me show that I have too."

Shaun shrugged. "You know what they say about a leopard and *his* spots."

"Good thing I'm not a leopard, right? Shauna, I hope I'm not too late, but shouldn't we finally see where these feelings between us go?"

"I don't know Michael, time is a luxury I don't have right now, and I don't want it wasted, you know what I mean. And I'm about three weeks out from launching my high end fashion line, so, if anyone walks into my life at this moment, he's going to have to be worth it."

"What does it mean to be *worth it*?"

"When I find out, I'll let you know," she said with a smile. "I really need to get going. I guess I'll see you at homecoming?"

"Or next week when we have lunch. I have a meeting in Charlotte and if you're free, I'd love to take you out for lunch."

Shauna tilted her head to the side. "Call me."

"All right, give me your number." Mike held his phone out to her so that she could type her phone number in. She did and then called herself so that she could save his contact information. "I don't answer unknown numbers, so I got you locked in." Shauna grinned at him and turned to walk away.

"Before you go," Mike said as he reached for her arm. "We should take a picture in front of Biddle, you know, for old time sakes."

"All right," she said as they linked arms and headed over to the oldest building on campus and the spot where they'd spent so much time together working in the computer lab.

Chapter Five

Two weeks after Clint's wedding, Shauna was going over samples for her new line and she hated all of them. Two of her jumpsuits didn't even look like the designs she'd sent to the seamstress.

Maybe her mood had more to do with the fact that she hadn't heard from Michael. No call, no text, just silence. It was like the blackout all over again. *Forget him*, she decided as she reached out to her backup seamstress. She had a show coming up and nothing was going to stop her from doing this. She wasn't the lady from *that* housewives show, and she wouldn't have a fashion show with no fashion.

"Shauna?" a voice called out from the front of her workspace.

She smiled, realizing that it was her not so silent partner Lily. "In the back," she said.

Lily sauntered in room and grinned at Shauna. She checked out her friend's black cat suit and shook her head. "Why do you always dress like you're auditioning for a superhero movie?"

"I just got off a twenty three hour flight and this is comfortable. Besides in this, TSA has no reason to feel me up when I walk through. Whew, it's been a time these past few weeks. But I have some great news." Lily tugged at her fresh braids.

"What's up?"

"My book is being optioned for a movie, a major motion picture with a huge studio backing the project! And your girl gets a screenwriting credit. I want to celebrate, but I'm waiting until my agent sends the contracts."

"Well, congratulations. I'm glad someone is having a good day because I'm not."

"What's the problem?" Lily looked at the sample designs.

"These samples are trash. This is a make or break moment for me."

Lily picked up one of the dresses and shook her head. "You let the Wish designers do this?"

"Not funny."

"I know. But there's a solution. There are a group of students at Smith who can help us and get these samples runway ready. I met them last year and they thought it was so amazing that I knew you."

"I'll take any help I can get."

Lily pulled out her smartphone and pressed a button as she nodded. "I'm not going to have you looking crazy. This isn't the *Real Housewives of Atlanta*."

Shauna hugged her friend as she talked to whomever she'd called.

Two hours later, three JCSU students, Zander, Alicia, and Wallace walked into the workspace. "Ms. Lily!" Zander exclaimed then clapped his hands. "I thought you were playing when you said you knew *The Shauna Carter*."

"Why would I lie to y'all about that? I just hope knowing y'all will help save this fashion show."

The students looked at Shauna with broad smiles on their faces. Zander raised his hand as if he was in class. "Does this count as an internship?"

"If you all can fix these samples, I'll write anything you need for internship credit," Shauna said.

"Can we get a real internship too?" Wallace asked. Alicia nudged him in the side.

"We need to get the work done first," she said. "Y'all don't have any manners."

Shauna smiled and set up the mannequins so that the students could start the work. Lily, who was standing in the corner texting on her phone, motioned for Shauna to come over.

"I know it's hectic, but umm, what's up with you and Mike Broussard? Have you seen him since the wedding?"

Shauna had been excited when she'd told Lily about Michael and their Mr. C's date and walk down memory lane. Now, she felt like a fool for believing something would develop between them. It was déjà vu. And not in the Beyonce' way.

"No and it's been two weeks and crickets."

"Somethings never change, huh?" Lily looked down at her phone and smiled. Now, seeing Lily with a smile that didn't resemble the Grinch was a rare occasion. Shauna had questions.

"Why are you smiling at your phone like that?"

"Business."

"You're telling a whole lie."

"I'm not. It's my business."

Shauna rolled her eyes. "Whatever. I'll find out sooner or later."

"Or maybe you'll read about it in my next book," Lily said then returned to her phone. "Listen, I have to go check in to my Airbnb, so send me pictures of what the end results are, and I'll see you later."

"Wait, you're actually staying in town for longer than five minutes?"

"Don't be a jerk, all right. Go tend to my investment," Lily said with a laugh. Shauna watched her friend leave and shook her head.

Switching her focus back to her team and Shauna knew two things for sure, they were miracle workers, and they could have any internship they wanted.

* * *

Mike pulled into downtown Charleston, South Carolina and he was beyond annoyed. For the past two weeks he'd been working nonstop with Sardis International trying to unlock their system

This ransomware was unique, a virus like he'd never seen. It was as if it had variants that adjusted to the different codes he used to try and unlock the system. If it wasn't such a fucking headache he'd be impressed. He hadn't been able to get anything other than work done and that meant he hadn't had a chance to reach out to Shauna or take her to that lunch he'd promised. Part of him wondered if she'd written him off. She hadn't called or text him since the wedding. She'd probably moved on with her life because there was no way that she was sitting at home alone thinking about him.

As he sat in the parking lot, he pulled out his phone and sent a text to Shauna. *Hey, do you remember me? Sorry I haven't been around; I've been super busy with work. Can I make it up to you?*

He waited for a beat, hoping she would respond. When she didn't, Mike was sure that he'd let her get away again. Heading inside, he decided that he was going to handle his business then head to Charlotte and spend the night. He needed to show Shauna that he may be late, but he's a man of his word.

The stars seemed to align for him today. The last program he ran to unlock the system worked like a charm and he was done in under an hour. Once the invoice was paid, Mike pulled out his phone and checked his notifications. Still no response from Shauna. His next move was to book a room in uptown Charlotte and hope that Shauna would agree to lunch with him when he called her. If she didn't, he would go visit some of his former teammates and explore the city looking around for office suites. Life would go on with or without Shauna in it. But he really wanted to see a future with her by his side.

After he confirmed his room at the Westin, Mike's phone chimed. She'd responded, making him burst out with laughter.

New phone, who is this?

"Oh, she got jokes," he murmured as he paired his phone with the car's Bluetooth and dialed her number.

"This is Shauna," she said when she answered.

"You're a real comedian, huh?"

"I'm sorry and you are?" When she laughed, his heart swelled. It didn't seem as if all was lost.

"It's the man of your dreams," he replied.

"I must have been sleeping for two weeks, because I haven't heard from you."

"And that's my fault, but I had a project that was giving me hell," he began. "I've been in Charleston for the last two weeks."

"Sounds like a vacation to me."

"Can't be a vacation because you weren't here. What do you have going on this week?"

Shauna snorted. "Just preparing for the biggest show of my life. But other than putting my reputation and everything on the line, I'm just sitting here waiting for lunch."

"Great, let me take you to lunch."

"How are you going to do that in Charleston because . . ."

"I was thinking fish and hush puppies from Mr. C's. If you have time, we can go tomorrow."

"So, you're passing through Charlotte tomorrow?"

"I have some business up there and I really want to see you."

"Umm, I guess I can make a little time for you, but I don't want Mr. C's. I think you owe me a more grown-up lunch after making me wait this long."

"What do you want?"

"Well," she said. "Something that says Charlotte and a place that won't have me wanting something else to eat an hour later."

"Chicken King," he said with a laugh.

"Now who's the comedian? And a bad one at that."

Mike chuckled. "How about you show me some good neighborhoods to live in and where the best restaurants are?"

"Sounds like you're trying to take over my whole day," she said.

"No, I know you're busy, but maybe later in the week if your schedule permits?"

"Thanks, Michael."

"Umm, you're welcome. But what did I do to deserve gratitude?"

"You're respecting my time and not trying to shoehorn your way into my week. I mean, I need this fashion showcase to be amazing and I'm over thinking a lot of things. Maybe hanging out with you can give me a little perspective. But listen, I got to go. Text me tomorrow and let me know what time we're meeting. I have a delivery I need to sign for."

"All right see you soon." Once they ended the call, Mike felt hopeful again. But it was time to step up his game if he wanted to make this woman fall for him.

Chapter Six

Shauna was beyond happy with the work the students had done to fix the samples and when the next round of designs came in they were perfect. And Michael had called. She was a little giddy about that.

Where did that come from? She was *giddy* as if she was still in college waiting for the cute guy to call her. This wasn't anything for her to get excited about. Besides, she ate lunch every day.

"Miss Shauna," Wallace said breaking into her thoughts. "Do you need anything else from us? I have class in an hour, but I can come back later."

"Oh, no, y'all did an amazing job. Hold on, let me pay you guys for your work, three hundred each good?"

The students nodded and quietly high fived each other. After Shauna paid them and was alone in her workspace, she took a deep breath. She had a lot to be proud of, her clothes looked damned good, and she had gotten RSVPs from everyone she'd invited. This was her moment. But what if no one purchased her gowns? Then she'd owe Lily more money than she could pay back in her lifetime. What was she thinking leaving a steady job with benefits to chase a dream that could easily become a nightmare?

Stop with the negativity. This is fear and you're better than that, she thought as she walked toward the front of the workspace. She turned off the lights and decided to head to her happy place, Amelie's French Bakery. A few French pastries and a large coffee would get her mind right. Or make sure she stayed up all night obsessing over the preview. Her phone rang, breaking into her jumbled thoughts.

"This is Shauna."

"Good afternoon, Ms. Carter, my name is Louisa Williams and I'm a buyer with Belk."

"Okay, how may I help you?" she asked wondering why Belk was calling.

"Well, I'd like to set up a meeting with you to talk about your clothing line and possibly selling it in our stores," she said.

Shauna blinked. Was this a joke? "What line are you talking about?"

"We've seen your casual wear in your online store and a lot of people have asked for that line in our stores. So, we'd like to talk about a potential partnership."

Shauna closed her eyes and pumped her fist. This was amazing. Belk had a significant market share in the Southeast. If she did well there, Macy's and other national department stores might come calling as well.

"I'd love to meet with you, but I do have partners who have to be kept in the loop about this," she said wondering if Lily was still holding a grudge with Belk because of that failed Cam Newton line. And then there were the financial issues that the company was experiencing these days. Her excitement started to wane. Was this a good business move for her when she was trying to break into high end fashion?

"That's understandable. Do you and your partners have anytime in your schedule next week to visit with us at the Belk headquarters?"

"Let me reach out to my partners and I can give you a call on Monday." Though Lily was her only partner, she added an 's' to sound a little more important. Shauna already knew Lily wouldn't attend the meeting because she held up the silent part of their partnership very well.

"Great, I look forward to hearing from you," she said.

Shauna hung up the phone and attempted a cartwheel but ended up falling on her butt. Still, she was over the moon with the fact that other people saw her work and the value in it. She called Lily. It went directly to voicemail. *Where is she?* Shauna wondered.

* * *

It was after seven when Mike arrived in Charlotte. As soon as he crossed into the city limits, he called Greg.

"Mike," his friend said when he answered. "What's going on, my guy?"

"I just got into Charlotte. What's for dinner?"

"Man, the way my kids ate all the baked macaroni and cheese that my wife made, all we have left is white bread and butter," Greg laughed.

"Damn," Mike said. "And I thought your low country ass ate crab legs with every meal."

"So, you trying to come over here for a low country boil? Nigga you ain't shit."

Mike laughed. "All jokes aside, can you meet me uptown for a drink? I want to talk to you about something. And for the record, I spent the last two weeks in Charleston, so I'm over seafood boils."

"Something or someone?" Greg asked. "And no one gets over seafood boils after two weeks unless you ate at those flavorless downtown restaurants."

Mike laughed again because that had been exactly what he'd done. "Why would you say *someone?*"

"I caught how you and Shauna were vibing at the wedding. I'm assuming you need to talk about her?"

"We're having lunch tomorrow," Mike said.

"Oh really? Making up for all those wasted years, eh?"

"Whatever, man. We're two adults reconnecting. People do it all the time."

"Bullshit, you were scared, for whatever reason. I don't get it, because there were plenty of girls on campus that you had no problem kicking it with. What was it about Shauna that turned you into an un-mighty mouse?"

Mike closed his eyes. Yeah, he had his share of one night stands and situation-ships while he'd been in college, but that was only because Shauna meant more than a fling and he hadn't wanted to mess things up. But he hadn't meant to allow decades to pass before he told her the truth about his feelings.

"Shauna was different. I mean, half the o-line was trying to hit," Mike recalled with a bitter taste in his mouth.

"And you scared them niggas off her. Shit, she could've been married and raising a family if it wasn't for your behind the scenes interference."

"Man, chill, that woman did what she wanted to do after college without giving me a second thought. And none of our teammates were going to give her the life she wanted or deserved. You know that."

"And you lived like a monk? How about you don't fuck it up this time," Greg said with a laugh. "Whatever happened during that blackout must have been deep."

Mike sucked his teeth. "Nothing happened."

"That might be the problem. I know we've all had lives, but maybe this is a sign that you two were made for each other and now is the time."

"You're meeting me for a drink or not?" Mike asked.

"As long as the first round is on you, I'm down. Where are we meeting?"

"The Westin. They seem to have a decent looking bar here."

"All right, let me ask the wife if she needs help putting the kids to bed, then I'm on my way."

When Mike hung up with Greg, he couldn't help but smile. He never thought *that guy* would be the family man of the year. Three kids and over a decade of wedded bliss he was living a life Mike could only dream about. Had he been smarter, that could've been him and Shauna. Mike's mind returned to senior year of college and the moment he knew he couldn't be what Shauna deserved – at that moment.

Midnight basketball was a must attend event at JCSU. Mike hadn't planned to go, but Greg and Clint wouldn't take no for an answer. Who cared that he had a test in the morning or that his friends with benefits situation could result in a baby. You need to get out of the room, *they said.* You should take your mind off everything and relax. *Hell, relaxing had gotten him into this mess.* You can pull out, *she'd moaned then tightened that thang around him and pulling out wasn't an option. He burst like a balloon falling on a floor covered in broken glass. Felt good for three seconds. Maybe it was because when he'd closed his eyes, he imagined she was Shauna that he'd lost control. Dumb. Just dumb.*

Mike didn't like to think of himself as obsessed with Shauna, but he thought about her a lot.

But knowing that he couldn't be what she wanted, he just hooked up with other girls who only wanted a good time. Mike knew Shauna was looking for a future that he wasn't ready to provide. Of course, she didn't tell him that, but he'd overheard her talking to her friends about life after graduation. A life that included wedding dress and destinations for honeymoons.

Shauna wanted told her girls that in three years she was going to be getting married on a beach in Honolulu and start a family. Mike knew he wasn't ready for that. And he really didn't want it to happen for Shauna either. What was the rush? And who in the hell was she going to marry?

What happened though? Why didn't she get her happy ending? He wanted to believe it was because they were each other's destiny. Now he sounded like that stupid soap opera his mama watched.

Mike had broken a lot of hearts in the name of sowing his wild oats. When he thought he was ready to settle down, Karma got her lick back. He wanted to believe that he and Shauna were finally getting their chance to love each other. He picked up his phone and sent Shauna a message.

I made it to Charlotte can't wait to see you.

* * *

Lily and Shauna sat in the corner at their favorite sushi bar going through the pictures of Shauna's samples. "This purple dress is amazing," Lily said. "I need that in my . . .Is that Mike texting you?"

Before Shauna could act, Lily grabbed the phone and read the message. "Ooh, girl, he is in town. You going to see him?"

"Give me my phone," Shauna said.

"Nope, I think you need to respond appropriately." Lily started typing. "Like, I'm glad you made it here safely, I take it that your announcement is a dinner invitation?"

"Did you send that? Lily, stop playing."

She held the phone up to Shauna, "Not yet, but you need to say something other than *K, glad you made it.*"

"Stop it."

"I'm already sick of you two." Before Shauna could stop her, Lily sent the text.

"Wow!" Shauna exclaimed. "That was so juvenile."

"Really? More juvenile than calling freshmen at Liston to see if they would come to the guard booth?"

Shauna laughed. "Whatever."

Lily smiled at her friend. "I hope you have the amazing sex that I'm going to have in two hours."

"Please, you need to relax. Michael and I are simply friends."

Lily laughed. "Sure Jan. But I smell bullshit. Y'all have been dancing around each other for decades. Are you going to pull the trigger on this or not? If your crush is single, maybe this is a sign."

"You're doing the most. And I didn't have a crush on him, because, according to you and Asia, Michael wanted me."

Lily waved her hand and rolled her eyes. "Anyway. When he gets you moist and you relax, I'm only accepting Cash App and Starbucks gift cards as apology gifts." She looked down at her phone. "I have to go."

"Wait," Shauna called out. "You don't get to keep secrets when you have been all up in my business."

"We'll talk about it later, I got to get ready for my date." Lily sauntered out the door with a smile on her face. Shauna was happy for her friend and this mystery lover. Maybe it was time for her to give Mike a try and see if she could find the happiness Lily seemed to be enjoying.

She looked down at her phone and read Mike's response. *Can't wait to see you. I'm at the Westin uptown and we can meet for dinner at Eddie V's if that works for you.*

Shauna exhaled and replied, *That sounds great. See you soon.*

Now she had to get ready.

* * *

Mike looked at his phone then downed his gin and tonic. "Greg, I hate to cut this short, but I got a date."

"That was quick. It is Shauna, right?" Greg asked.

"It is. I'm surprised that she responded so quickly. We're going to have dinner. Guess I should thank your kids for eating all the mac and cheese."

Greg drained his drink and smiled. "Get your woman, man. But the next time you invite me out, you owe me two hours of no kids."

"Bruh, stop it. I'm trying to get like you and have my happily ever after. I waited too long, got to strike while I still have the chance."

"But why did you wait? You had a chance to lock Shauna down and then there was Rayne."

Mike shook his head. "Rayne was never an option. She wanted the sun, moon, stars and the ocean."

"Newsflash, all women want that."

"I couldn't give it to her fresh out of college, so she decided to walk away. That shit was painful."

"I understand that. And she never tried to come back after you got all *Good Morning America* famous?"

Mike snorted. "Tried and failed."

Greg nodded. "I hear that. I hope you and Shauna get your shit together. I got at least one more wear of that suit I wore at Clint's wedding before I donate it."

"As much as you're in church, you'll have plenty of times to wear that suit."

"You're missing the point. I'm not wearing it again until I get an invite to the wedding of the century." Greg rose to his feet and Mike did the same. "Don't fuck it up this time."

"How did I fuck it up in the past?"

"Sitting there like a bump on a log not telling her how you felt."

Mike shook his head. "You're still country as hell, man."

"I'm never changing but thank goodness you have. See you later," Greg said as he grabbed his keys.

Mike was wondering if he had changed enough to be the partner that Shauna wanted and deserved? Could he be a help mate, support her dreams and make her feel protected? Could he love her forever, through the ups and downs of life?

Chapter Seven

Shauna walked into Eddie V's wearing one of her designs, a black and silver halter jumpsuit. She'd originally designed it for Lily, since that girl was determined to dress like Catwoman every chance she could, but it was the perfect date night outfit. It didn't hurt that the jumpsuit showed Mike what he'd miss if he kept disappearing on her. This wasn't college and she was no longer going to wait for him to get his shit together. Either he was going to get on board or get left behind. It wasn't as if she hadn't Googled him and knew how successful his technology security company was. She also knew he'd never been married, which was a surprise. But there was an ex fiancée. A Miami model who didn't mind dating multiple men at the same time, according to *Media Take Out*. Shauna wasn't even mad at her. She was single and beautiful. Maybe Michael thought he could tame all of that. Seemed as if she had been the code he couldn't crack.

Shauna glanced at her watch, it was five after eight and there was no sign of Michael, no text saying he was running behind or anything. She was perturbed. Wasn't this history repeating itself? She headed to the bar and plopped down on an empty stool.

"Now what if I was waiting for someone?" the man next to her asked.

"Then I guess she's late and we're in the same boat." She glanced at him then smiled. "Corey?"

"Shauna Carter, what are you doing here? Stalking me?"

"You wish." She reached over and squeezed his hand. "Nice to see you, though."

Corey McMillian was one of Charlotte's most prosperous lawyers and he used to be Shauna's crush. That's until he made it clear that he was looking for a good time and not a lifetime. She respected that, but she wasn't going to be one of his many bedfellows. He had every right to do what he wanted. And she was well within her rights to decline his offer.

"You too," he said giving her a slow once over. "Nice outfit. One of yours?"

She nodded then waved for the bartender. "If I don't wear my clothes and look good in them, how can I expect others to do so?"

"You look good. Very good. I know how you can make that suit look even better," he said with a devilish gleam in his eyes.

"And what design suggestions to you have for me, Lawyer Corey?"

"Take it off and let it land on the floor at my place."

Shauna rolled her eyes. "You're a pig, you know that."

He placed his hand on the small of her back. "Well, I can only be me," he said. "You wouldn't like me any other way. What are you drinking? It's on me?"

Shauna looked over her shoulder and saw Michael walking in the restaurant carrying a bouquet of roses. This was awkward.

* * *

Mike tried to keep it together when he saw Shauna and *that man* at the bar. She couldn't give him a fifteen minute grace period before latching on to the next dude? Was this her man or . . .You know what, it didn't matter. Mike walked over to the bar. "Shauna," he said. "Sorry I'm late."

"I really thought you stood me up." She rose to her feet and gave him a hug and a quick peck on the cheek. That made him feel good. Obviously this guy wasn't important. "Corey, this is my friend from college, Michael Broussard."

Corey gave Mike a cursory glance. "You played defensive end at Smith, right?"

Mike nodded. "Sure did."

"Corey McMillian, tight end from Winston Salem State."

The men shook hands but smirked at each other as if they remembered the same battle on the field. "And I still say y'all cheated in that 96 game," Corey said.

"Brother please, y'all lost a game everybody thought y'all were going to dominate. Don't you think it's time to let it go?"

"As soon as you all do. That win is the only thing y'all got going for you this year."

"Hey," Shauna interjected. "You're not going to sit there and talk about my school like that."

Mike laughed. "Shauna goes hard for the blue and gold, you might want to watch yourself."

Corey threw his hands up. "You two Bulls have a good night. And we'll see y'all in October. Remember there is no crying in football."

"Except for that time when I took you out on the 40-yard line. You cried that day," Mike quipped before he and Shauna headed to the hostess stand.

"I didn't know you and Corey knew each other," she said once they were out of his earshot.

"You two looked pretty cozy. Something I need to know?"

"Yes, when you're running late a text, or a phone call would be appreciated." She rolled her eyes as the hostess led them to their table.

"My apologies. The phone died on my way over here. I'm just going to keep it real with you, I didn't expect to see you tonight and I got overly excited. I should've charged my phone."

"Why are we like this?" she asked.

"What do you mean?"

"We're acting like children. We're not in college anymore, Michael. What are we doing?"

He took a deep breath. "Shauna, I'm trying to make up for missing the opportunity to tell you how I felt all of those years ago."

"And you think this is the right time now?"

"You tell me."

"Honestly, I don't know. But I wouldn't be here if I didn't think there was a spark between us."

"Since we're being honest, what's the deal with you and Winston-Salem State?"

"Corey?" Shauna laughed. "That's just my friend."

"You have a lot of friends."

She tilted her head to the side. "Say what you mean."

"I'm wondering am I just *your friend* or does that spark mean we can be more?"

"You have yet to give me a reason to be all into you. One minute you're here, the next you're gone. I don't have time to play games, we're too old for that. Either you're all the way in or stay in the friend zone."

"I don't want to simply be your friend," he said. "We've tried that already and it's not enough for me. But if you don't feel the same way, I'll accept it." Mike stroked her cheek and she smiled. That breathtaking smile making his heart skip a beat. He inched toward her. "Do you mind if I kiss you?"

"I've been wondering what was taking you so long."

Mike covered her mouth with his, kissing her with tenderness. But when he felt her tongue brush across his bottom lip, he went in with heat. He sucked her tongue until she moaned. Then they pulled back from each other. "You know," she said breathlessly, "we can take dinner to go and eat in your room."

"That sounds like a great plan, I guess we should order first."

"Or we could order afterward. The Westin has room service, right?" she asked then stood up and held her hand out to him. A flustered waiter crossed over to their table.

"Is there a problem?" he asked. "I was coming to take your drink orders and. . ."

Mike shook his head then pulled a fifty dollar bill from his wallet and handed the young man the money. "We just had a change of plans. Sorry for the inconvenience."

The waiter smiled at the tip. "Well, thank you and have a good night."

It took every ounce of self-control for Mike not to pick Shauna up and sprint to the hotel. But he played it as cool as he could while holding her hand. Her hands were soft as Italian silk. Was she that smooth all over?

"Michael," she said.

"Yes?"

"You better make this worth the wait."

"No pressure huh?"

"Oh, I want all the pressure," she said with a low moan. Shauna pressed her supple body against his. Mike's dick spang to attention. Then she kissed him deep. So wet. So hot. Mike was the one moaning this time when her tongue tangled with his. He gripped her ass and pulled her closer to his erection. She gasped when she felt his hardness against her.

"Get a room, damn," someone called out causing the couple to break their passionate embrace.

"Umm, shit, Shauna, we'd better get moving," Mike said once he caught his breath.

"Lead the way," she said, her voice sounding like a seductive song. He didn't care about how he looked when he scooped her up in his arms and took off down the sidewalk.

* * *

Shauna had never been this bold with a man, but Michael had unlocked something in her that she was ready to explore. After all, it had been a long time coming. And she didn't want any regrets.

When they walked into the hotel and stepped on the elevator, she kissed him again grabbing his belt buckle. Michael broke the kiss and moved his mouth up and down her neck. "I want you so bad," he groaned.

"Maybe you shouldn't have gotten a room at the top of the building."

He glanced at the elevator keypad and realized he hadn't pressed the button for his floor. "Hit four," he said.

Shauna pressed the button then returned to Michael's trousers. "What if I . . ." Before she could finish the doors opened on the second floor and a mother and her son stepped on the car. She shot them a disgusted look as if she knew what was about to happen. Honestly, it wasn't hard to figure it out, since Shauna was holding Michael's belt, and his fly was unzipped.

They couldn't get to the fourth floor fast enough.

Finally, they'd reached their destination, and they rushed off the car. "That lady was mad," he said as he pressed the key card against the door's lock.

"Who cares," Shauna breathed once they were inside. "It's not as if she walked in and saw me doing this." She slipped her hand inside his pants and stroked his erection. "You think this would've gotten her upset?"

He tossed his head back and moaned. Shauna used her free hand to tug his pants down to his ankles. Michael blinked when she eased down his waist with her hands. "Or would she had lost her shit when I did this?" Shauna dropped to her knees, pulled his dick through the front slot of his boxers and licked the head as if he was a melting popsicle.

"Shit, shit, fuck! Damn!" he exclaimed as she took him deeper in her mouth. Michael's knees went weak when she cupped his balls while deep throating him. Shauna looked at the pleasant look on his face and knew it was time for him to return the favor. Pulling back, she looked up at him and smiled.

"Still thinking about that lady?" she asked as she crossed over to the king sized bed. He kicked out of his pants and boxers.

"There's only one lady who matters and she's right here," he said then joined her on the bed. "That mouth of yours is magical."

"Your turn, you need to show me what your mouth can do." "Take your clothes off."

"The zipper is in the back, you do it." Shauna flipped over on her stomach. "Just be careful with the fabric." Michael carefully unzipped her jumpsuit and peeled it from her body. Then he stroked her shoulders, moved down her back and cupped her cheeks. He kissed her left cheek, then her right. Shauna arched her back against his lips and he didn't disappoint as his tongue slid down her crack. Then he licked her into submission. Shauna's thighs quivered as he flipped her on her back and spread her legs apart.

Michael ran his hand across her wetness, and she inhaled with anticipation. He started with one finger, pressing inside her. Shauna closed her eyes when his finger found her clit. He stroked her until her screams filled the air.

"Oh, you like that," he said before replacing his finger with his tongue. Shauna gripped the back of his neck, arching her pussy closer to his lips. Shauna came fast and hard. He didn't let her pull away when the first wave of her orgasm struck. He held on to her hips tighter, watching her as she gripped the sheets and struggled not to scream.

"My. God! Michael." Her body spasmed then went flat. She'd never felt an orgasm so intense, so soul snatching. He did that.

When she opened her eyes, Michael was lying beside her with a grin on his face. "Are you all right?" He ran his index finger down the side of her arm.

"Ask me again in five minutes," she said as she turned to face him. Her eyelids were heavy like winter drapes. There were things she wanted to say, but her brain and her mouth weren't cooperating.

"Close your eyes, baby," he whispered as he wrapped his arms around her. A few seconds later, Shauna was sleeping in his arms.

Chapter Eight

Mike watched Shauna while she slept. She was even more beautiful when she came. Her taste was still on his lips, and he needed her more than he did when she'd walked in the room but holding her was enough for now. It felt good. Felt like a future was growing. And his dick was getting hard with each breath she took. Okay, it was time to wake her up. He stroked her cheek, then kissed her soft skin, she stirred under his touch and inched closer to him. Mike dropped his hand to her thigh and stroked her until her eyes opened.

"Michael," she intoned as his fingers danced up and down her inner thigh. "What are you doing?"

"Warming you up," he said then spread her legs apart. He tapped his fingers across her wetness, relishing in her moaning. He slipped his index finger inside her, the pad of his finger rubbing her clit as if it was a genie lamp.

She was gushing, it was time. Mike spread her legs apart and planted his face between her thighs.

She exploded in his mouth as he licked and sucked her clit. Shauna howled with pleasure as he continued his sensual tongue lashing. Shauna threw her hands above her head as if she'd granted him total control over her body. Mike was happy to accept. He pulled her hips closer to his face and darted his tongue in and out before clamping down on her precious pearl and sucking her like the delicious lollipop he'd always thought she was.

"Michael!" Shauna shrieked as she released her orgasm. He locked eyes with her and damn near came himself from secondhand satisfaction.

Pulling away from her, he smiled. "How are you feeling?" Mike asked.

She shook her head. "I need a minute."

"Take all the time you need. I'm going to be right here," he said then leaned in and kissed her lips. Shauna gripped his cheek as their kiss deepened. She threw her leg over his hip and as much as he wanted to dive into her wetness, he knew he had to protect them.

"Wait," he said. "Condom."

Shauna nodded with her eyes closed. "Hurry up."

Mike grabbed a gold foil package, ripped it open and slid the condom in place. Shauna opened her eyes and smiled at his length and girth. "Come here, woman," he said as he opened his arms to her. Shauna wrapped her arms around his neck then lifted herself on his dick. He wasn't expecting that. She gripped his dick with her lips and rocked slow. Damn, she was tight and hot. Shauna damn near brought him to climax when she rocked her hips side to side.

He pulled her closer to his chest, just hoping to slow her down and extend his climax. There was no way he could come this fast. But Shauna wasn't taking his hint. She dropped down on him and ground against him. Mike felt as if he was about to explode if she moved five inches to the left. She grabbed his chin and pressed her mouth against his. Mike sucked her bottom lip and that slowed her down as if she had too many sensations flowing through her body at once. Now she knew how it felt. Mike traced her lips with his tongue and gripped her ass. "Oh, shit," he groaned. "Shauna."

"Don't stop," she moaned. "Don't move. I'm about to come."

"Let it go, babe, come for me." He smacked her cheeks, and she screamed before tightening around his dick. Mike threw his head back and finally allowed his explosion to happen. He and Shauna matched screams as the waves of their orgasms washed over them.

He fell back on the bed and Shauna collapsed against his chest. He didn't want to let her go; he didn't want her to move. This was more than anything he'd dreamt about or fantasied about. If good things came to those who waited, this was what it meant. Looking into her eyes, he couldn't help but wonder what was going to happen next.

"Oh, Michael, this was . . .Oh my God."

"So, you're going to stay with me tonight to make sure it's just as good in the morning?"

Shauna laughed and squeezed his cheek. "I wish I could, but I have a meeting first thing tomorrow."

He was disappointed, but how could he say it without looking like a desperate loser? "Oh, all right, maybe we can have lunch after your meeting?"

"Absolutely," she said as she stood up and began collecting her clothes. "I'll call you when I'm done."

Mike rose from the bed and crossed over to Shauna, who was now in her bra and panties. She was still sexier than the law should've allowed. She looked up at him and smiled as she slipped her heels on.

"You know," he said. "I'm wondering how you're going to put that suit on with those shoes on."

"Maybe I don't want to get dressed right away," she said then she pressed her body against his. "I don't want you to think I'm leaving because I didn't enjoy every second we spent together. And I don't want you to lay in that bed wondering if something is wrong when everything was right." She stepped back from him. "So, when I meet you for lunch, make sure you have everything in here, because I'm probably going to wear something like this."

"Lawd, have mercy."

"Make sure there's some strawberries and whipped cream with that lunch, okay."

She picked up her jumpsuit and Mike watched as she slid it on without having to take off her shoes. Shauna definitely knew all the right moves no matter the situation he surmised as he watched her.

"Michael," she said, breaking him out of his lustful trance. "You're going to walk me downstairs naked?"

"Give me a second," he said, catching her glance at his erection. How did watching her put her clothes on make his dick hard? Shit. She had him hooked. And he didn't mind.

He grabbed a pair of grey sweatpants; a white tank top and a pair of Nike slides then dressed quickly. Shauna stood at the door watching him. When he crossed over to her, she grabbed him by his tank top.

"Don't you ever put these sweatpants on again when I'm trying to leave," she said.

"What's up with you ladies and these grey joggers, they're just pants."

"Yeah, whatever. Only men built like you say that." She brushed her lips against his and Mike devoured her mouth, kissing her full, sweet lips as if it was the first time all over again. Their tongues danced a wet samba and when she moaned, he did everything in his power not to pick her up and carry her back to the bed. Shauna pressed her hand against his chest.

"And that's why you men put on those pants because you get this kind of reaction, and you love it."

"You got me. Because if you're going to kiss me like that, then all I'm wearing around you will be grey sweatpants."

"Whatever. But you did give me an idea. Maybe my next line should be a male line," she said. "And you can be the spokesmodel."

"Nobody wants to see my face."

"It's the . . .It's not your face that I'm thinking about," she said with a laugh. "I'll see you tomorrow."

Mike shook his head and opened the door. "You're a trip, you know that."

"Don't act like you don't like it," she said as they headed for the elevator. "You better put that thing away before you get in trouble for being armed and dangerous."

Mike pulled her in front of him as he leaned back on the mirrored wall. "I'm just going to hold you hostage with it," he said then thrust against her backside.

"Stop it," she moaned as the doors to the elevator opened and a group of people stepped on.

Mike wrapped his arms around her waist and kissed the side of her neck. "What if you go home and bring your *spend the night bag* over here and go to your meeting from here?"

She turned to face him and shook her head. "It's not that simple. But I'll be sure to bring it after my meeting," Shauna said then stroked his cheek. As the elevator came to a stop in the lobby, Mike held Shauna's hand as they exited the car.

"Where did you park?"

"In the lot across from Eddie V's."

"Okay, let's go."

"Mike, I can walk two blocks by myself."

"I know you can, but you're not going to. Safety first." He squeezed her hand.

"And who's going to walk you back to your hotel?"

"Really?"

"Yes, these streets are dangerous for everybody," she quipped.

"You could always take me home with you."

"Not tonight," she said then stroked his cheek. "But soon."

When they made It to her car, Mike gave her a smoldering kiss good night and waited for her to get behind the wheel and lock the door before he headed back to the hotel.

* * *

Shauna headed home driving slower than usual. Part of her was savoring the amazing sex she and Michael shared, but then there she was overthinking everything that had just happened. Had he wanted her to stay tonight so that tomorrow he wouldn't have to be bothered with her?

What if he still had an erection and was going to call some other old flame from college and . . .

"Stop it," she chided as she came to a stop at a red light. If Shauna needed to change anything about herself, it was always waiting for the other shoe to drop. She couldn't live in a moment of happiness without wondering when it was going to turn tragic.

That had been one of the reasons why she tried to hide her feelings about Michael when they were in college. But the night before graduation she had planned to lay everything on the line.

Lily walked into Greenfield Hall with two bottles of champagne, a bottle of whisky and a bottle of gin. "What did you do, rob the liquor store?" Asia asked.

"You know you're not supposed to have that stuff in here," Shauna whispered.

Lily sucked her teeth. "In 24-hours we're going to be alumni, who's going to stop us? Besides, we're taking a tour of our greatest hits." Lily reached into the bag and pulled out three plastic champagne flutes. "First, a toast to the good times." She handed the glasses out then popped a bottle of champagne. She filled their flutes, and they clinked the plastic glasses together.

"I'm happy we met freshman year and we're ending our college journey together," Lily said.

"You girls are the best and our late night trips to Walmart were unforgettable," Asia said. "Just like a therapy session with good music."

Lily and Shauna burst out laughing.

"Well, I have to say that having you nuts in my life taught me to believe in myself more and I will never forget that," Shauna said then reached out to hug her girls. Before they started crying, the ladies took a sip of the cheap champagne and for a moment, it tasted as if it was really French and expensive.

"Oh god, that's awful," Asia said.

Shauna nodded in agreement. Lily took another sip and shook her head. "Trash. But let's go. We must do something that we wish we could've or should've done last month, last year or yesterday," Lily said.

When Lily looked at Shauna, she knew this was about to be some bullshit. "What does yesterday mean?" Shauna asked.

Asia and Lily exchanged a sneaky look. "Nothing," Asia replied. "Let's go."

The trio headed out the door and Shauna wasn't surprised that they ended up at the front door of Carter Hall.

"What the hell, y'all?" she snapped.

Asia shrugged and Lily did a crude dance move. "It's a graduation party over here and we were invited. Hence the whiskey and gin."

Asia knocked on the door as Shauna glared at her friends, she knew who was probably behind that white wooden door and . . .

"Ladies," Michael Broussard said when he opened the door. "Welcome." His eyes were fixed on Shauna as they walked in. While Lily handed over the liquor she'd gotten for the party, Shauna pinched Asia on the arm.

"Why are we here?" she asked.

"Because it's our last night on campus and you need to go ahead and tell that man how you feel about him," Asia replied.

"I feel nothing," Shauna whispered. "And he's proven that he feels the same."

Before Asia could reply, Lily and Michael were walking in their direction and the DJ just started playing Monica and Usher's Slow Jam.

"Y'all going to dance or not?" Lily asked then pushed Michael in front of Shauna.

"Damn, girl, you lift weights or something?" Michael asked before placing his hand on Shauna's shoulder. "Hi."

"What's up?"

"Want to dance?"

She shrugged as she watched her friends walk away. "Why should I even waste my time fooling with you, Michael?"

"I don't want us to graduate and never speak again. I'm sorry that I stood you up for the movie, but something came up."

"Yeah, your AKA girlfriend? Rayne, right? It's cool, Michael. We started as friends, and we can end that way. No harm, no foul. And don't touch my ass when we dance, okay."

"I make no promises."

"Well, I promise to knee you in your nuts if you try it, okay," she said with a surly grin. As they made it to the makeshift dance floor,

Shauna closed her eyes while they danced, pretended that she and Michael could move on as more than friends.

Maybe the end of college would be the beginning of something special between them. She lifted her head and opened her eyes. He smiled at her and looked as if he was about to say something. Then the music came to a screeching halt.

"What the hell is this?"

Michael and Shauna looked into the angry face of Rayne. Shauna shook her head and walked away. She wasn't going to spend her last night at JCSU in some fucking drama she didn't ask for.

Lily, who'd seen the exchange, crossed over to the table where the liquor was and grabbed her two bottles. "They won't be drinking my shit tonight."

Now that they were real adults, would this chapter in their lives play out differently?

Chapter Nine

Shauna woke up at 5:30 a.m., half expecting Michael to be beside her. Last night's dreams were more like flashbacks of making love to him. What would later today look like? Would they have as much pleasure as they'd shared last night? However, as she sat up in the bed, she knew her attention needed to be on the meeting with Belk, not Michael Broussard's dick, even if it was a lovely and amazing dick. *Focus!* Shauna ran her hand across her face and shook her head. She was happy Lily had been behind the potential partnership with Belk. Lily was clear about a few things: this deal couldn't encroach on their company goals and Shauna's couture line was not included.

It was times like this when Shauna was glad her bossy friend was her partner. She understood her vision and supported it fully.

When her phone rang, Shauna wasn't surprised it was Lily. Did she ever sleep?

"Lily, you know you could text this time of morning."

"I knew you were up because you're probably overthinking this whole meeting situation."

"And?"

"You know I'm always thinking ahead and because I know you and I want this to be a success, I'm sending one of the best lawyers in the city with you."

"Who?" Shauna asked, feeling the pressure starting to ease off her.

"Corey McMillian."

If she'd been standing, Shauna would've fallen to the floor. "Wait, who?"

"Stop acting like you don't know him, we both know that you do. But Corey has a lot of corporate law experience and I've retained his services for the company."

"You didn't think to talk to me about this first?" Shauna asked.

"Are y'all fucking? Please don't tell me you and Corey are smashing. I don't believe in mixing business and orgasms."

"No. You're not are you? This isn't your. . ."

"What did I just say? But if that's your flavor, wait until the Belk deal is done. Attorneys are great in bed when they win a case. Ask me about my divorce lawyer one day."

Shauna sighed and laughed. "Well, Corey isn't the one I need to keep my legs closed to."

"You and Mike Broussard finally bussed that nut together?" Lily exclaimed.

"Is this how you sell all of those books, being nasty?"

"Don't worry about how nasty I am. Just tell me, was it worth the twenty-year wait?"

Shauna closed her eyes and sighed. "It was. God knows it was.

We did some things that I can't stop thinking about and then..."

"Nope, I don't want to hear the details but I'm glad it was good. Just for the record, I did a little background on Mike Broussard, he's not married, he doesn't have any pending criminal cases or child support claims."

"Lily!"

"What? I think the words you're looking for are *thank you*."

"This isn't *Moana* and you're not The Rock. I'm not going to thank you for violating that man's privacy."

"It's on the internet, so it's not that private. Also, who wants to get caught off guard?"

Shauna knew Lily was speaking from personal experiences and she was going to leave that alone, because this was a dark rabbit whole she didn't want to go down today.

"Thanks, Lily," she said. "You know, I saw Corey last night before Michael and I had dinner, and he didn't say anything about us working together."

"That's because he thinks he's working for me, which he is. Just know that he has our company's best interest at heart and no matter how good that deal sounds, don't say yes until he tells you it's okay."

"Got it. Lily, this is really happening, I can't believe it."

"Why not? You're talented, you've worked for this and you're good at it. If we sign this deal before the fashion preview, just imagine all the free publicity for your show. Your gowns and formal wear will sell like candy bars.

Then I can be a true silent partner and simply collect my checks while I travel."

"Here you go. You have yet to tell me about your Mr. Right Now, who I assume is going to be on these trips with you."

"False alarm, he couldn't fuck," Lily said with a snort. "I don't have time for one orgasm, and he wanted to follow me to San Juan and I'm like, slow down partner it's been two weeks."

"Wow, Lily, you sit here and tell me to give Michael a chance, but you cut motherfuckers off like a barber."

"I live by the rule of do what I say and not what I do."

"Wow," Shauna said. "That makes no sense."

"What are you talking about? I'm here for a good time and never a long time with a man. Been there, done that. Will never do it again."

"So, you're having marriage flashbacks, huh?"

"More like nightmares," she said. "Anyway, my corporate attorney is going to meet you at the Belk headquarters."

"But how do you know Corey?"

"You sound like you *know* him," Lily said. "Have you been holding out on me?"

"We had one drink together a few years back, nothing ever came of it. We're cordial."

"Damn it, he's really one of the best contract attorneys in town and I need to keep him on retainer."

"It's not a problem. I know how to be professional."

"Huh, you better. Let me know how everything goes and let's grab some lunch."

"Only if you tell me about Mr. Not Right Now over pho and noodles."

"Not pho. I need some spicy tuna rolls in my life if you want me to spill my guts."

"Okay, sushi queen. Our regular spot?"

"Akahana for the win. One-thirty?"

"Sounds like a plan. I'd better get ready for this meeting. Oh, no, wait. Michael and I have lunch plans."

"Go little rock star. And please blow his back out!" Lily said then ended the call. Shauna was sure of two things as she headed for the shower, Lily spent too much time on TikTok, and this meeting was going to be step one on her way to fashion world domination.

After she dressed in a pair of taupe pants with a matching seersucker jacket, white ruffled shirt and a pair of nude heels, Shauna grabbed her iPad and headed out the door. She wasn't sure how she felt about having Corey in the meeting with her. Yes, they had a brief flirtation in the past, but that didn't mean they wouldn't be professional in this new situation. After all, Corey worked for her. She turned the ringer off on her phone before starting her car and said a silent prayer for success and strength. *Please let this be what I need to move my company forward.* She opened her eyes, put on her game face, and headed for the Belk headquarters.

Shauna was glad she'd left her house early because traffic was hell getting to south Charlotte.

There was an accident on Interstate 77, which added another twenty minutes to the trip. But she was still going to be on time. When she arrived at the office, Shauna smiled as she spotted Corey getting out of his car, a black Porsche 911. Mid-life crisis, maybe? He looked good in his dark grey suit and oxford purple shirt.

"Good morning," he said when he spotted Shauna.

"Morning, Mr. McMillian," she replied. "You could've told me that we were going to be working together."

"I had no idea," he said as they started walking toward the entrance. "When Lily called me, I thought she was talking about the movie that she's doing. Had no idea you two were business partners."

"How do you and Lily know each other?" Shauna asked, secretly double checking her friend's story.

"My partner handled her divorce. Then, like most divorce lawyers do, he fell for her. She must have broken his soul

because he handed her off to me." Corey chuckled. "Lily is hell, I will say that. But she's sharp when it comes to her business."

Shauna nodded in agreement. "When she sets her mind to something, she makes sure the odds are always in her favor."

"And now she's working in fashion." Corey gave her a slow once over. "One of your designs?"

She struck a pose as if he was taking a picture. "You know it."

Corey glanced at his watch. "Let's get moving so that we can close this deal."

"I like the way you think," she said as he opened the door and held it for her. They walked over to the elevator and headed up to the executive offices where they were scheduled to meet with Louisa Williams.

When the doors of the elevator opened, a tall woman with straight black hair dressed in an oversized pinstriped suit that Shauna wanted to tailor for her so bad, greeted them. Of course, it was Belk blue, but that wasn't her color. "Good morning, it's great to see you both. I'm Louisa Williams."

"I'm happy that you invited us to meet with you," Shauna said as she extended her hand to Louisa. Shauna nodded to Corey. "This is Corey McMillian, my company's attorney."

Louisa smiled at him as they shook hands. "Nice to meet you, Mr. McMillian. Let me take you all to our conference room. We have coffee available as well as a few breakfast pastries."

"We've already had breakfast, we're ready to get down to business and hear the offer," Corey said in a firm, yet professional voice. Shauna shivered inwardly because that shit turned her on. *Stop it,* she thought. *This is business.* Louisa led them into the conference room where three other

people were seated around a round table sipping on coffee and eating pastries that looked dry as sand. It wasn't lost on Shauna that all these decision makers were white men. What did these men know about women's fashion? Maybe that's why Louisa was dressed in the oversized blue suit.

"Good morning, Ms. Carter," one of the men said as he stood up and wiped icing from his fingers. "I hope you and..."

"Attorney Corey McMillian," Corey said introducing himself with that voice again. Why in the hell were her knees quaking?

Pull it together, Shauna!

"Mr. McMillian, thank you for joining us. I'm Russell Waters, the lead buyer for our women's lines." He extended his hand to Shauna and as much as she didn't want to shake his sticky hand, she knew she had to as a professional.

"Nice to meet you," she said, wishing she had a Clorox wipe for her hand.

"Well, we have seen your sportswear designs, and they are fresh and amazing. Let's sit and talk."

The other two men were introduced as Josh Smith and Daniel Porter. It seemed clear to Shauna that had she come in alone, these men would've been considered Russell the muscle. Now she was even more grateful that Corey was there.

She looked toward Louisa who seemed as if she'd become a part of the wallpaper. This was exactly why Shauna had avoided corporate jobs like the plague. Women were always expected to sit back and be quiet. Shauna had no doubt that Louisa was the one who'd presented her line to these suits. She doubted they followed her on Instagram.

She glanced at Corey as he set his briefcase on the table. "Gentleman and lady," Corey began. "My understanding is that Belk Corporation is interested in the casual wear line by

Ms. Carter, and we're interested in having the distribution that a partnership with Belk would offer my client, however before any agreements are made or considered, we're not entertaining any exclusive deals."

Russell seemed to blanch. "But. . ."

Corey shook his head. "That's non-negotiable."

Shauna hid her smile by pretending to sneeze and covering her mouth. It wasn't what he'd said, but the way he started the negotiations from a position of power. Hell, she and Lily had always said their business would belong to them and no other corporation.

"That's an interesting way to start things. With niche brands, we'd like to make Belk the home for them."

"And that's great for Belk," Corey said. "But it limits my client's growth. We want everyone to be successful, right?"

"What if we compromise and do a year of exclusivity, then your client is free to work with other department stores?"

Russell asked.

"We're getting ahead of ourselves," Corey said. "You haven't even shown us the original offer."

Shauna eased back in her chair and watched the men across the table from her. The looks on their faces told her this wasn't how they expected this meeting to go. Russell passed a folder over to Corey. He opened it and nudged Shauna to review the contact. It was everything she didn't want, a five-year exclusive deal with Belk, a right of first refusal on new designs before she could sell them herself. Oh. Hell. No.

"What is this bullshit?" Shauna whispered.

"The exact reason why you need me," he replied with a wink.

Corey closed the file folder and slid it across the table. "Thank you for your time," he said as he reached for the handle of his briefcase.

"Wait, wait," Russell said. "We can talk about this."

"We're going to have to do a lot more than talk," Corey said. "If you will allow us sometime to go over the details of this contract, we can meet again next week." He nodded toward Shauna, and they rose to their feet. Corey handed Russell his business card. "Email me your best offer."

"I'll do that Mr. McMillian. Ms. Carter, we hope to develop a partnership that will benefit both of us."

"That's the plan," she replied. "Louisa, thank you for reaching out and recognizing that your customer base can benefit from my designs."

She smiled at Shauna. "Thank you for meeting with us."

Corey and Shauna left the conference room and rode the elevator in silence. But once they made it outside, she turned to him and smiled.

"Remind me to never go up against you," Shauna said. "You shut them down from the start."

"That's why I'm the best at what I do. You better keep me on your team."

"Why don't you let me buy you breakfast and not some damned Danishes?" Shauna suggested. "And as far as the team goes, you better keep making Lily happy. She's the GM for now."

"That's scary. You're going to have to treat me to Tupelo Honey after dropping that on me."

"I'll meet you there," she said then shook his hand. Corey held on to her hand for what felt like a touch too long. What in the hell was going on right now? Maybe it was just her imagination.

* * *

Mike would've been happy sleeping until noon after his night with Shauna, but when Clint found out he was in town, thanks to Greg's big mouth, he had to meet his friend for breakfast.

Clint was that person who could eat breakfast for every meal, and it made sense, because his breakfast dishes always included some form of steak. The restaurant he'd chosen for them to meet at wasn't far from the hotel, so Mike decided to walk. Uptown Charlotte had changed since he was a student at JCSU. The abandon buildings that littered the area were now high rise apartments and office buildings that the Black folk who used to live in the neighborhood couldn't afford. The gentrification was real and scary. So much history was gone from the city, even around Johnson C. Smith's campus. That didn't sit well with him, no matter how pretty the city looked now.

It was a fifteen minute walk to the restaurant, but it was worth it to get some fresh air.

"It's about time," Clint said when Mike walked into the restaurant. "Our table is ready. Another five minutes we would've gone back on the waiting list."

"Good morning and hello to you as well," Mike said then laughed.

"What brings you to town or is Greg telling the truth?"

"And what truth would that be?"

"That you're still chasing Shauna Carter. You know, y'all could've been together a long time ago."

"I wasn't ready and that would've been unfair to her. You know how that goes," Mike said in a not so veiled reference to Clint's first marriage.

"I can understand that. But what's changed now? How do you know that she hasn't settled into her career and doesn't want that ring anymore?"

Mike's mind went back to last night and being wrapped up with Shauna. He didn't know what she wanted, but he knew he needed and wanted her.

"Yo," Clint said. "You good?"

Mike realized that he hadn't moved since Clint said that about Shauna. "Yeah, yeah, yeah, let's eat."

After the host sat them at a table, Mike focused on Clint and told him that he and Shauna were getting closer.

"Seriously?"

"Yep. We had dinner last night and we're going to hang out later today."

"Maybe I was wrong," Clint said. "Both of y'all could be. . . Wait a minute, is that Shauna up there with some dude?"

Mike turned and faced the host station. And there was Shauna with the same guy from Eddie V's. The motherfucker who she said didn't mean anything to her, but they were having breakfast. Is that why she had to rush off last night? Had she run into his arms and his bed after leaving his? Mike couldn't and didn't want to remember his name. Was Karma punching him in the face again?

"That looks like her," Mike said flatly.

"I'm going to go say hello," Clint said. "I hadn't seen her since the wedding."

"Man, sit your ass down," Mike snapped.

"Nope. And why are you so upset?"

Mike narrowed his eyes but didn't say anything. Clint glanced at his friend then sat down. "Man, y'all fucked and now she's in here with another man?" Clint whispered.

"I didn't say that," he replied.

"Your crestfallen face says it all."

"You got a word of the day calendar or some shit?" Mike retorted, not taking his eyes off Shauna and that jackass. Okay, he couldn't be mad at that guy because maybe she lied to him too. Didn't she tell him that there was nothing going on between them, yet here they are. Mike rose to his feet. "There's no reason why I shouldn't go speak."

"Don't do that. You're going to mess around and cause a

scene in front of these white people." Mike ignored his friend and crossed over to Shauna and that guy.

"Fancy meeting you here," he said instead of hello.

"Michael, good morning," she replied as if last night had never happened – at least in his mind.

"Yes, it was."

The guy touched Shauna's elbow. "I'll meet you at the table," he said then nodded at Mike. Mike shot him a cold glare before returning his head nod.

"So, this was your important meeting?" Mike asked once they were alone.

"Excuse me?"

"Shauna if you want to play around, just let me know so I don't waste my time. You made it clear how important your time is, you can't think I don't deserve the same consideration."

"You have a fucking nerve," she whispered. "And I'm not doing this with you in front of these people. And for the record, I don't owe you an explanation, but Corey is my lawyer."

"Oh, so . . ."

"Michael, you can go fuck yourself." Shauna smiled as she sauntered away. Okay, he'd fucked up and he should've sat there and ordered his food. She didn't owe him an explanation, nor did she deserve his judgement.

Chapter Ten

Shauna took a deep breath before walking over to the table where Corey was sitting. Had Michael lost his damn mind? Yes, they were trying to get to know if there was something for them to grow with, but now he was fucking with her business. No, she wasn't going to allow him or her feelings to compromise her business decisions. Did he think that giving her a couple of orgasms meant he had control over who she could eat with? What the hell was he thinking? Just because they'd had an amazing night together, it didn't mean he had control over her life.

"Everything all right?" Corey asked when she sat down.

"Just fine," she replied with a plastic smile.

"That's not what I saw, but we'll go with your story."

Shauna laughed. "What did you see?"

"A man who wants to be more than your friend. But who can blame him?"

Shauna rolled her eyes. "I don't live my life by what men want or expect from me."

Corey threw his hands up. "Sorry I asked."

"What's good here?" Shauna asked as she opened the menu. "This is the first time I've been here."

Corey cocked his right eyebrow. "Umm, wasn't that the same friend you saw last night when we were at the bar at Eddie V's?"

Shauna expelled a frustrated breath. "You want to order or talk?"

"I'm not turning down free food, so I'm going to shut up. By the way, the chicken and waffles are amazing."

Shauna covered her face with the menu thinking that Michael had no right to question her. They hadn't made a commitment to each other and just as she'd told him, she didn't owe him shit. Why did men believe an orgasm offered them ownership of a woman?

"Oh, look," she said. "They have Charleston styled shrimp and grits. I think I'm going to order that."

"Sounds good. I have a question," Corey said. "How much money do you and Lily want to make from Belk? That initial contract, though we didn't like the terms, was lucrative."

"How much were they offering for me to sell out my brand? I want to make sure I don't lose the ownership of what I created, so if they aren't offering five billion dollars, it's not enough."

"And I thought I was a tough negotiator," Corey said with a laugh. "It wasn't that much. They were offering five hundred thousand dollars."

Shauna folded her arms across her chest. "I'd accept that without an exclusive deal. Send me and Lily a proposal and I'll let you know what will work for our company."

"And you're accepting the terms without Lily's input?"

"She's the alleged silent partner, so I make the final decision about my brand, okay," she said. "But of course I'm going to talk to her about it. She told me to trust you, so if you think Belk's offer has merit, then we'll go with it."

"All right, boss lady," he said. "I'm beginning to see why you and Lily are partners, both of y'all are hell on wheels."

Shauna blinked then laughed. "So, what you're saying is you have a problem with strong women."

"Not at all, but your friend might," Corey said. "I could tell there was something going on there."

"That was nothing but a misunderstanding and there's nothing to talk about." Shauna looked over her shoulder to see if she could spot Michael and there he was sitting with Clint staring at her. Did he tell Clint what happened between them last night? It didn't matter, but for a moment, she felt as if she was in college again, worried about what other people would think of her.

"Y'all dating or something? Because he keeps looking over here like he's ready to throw hands."

Shauna focused on Corey and started to be petty and stroke his cheek just to get under Michael's skin. But there was no need to play games with someone who she wasn't going to fool with anymore. Dating was totally overrated.

* * *

"You're going to eat or keep staring at Shauna?" Clint asked breaking into Mike's angry thoughts.

She played him like a game of checkers. Or a bad hand of spades. "Kind of lost my appetite. I'll probably take this to go."

"Man, if you don't suck it up and move forward. I mean all y'all did was have sex unless you confessed your undying love to her."

"Shut up."

"Wait, you're in love with Shauna? Seriously?"

"No. I just thought that we were . . .I got lost in what could've been, so that was my mistake."

"What did she have to say for herself?"

Mike shrugged and stabbed his eggs with his fork. "Something about him being her lawyer."

"Wow, you went over there and made a fool of yourself?"

"Maybe. Shauna told me to go fuck myself, so I guess that's the end of that."

Clint broke out into loud laughter. "I wish I could've heard that. I don't think I've ever heard Shauna curse like that before. Tell me something, are you one of those people who believe every time a woman is with a man she's going to sleep with him? That lady has been working to create a brand for years and you know what that's like, being that you own your own company. How many women have you shared a meal with in the name of business?"

"Shut up," Mike said. He felt bad enough that he'd accused Shauna of . . .what was he accusing her of? They didn't have a commitment and as much as he didn't want to acknowledge it, he couldn't expect anything from her. But he wanted and needed more. Maybe one night was enough for her. He wasn't dumb enough to believe that she didn't know this guy was her attorney last night. Why didn't she say something then? "You know," Mike said. "She was talking to that nigga last night before we had dinner. So, if that is *just* her attorney and she's just working with him, then why didn't she say that last night?"

"Dude, you're tripping," Clint said. "She probably wasn't even thinking about nothing but your dumb ass last night. Why do you find it so hard to trust people? You've been like that since I've known you. That's why you keep losing everything."

Mike rolled his eyes, even though his friend was right. Trusting people was something Mike was taught not to do at an early age.

The people who claimed to love you the most were also the ones who betrayed you and left you broken. If he would go back to his overdue therapy session, he might get to the bottom of it all.

"Anyway, I guess I can check out of the hotel when I get back to Raleigh. No need to stay here any longer," Mike bemoaned.

Clint shook his head and finished his breakfast without saying another word.

* * *

When Corey and Shauna left the restaurant, she made sure Michael and Clint had left first, because if Michael Broussard thought he could talk to her like she didn't have thick thighs,

an air fryer and Amazon Prime, he was out of his damned mind. When she got in her car, Shauna immediately called Lily.

"Well, it's about time," her friend said when she answered the phone.

"Does it really hurt to say hello?" Shauna asked.

"I know y'all aren't just now getting out of the meeting. How did everything go?"

Shauna sighed and told her the basics of the meeting at Belk and how they were looking for an exclusive deal and that Corey was going to offer an alternative proposal for them to look at. "But are you ready for the second part of my shitty morning?" Shauna asked.

"Oh, it gets worse?"

"It does and it's because Michael Broussard is a fucking dick."

"Ouch. What did he do? Did you put it on him that bad that he's looking for that ass in the daytime with a flashlight?"

"Are you done? Because this isn't funny, and neither was your fake ass SNL monologue."

"Okay, sorry. What did Mike Broussard do?"

"I took Corey to breakfast, and we ended up at Tupelo Honey, Michael was there, and he came up to us acting like a jealous boyfriend. He had the nerve to tell me I was wasting his time."

"When did you and Mike become a couple? And he said all of this in front of Corey? That's embarrassing as hell."

"It would've been had Corey not walked away. He had no right to assume the worst about me or to expect anything from me."

"And you wonder why I treat people the way I do. Give a fool an inch and they want a mile. He was wrong for doing that shit. Acting like a child when you and Corey just had a business meeting."

Michael didn't understand or appreciate how dedicated she was to making her dreams come true. He could be a part of that, or he could get the hell out of her way. It looked as if he was going to be getting out of the way. And if she was honest with herself, this made her sad because she thought Michael was special.

"Sounds like we need to have a drunk lunch instead of sushi." Lily said breaking into her thoughts. "Because I'm guessing your lunch date with Mike is off."

"That would be correct. I could use a few drinks after this morning," Shauna said. "But let's just order food at my workspace so we can talk freely."

"And we can make a voodoo doll too, because I . . ."

"We're not doing that! What do you do on your research trips? Come up with new ways to get revenge on people?"

"I never know when I'm going to need things for a book. Don't judge me. My readers love my authentic story telling."

"If you ever write about me, I'm suing."

"Whatever. I had already written the Shauna and Mike story and now he's fucked that up. I guess I can make it a murder mystery, since my agent says that's hot now."

"Bye, girl. I'm going to place our lunch order, okay?"

"Don't do that, I'll bring over Akahana and then we can plot Mike Broussard's down fall. Just have some vodka delivered from that booze app and I'll bring the ice."

Shauna laughed as she ended the call.

She wondered if Michael would call and apologize for being an ass or if this was the real Michael and she'd dodged a bullet. Too bad he didn't reveal himself before he gave her the best head of her life.

After she drove home and still hadn't gotten a call or text from him, she knew that it was time to move on. Even if he didn't think he should apologize, which he should, he did owe her an explanation for his actions. She was going to pull from Lily's playbook and cut him off. Shauna pulled out her phone and blocked Michael Broussard. She was going to leave him in the past where he belonged.

* * *

Mike sat in his hotel room wondering if he had made as big of a mistake as he knew he had. Part of him wanted Shauna to call him and cuss him out so they could work through what happened. Then he knew he should reach out, but he didn't know what to say. Sorry didn't seem appropriate because he had jumped to conclusions that didn't make sense. He reached into his pocket and pulled out his smartphone then dialed Shauna's number. Straight to voicemail. He called again, same result.

Had he been blocked? Was she really that mad? Maybe he had been right not to trust that *he* was just her lawyer. Fuck it, if that's how she felt then what could he do about it?

Well, he could pack his shit and go home. He still had to research where he wanted to set up shop in the city he loved, but it was clear to him that Shauna wasn't going to be a part of his life when he moved to Charlotte.

And that sucked. He started packing and saw one of Shauna's earrings on the floor. Picking up the diamond hoop, he wondered if she missed it and who'd given it to her? Why was he spiraling? He tucked the earring in his bag and called Shauna again. Voicemail. She was definitely ignoring his calls.

"So, this is how it ends," he muttered as he zipped his bag, then tossed his phone on the bed. He was about to call the front desk to request an early check out when his cell phone rang. As much as he hoped it was Shauna, it wasn't. It was Clint.

"What's up, man?"

"You got your life together yet?" Clint asked with a laugh.

"Glad you're finding humor in all of this. I'm about to head home," he said.

"Don't do that yet. We're having a dinner party tomorrow night and I'm going to do you a solid."

"What are you talking about?"

"I'm going to invite Shauna."

"No."

"Bruh, you need to have a conversation with her, and I have no problem locking y'all in a room until you two hash this shit out. See, I know you have real feelings for this woman."

"I'm not doing all of that. If she wants to talk to me, then she has my number. Because I believe she blocked me."

"Wow, you really pissed her off. MB, you've been wanting her for a long time and now you have the chance. You can't give up without a fight, again."

"I can't force her to. . .What if I was wrong about Shauna all of these years and built up this image of who I thought she was, but that's not the reality?"

"Don't you think you owe it to yourself to find out? You have to make sure you're wrong before you give up."

"I got somethings I have to work out before I try to make sure Shauna and I have a future. So. . ."

"Nigga, you're coming to my dinner party and you're going to see what happens. Not taking no for an answer."

"You know this isn't a movie, right?"

"Yeah, because if was I would've walked out of the theater already. This shit is drawn out and boring."

"I'm glad that you see my life as entertainment."

"I didn't until I saw how wild you went for Shauna. I mean, was it worth the twenty-year wait?"

Mike chuckled to keep from answering. Was it worth the wait, hell yes.

But now it still felt like a dream because Shauna made it clear that they were done – before they even got started.

"What if she doesn't show up?"

"Then there will be other single women looking to be chose at the party. Stop putting all your eggs in one basket, my dude. If you're single, be single and play the field like you're still returning interceptions for touchdowns. You don't have to belong to one woman."

"You don't sound like a man who just got married," Mike said. "Everything all right over there?"

"We're fine, but my life isn't for everybody, and somebody got to be the dog in these streets, I guess the question is it you or Shauna."

Mike rolled his eyes even though Clint couldn't see him. "I guess I can come to your little dinner party and see what happens."

"I knew you would. I'm going to text you my address. Maybe you should pull up on Shauna with flowers and an apology. Women love that shit."

"I'm not trying to look like a stalker, I've never been to her house."

"The address to her showroom is on the internet. What kind of IT professional are you if you don't know that shit?"

"The kind that's about to hang up on your ass."

"Listen, y'all should figure this out and decide what the next move needs to be. Maybe it's time for you two to move on. Once y'all figure this shit out, I'll know who to leave off my party invite lists."

"Really? It's all about your parties? That's pretty fucked up."

"I'm being Switzerland over here, listen, Shauna is a good friend and so are you. I'd love to see you motherfuckers together. So, whatever this beef is, go on and grill it up and eat it."

"Any tips on getting her to listen to me after I made a total ass of myself?"

"Honesty, bro. You're going to have to tell her what you want and hope that it's the same thing she's looking for."

"Maybe she found what she wanted with the lawyer dude."

"Then fuck it, just come to the party and ignore her. Although, I know you're not going to do that. Don't miss out on your second chance because you're scared."

"I'm not. . ."

"Bullshit."

"I'm going to unpack and extend my stay for your little party."

"While you're at it, call Shauna and apologize for acting an ass this morning. Maybe she will listen, and I won't have to lock y'all in the pool house."

"First of all, you're not doing that, whether I call or not."

Mike ended the call as memories of being with Shauna

flashed through his mind. Forget calling her, he needed to see her. Was he going to use the earring as his excuse, yes. But at least she wouldn't be able to send him to voicemail when he showed up at her showroom.

* * *

Lily handed Shauna a box of California rolls and a bottle of Jack Daniels Honey without even saying hello. Shauna accepted the items and shook her head.

"I took an Uber over here so that bottle is going to be finished before we leave. Did you order the vodka?"

Shauna shook her head. "I drove here."

"You have a gate, lock your Jag in," Lily said. "You okay?"

Shauna shrugged as they settled in the workspace. She opened the box of sushi and sighed. "Why am I letting this bother me so much?"

"Because you thought this was one of those Hallmark movie moments or maybe you've been sitting on your feelings for

him and now their hurt because you wasted all that time?"

"Don't act like I've been sitting around thinking about Michael Broussard for years."

"No, but we've both been in some shitty situations and here comes a man not covered in poop."

Shauna stabbed at one of the rolls with her chopsticks, "Yet he was. Like why he would think that I'd roll out of his bed and hop on another dick that quick?"

Lily passed Shauna a cup of shrimp sauce. "It often has something to do with their own guilt. Nic swore up and down that when I was at a book signing I was sleeping with someone else. But surprise, surprise, it was his sorry ass all along."

"Have you seen him since the last time?"

Lily rolled her eyes. "I told that man four years ago he was dead to me, and I meant it. No looking back."

"Then I should be like you. No looking back at Michael and just see what. . ."

"Pause, we are not the same here." Lily pulled two 32 ounce ice cups from her bag then reached for the Jack Daniels.

"You better not fill those up."

"It's mostly ice, chill out. See what I did there."

"Have you been drinking already?"

Lily nodded. "Just a couple of shots. But today is the last day of day drinking. Corey and I are meeting with the producers for the company who will be filming the movie tomorrow, I have to be sharp."

"And I was going to ask you to be my plus one at Big Boy's dinner party."

"Clint's having a party? What time?"

Shauna pulled up the invitation on her phone, "It's at eight."

Lily picked up a California roll with her chopsticks and shrugged. "I think we should be done by then. And I want to give Clint and his new wife a gift."

"Okay, Maleficent."

"Stop it. Had I been around when he got married again, I would've been there as your plus one," Lily said with a laugh. "Who knows, maybe I could've pushed you toward the bouquet and you and Mike Broussard could be picking out engagement rings now."

"Whatever. You know my end game isn't being a wife. You tried that and look at how that worked out for you."

"Ouch. How about you make better decisions than I made? I knew I was in a relationship with a man who was jealous of my career and success. But he was cute with a big dick. I thought I was going to have something that my parents had. Once upon a time, I believed love conquered all. I was a fool."

"Damn it," Shauna said as she burst out laughing. "I could've gone my whole life without knowing that much about Nic."

Lily shrugged. "I'm just speaking my truth. Besides, what didn't work for me doesn't mean that's going to be the same for you. Call me a sucker, but I believe you and Mike have a chance. At this point, y'all just need to have a conversation."

"I thought this was going to be a fuck Michael Broussard session filled with liquor and sushi. Why are you championing for him?"

Lily winked at her friend. "I had to trick you to be able to speak truth to power."

Shauna rolled her eyes and stood up. "I'm going to turn the lights off up front. When I come back, I need my mean friend who talks a lot of shit to be here. Pour up another drink or something."

Lily grabbed the bottle and refilled her cup.

Shauna reminded herself to get the smart switches installed in the front of her workspace. On a day like today, she could've turned the lights off from her smartphone while eating sushi. When she made it to the front door, Shauna almost fell when she saw him standing there. What had Lily put in that drink? Had the sushi rolls she'd eaten been an edible? Perhaps she was dreaming? How. . .

Michael tapped on the door and held up a bouquet of roses. She crossed over to the door and unlocked it.

"What are you doing here?" she snapped.

"I want to apologize. May I come in?"

"No."

"Shauna."

"No, Michael, you were disrespectful this morning. I don't think words of 'I'm sorry' are going to be enough to make up for you being an asshole."

"The roses don't help at all?"

Shauna sighed. "No, but I'll take them anyway." She snatched the flowers from his hand and tried not to laugh. "Seriously, though. What was that all about? Who hurt you, because it wasn't me."

He nodded as she sniffed the roses. "You're right and I'm sorry for how I acted. You didn't deserve that. It was about me and not you."

Shauna cocked her right eyebrow at him. "Is that how you work life? You allow your past to influence how you interact with people in the present? Because if the past is prologue, you shouldn't be in my presence."

"Not making an excuse for what happened, but if the situation was in reverse, how would you have reacted?"

"Honestly, I would've said hello and moved on. We weren't in the café after a blackout in the computer lab," she said. "Remember that? You walked the cafeteria with your AKA girlfriend and made sure I knew she was your number one choice, and I was just. . .For you to make a scene in front of my attorney, who is in the middle of negotiations for my company, makes me wonder if this is even worth my time."

He dropped his head. "I understand, I'm sorry."

Shauna rolled her eyes. "Lily and I are having lunch and she brought way too much sushi and Jack Daniels. Would you like to join us?"

"Are you sure that's okay?"

Shauna nodded, thinking that Lily would probably tell him off or make him uncomfortable. "Of course," she said.

Michael shook his head. "I really feel like this is a set up."

"Why would you say that? We're just three Smithites sharing a meal. Come through, buddy."

He placed his hand on the small of her back making Shauna stop and turn to face him. "Shauna," he said pulling her close to his chest. "I need you to know if you're going to forgive me and let me show you that I'm worth your time."

"You have a lot of work to do," she said as he stroked her cheek. Michael leaned in and brushed his lips against hers. Shauna moaned and closed her eyes, expecting a hot and wet kiss.

"I'm a hard worker," he breathed, and Shauna was wet. Why was she mad again?

Chapter Eleven

Mike wondered if he was being set up. Would Lily and Shauna jump him and beat his ass for his dick move earlier today. He didn't really know Lily, but he'd heard stories about her. Smart girl with thuggish tendencies.

"Hey, Lil, we have a guest," Shauna called out as they walked into the backroom.

"Is that Mike Broussard?" she asked. "How are we supposed to talk about him if he's in the room?"

Mike laughed. "So y'all were talking about me?"

Lily looked down at her watch. "Oh, my goodness, look at that. I have a meeting."

"Really?" Shauna snapped.

Lily nodded and grabbed one of the takeout boxes. "Totally slipped my mind, but there's enough food for you guys to share." She picked up her purse and the half bottle of Jack

Daniels, making Mike wonder what kind of meeting she was heading to. "Have a good lunch and I'll see y'all at homecoming."

"Wait, where are you going?" Shauna asked.

"First, the airport, then Washington. But don't worry about me. Have your lunch," Lily said then turned toward Michael. "How about you don't fuck this up this time? Oh, Shauna, I can't be your plus one tomorrow, sorry."

Mike shook his head as Lily walked out the door.

"So, you and Lily were talking about me?" he asked when they were alone.

"Maybe, actually, yes. I was telling her how I should beat your ass," Shauna said.

"I deserve that."

"Yes, you do. But why did you think I deserved that drama this morning?"

"I was wrong."

"Not an answer to my question," Shauna snapped.

"Shauna, just follow me for a minute. You were sitting at the bar with that man last night. Then I asked you to spend the night and you said no. . ."

"So, after we made love, you thought I was just going to fuck someone else? If you feel that way about me, why are we here? I told you I didn't have time for this shit. Yet here you are dragging me down with the bullshit."

"Shauna, I don't. . .Maybe I'm projecting because I know that. . ."

"Michael, my name isn't karma. I'm not here to make you pay for your past mistakes. But you're really taking a chance on messing up a future that could've been amazing."

"So, that's it?"

"Maybe. I mean you haven't given me any indication that I should be looking for a happily ever after with you." Shauna

rose to her feet and walked over to her design desk. "Michael, we've been friends for a while, maybe we should just leave it there."

Mike crossed over to her and touched her wrist. "We left things alone a long time ago and I've regretted that because I know you and I have something between us that burns slow. Shauna, don't make me wait another twenty years."

* * *

She turned and faced him, the heat in his stare melted the ice she'd pretended to build around herself. Or maybe she was drunk and simply wanted to ride his dick again. Shauna knew she would never drink another thing Lily ever handed her. Because the moment she found herself between Michael's legs and holding his face, she knew she'd had too much to drink. She pressed her lips against his and Michael knew what to do next.

Their tongues touched, then danced as if they'd been waiting for this moment. He drew her body closer to his and Shauna moaned when she felt his erection against her heat. Was she going to let him inside her this easily? When she had more questions about where they were going and what they were supposed to be doing?

She forgot all about that when he tugged at the waistband of her pants and tugged them down. To hell with talking.

* * *

Mike wasn't going to lie, this wasn't the way he'd expected things to go when he saw Shauna this afternoon, but he was going to take it. He needed to feel her around his hardness and when she stepped out of those pants and hopped on his dick, Mike could do nothing but moan with delight.

"Shit," he moaned as she ground against him and bounced her ass against his thighs. When she ran her tongue up and down his neck, Mike nearly buckled under her touch.

She held on to the metal bar behind the desk and continued to grind on him until Mike screamed. He exploded inside her. Shauna collapsed against his chest and sighed.

"We have to stop doing this," she said.

"Why?"

"Because this makes everything between us so complicated."

"Shauna," he gritted. "I don't want to just have the most amazing sex with you. I want every part of you. I want you, I need you."

She inhaled deeply. "Really?"

"Yeah. But what do you want?"

Shauna stroked his face and smiled. "If I'm honest, I don't know. But I can tell you what I don't want. I don't want the drama and the bullshit. If you ever do what you did to me this morning, you can forget we ever met."

"I understand. But, you know I still have some making up to do right."

"You certainly do and I'm going to accept every apology you want to give me."

"Let's start by getting out of here," he said with a wink. They adjusted their clothes and Shauna smiled at him with a wily look in her eyes.

"Where are we going?"

"I can take you back to my room if you like. We can finish the sushi, or we can order some real food."

"Sushi is real food, but I could go for an apology steak and some home fries."

"Sounds good to me," he said then leaned in for a kiss. Shauna pressed her hand against his chest.

"But you have to serve me that meal, in bed, naked."

Mike laughed. "I thought you were going to make a request that I couldn't live up to."

After they had gotten themselves together, Mike led Shauna to his vehicle and headed back to the hotel.

He was happy that he was getting another chance with her, because he felt as if she deserved his everything.

As they got on the elevator, he pulled her closer to him. "Thank you," he whispered.

"For?"

"The opportunity to finally get it right."

Shauna brushed her lips against his. "Just realize, this is it. No more chances. So, if it doesn't work this time, then we're going to have to accept that we weren't meant to be more than friends."

"Really?"

She stroked his cheek. "I told you I don't have time for this and if you're going to waste anymore of my time, we're going to end things before it's too late."

Mike looked down at her and smiled. "From now on, every minute that you spend with me is going to be worth it."

"It better be," she said as the elevator opened on his floor. They sauntered into his room and made a bee line toward the bed. Shauna kicked off her shoes and Mike did the same with his. He smiled at her as they leaned against the pillows. "I want to do something you probably haven't done in a long time."

Shauna raised her right eyebrow. "Do I even want to know?"

Mike stood up on the bed and held his hand out to her. "When's the last time you got to be a kid?"

She took his hand and shook her head. "So, we're going to jump on these people's bed?"

"But first, take the outfit off," he said.

"Why don't you do it for me?" she said with a wink.

"Don't tease me with a good time," he said then tugged at her tunic.

Her body mesmerized him as he pulled her leggings off. Shauna was a work of art, and he needed her more than he'd ever thought he would. She was imprinted on his brain, and these were memories he'd never let go.

"Nice panties," he said as he began stripping his clothes off. "You always wear a matching set?"

"I sure do. It makes me feel powerful no matter what I'm wearing. And just FYI, you're taking too long to get out of those pants," she said as she ran her hand across his bare chest. Mike closed his hand around hers.

"So, you just want me for my body?" he quipped.

"And you're telling me it's different over here?" She took his hand and slipped it between her thighs. "The only reason you were all up in your feelings as because you know how good it felt to be right here." She pressed his hand against her wetness. "What you should be doing is thanking me for letting you visit."

"Umm. All I can do is visit? I want to take up real estate here," he said then dropped down and covered her pulsating pussy with his mouth. To hell with jumping on a bed, he wanted to drown in her sweet nectar. He gripped her hips as he positioned himself underneath her. Without needing much coaxing, Shauna sat on his face, giving him the green light to devour her.

Mike lashed her clit as if he wanted nothing more than to make her scream. And she did. Loud, deep, guttural.

"Michael, Michael, Michael," she intoned like a mantra.

"Come for me, baby," he whispered before sucking her again. "Tell me you like it."

"I'm-I'm coming!" Shauna nearly collapsed as he flicked his tongue against her swollen clit.

The moment she exploded. Mike knew he'd gotten a little bit of forgiveness. She collapsed against his chest and sighed.

"I've never jumped on a bed like this before," she said after a beat.

"Glad I could give you a new experience," he said.

"You're going to stop playing with me, okay," she said. "I need some clarity about what's happening here."

"What do you need to know?"

"Everything, Michael. Is this just sex because that's fine. But don't try to sell me something you can't deliver."

"Shauna, tell me what you want," he said.

She propped up on her elbow and focused a deep stare on him. "I want everything," she said quietly. "I want someone who only wants me. I want consistent loving that I don't have to question. I want to be with the person who can support me and my future without question. Can you handle that?"

"I can. But can you do the same?"

"I wouldn't ask you to do anything I wasn't willing to do, but I told you, I don't have time to play games with you or anyone else's son," she said.

Mike cupped her face in his hands. "I'm not playing any games. You're all that I need and want."

"Disappear on me for two weeks again and it's a wrap for you."

"Understood."

"And you should probably make plans to be here for my fashion show, you know, if it's real."

"I'm going to be on the front row."

She ran her finger down his chest. "I really like the sound of that," she said as she straddled him. Shauna ground against the tip of his dick and he almost let her draw him in.

"Umm, damn that feels good, but I got to protect us," he moaned.

"Yes," she resigned and rolled over on her side.

Mike rose from the bed, remembering that he'd packed his condoms when he thought he was heading back to Raleigh. Shauna sat up and watched him as he fumbled through his bag.

"Were you leaving?" she asked as he padded back to the bed with the box of condoms.

"Didn't think I had a reason to stay. Thank goodness I was wrong," he said then climbed in the bed.

"You brought it on yourself, now come on and make it up to me," she said as she ran her hand down her thighs.

Mike placed his hand on top of her wetness, stroking her until she arched her back into his fingertips. "Let me taste it," he said.

"Please do," she moaned as his finger tickled her clit. Shauna's thighs quivered as he replaced his finger with his tongue.

Long lick, suck, lick. Shauna screamed and he did it again and again until she exploded. She gripped the back of his neck and held him against her vibrating pussy. Mike licked her sweetness until she pushed him away. "Damn," she moaned. "Your tongue is magical. Amazing. I can't move an inch."

"So, you're just going to leave me here to watch you bask in the afterglow?"

"Yes, I think you deserve that for putting me through that shit this morning, but it'll be so worth it."

Mike drew her into his arms, "Let me apologize again and hopefully, you will believe me this time."

"Umm, you still have some convincing to do, but I'm willing to listen," she said then kissed his chin.

He held her closer. "Shauna, let me love you."

"Prove to me that I'm not wasting my time."

"I will. Trust and believe that."

Shauna wrapped her leg around his waist and thrust her hips forward. "You can start now," she said.

He gripped her hips and dove into her wetness. Shauna moaned as he pumped in and out. Mike knew what they were doing at the moment was reckless, he didn't have on a condom, but it felt so good being inside her that he couldn't stop, and he dove deeper and deeper until he was on the brink of an explosion. He pulled out and sighed as he came on her thighs. Shauna sighed and closed her eyes. "My goodness," she moaned.

"Shauna," Mike breathed against her ear. "You're amazing."

"Is that all you can say?" she asked.

"What more can I say?"

She stroked his face and smiled. "Michael," Shauna moaned. "You better be everything you claim to be, because I like this."

"Then let me keep it up."

"Can you?"

He brushed his lips against hers. "Absolutely."

"Then tell me you're going to be here for my fashion show."

"Whatever you need from me, I'm going to be here."

She smiled and held on to him tightly. "Please don't disappoint me," she whispered before drifting off to sleep.

Mike held Shauna as she slept and knew this was everything he needed.

Chapter Twelve

The next day, Shauna woke up in Michael's arms and sighed. She had so much she needed to get done, but she didn't want to move from the warmth of his body. This felt so good and so…

"Good morning," he said huskily.

"Morning," she replied as she turned to face him. He brushed a kiss across her cheek.

"Want to get some breakfast?"

"No, I just want to stay right here until I have no choice but to leave."

"Then you're trying to be here forever? Because…"

"Slow down, Michael. I have stuff I need to do today. Remember, I have a fashion show to prepare for."

"How can I help?"

Shauna smiled and considered how to answer that question. "Well, you're going to have to do some heavy lifting and possibly take off your pants," she said.

"Guess it's a good thing I don't have any on now." He took her hand in his then dropped it on his thigh.

"I need a model, okay, not this," she said then stroked his penis. "At least not right away." Shauna knew that if she didn't get out of the bed, she wasn't going to get anything accomplished. So, reluctantly, she sat up and swung her legs over the side of the bed.

"You know you're so wrong to leave me in this state," he said.

"You'll be fine, and I'll make sure of it," she said with a wink. Shauna headed for the bathroom and took a quick shower. She returned to the bedroom, wrapped in a towel and Michael released a low whistle of appreciation. "Do we really have to leave? Because…"

"Yes, we have to leave and I need to stop by my house and pick up somethings," she said.

"Aww, I get to see the castle."

Shauna rolled her eyes as she picked up her clothes from the foot of the bed. "You're going to stand there and stare or are you going to get ready?"

"The view is amazing, why should I move?" he asked.

"Not to sound like a broken record, but I got shit to do and you volunteered to help." Shauna dropped her towel and dressed. Michael headed for the bathroom and Shauna put on her shoes. It was time for them to explore what they meant to each other, right? But why was she feeling so nervous about everything?

You deserve to be happy and hopefully, he will be a part of that. If not, just choose yourself.

"Hey," Michael said breaking into her thoughts. "You're good?"

She nodded. "I was just thinking." Shauna smiled, seeing that he was already dressed. "Let's get going."

"After you, my dear."

They headed to the parking lot and got into his car. Shauna gave him directions to her south Charlotte townhouse. Michael smiled as he pulled into her driveway, "Oh she's fancy, huh?"

"Yep, my home is my castle," she said as they got out of the car. "Come on, I'll give you a tour."

She walked to the front door and opened it. Shauna's home was trimmed in gold and exuded warmth. She didn't make a habit of bringing people to her place of peace.

"Your house is beautiful," he said. "But I wouldn't expect anything else but beauty from you."

"You can stop being so sweet."

"I'm just trying to make up for all the times I wasn't," he said.

"Starting right now, we're looking forward, not back. Whatever happened twenty years ago or yesterday is water under the bridge."

"All right," he said then closed the space between them. "So, what did you need to get from here?"

"Some materials I need and then we're going to my workshop and start the preparations for the show."

Michael nodded and followed Shauna as she headed up the stairs.

She led him to her second bedroom that doubled as a storage facility. "So, when I spend the night, I guess I have to sleep with you, huh?"

"As if you would sleep anywhere else."

"That's true. So, your fashion show, is this the first one for your new line?"

"It is," she replied with a smile. "Look at you paying attention."

"Kind of hard not to when you're so dedicated to this. What are you doing for your online shopping security? When you drop those new designs, your site is going to blow up."

Shauna stroked her chin. "If only I knew a cyber security specialist."

"Aren't you the lucky one," he said.

"When we get to the workspace, you can check out my system. Let me know the strengths and weaknesses. And please send me the invoice."

"I'm not charging you."

"You run a business, right? I'm not asking you to work for free," she said then grabbed two rolls of fabric.

"My consultations are free," he said then took the fabric from her hands. When Shauna grabbed more fabric, he reached for those rolls as well.

"You know I do this all the time, right?"

"That's because I'm not here when you're doing that, today is different. And something you should get used to."

"Don't play with me, Michael. Because when I get used to it, I'm going to need it all the time."

He winked at her. "Anytime you want it, it's yours."

"I'm holding you to that, all right. Now, let's go."

After loading his car, they headed to Shauna's workspace, and she couldn't stop smiling. For once, she wasn't thinking about another shoe dropping.

* * *

Mike watched Shauna as she draped her mannequins and touched up hems on her gowns. She was in her element, and it looked good on her. "When is the show again?"

"In five days."

"Let me extend my stay uptown so I can be here to see that. Where's your server?" he asked.

She pointed to a door in the back of the studio. He stood up and headed back there. Shauna was focused on getting her show together and he wasn't going to disturb her groove. Checking out her servers and cloud security,

Mike wasn't surprised that things were in good shape. It wasn't as if she'd forgotten her computer science lessons. He did think expanding security features on the encrypted checkout feature of the website would be a good investment for the future. If that was what she wanted. But he knew she was going to need it because her show was going to blow people away. Every time she put one of her samples on a mannequin to tweak it, all he could do was imagine how amazing she'd look taking it off. He knew that wasn't how fashion shows worked. Shauna walked into the server room.

"So, am I at the risk of being hacked and held up with ransomware?" she asked breaking into his thoughts.

"Honestly, no. But you might want to review your

encryption for check out on the site since your sales are going to increase."

"How do you know that?"

"I believe in you and your talent. And I have eyes. These gowns are beautiful."

Shauna smiled and flung herself into Mike's arms. "Thank you for saying that. The closer I get to the show, the more imposter syndrome sinks in."

"You're an amazing designer and you aren't an imposter. Soon everybody is going to know what I know."

"And what do you know?" she asked then brushed her lips against his.

"That I'm holding the next fashion star in my arms right now and I'm never going to let her go." Mike kissed her slow and deep. That was the exact moment that he knew, he was ready to love Shauna the way she deserved to be loved.

* * *

The morning of the fashion show, Shauna woke up at four a.m. and wished she was still wrapped up in Michael's arms. But she couldn't sleep. Every thought was about something she hadn't done and how that one missing piece was going to unravel her entire show. Shauna sat down at her desk and pulled up the show's outline and soundtrack. Of course, everything looked great on the laptop, but what if things didn't work out in reality?

She reached for her cell phone to call Lily when she felt his hand on top of hers.

"Babe," Michael said. "Come back to bed."

"I didn't mean to wake you."

"If that were true then you wouldn't have gotten out of bed."

Shauna turned around to face him. "Michael, I have a lot riding on this show and. . ."

He kissed her lips and reached behind her to close the lid on her laptop. "Your show is at six p.m., come back to bed and get rested."

She sighed and stroked his cheek as she rose to her feet. "Yes, sir," she said. "But sleep is the only thing on the menu."

"Yes, let's sleep because nothing is going to stop your shine today, Shauna." Michael kissed her on the forehead. "I love you."

She took a step back and looked into his eyes. Love was unexpected. But she was on her way to feeling the same way for Michael. He cupped her cheek. "You don't have to say it back now, but I'm glad I have the chance to be here with you at the right time, a time when I can be everything you want and need."

"Stop, stop," she said before covering his mouth with hers.

Michael pulled her against his body as their kiss deepened and caught fire. Shauna broke the kiss and smiled at him.

"Sleep," she said. "We're going to sleep."

"You sure about that?" he asked as he stroked her ass. Shauna groaned.

"Yes, because after the show, it's going to be on," she said then broke away from him. Shauna started for the bedroom and Michael followed with a smile on his face.

Four hours later, Shauna woke up with a start. It was time to get her life together because she had to make sure everything was ready for the show. But how did she end up alone in her bed?

* * *

Mike tried to move quietly in the kitchen. He wanted to fix
Shauna breakfast in bed. Since she had some almost overly

ripe avocados, he decided to make avocado toast, bacon and eggs. But there was a slight problem, he didn't know where anything was in her kitchen. At least the coffee maker was easy to find. He started brewing coffee while looking for a frying pan. While he appreciated her cast iron skillet, he wasn't trying to use that pan for a simple breakfast.

"What are you doing?" Shauna asked, causing him to bump his head as he looked up at her.

"Well, I was trying to surprise you with breakfast," he said. "But I see you're up now."

"I am and that's so sweet," she said. Shauna crossed over to him and kissed him on the cheek. "Had no idea you could cook."

"Breakfast is my jam," he said. "That is when I can find the right pans."

"Above the stove," she said. "What are you cooking?"

"Avocado toast, eggs and bacon," he said.

"Ooh, I'm glad you didn't find the pans. I'm not a fan of eggs. But avocado toast, I'm here for it. Get to cooking, sir," she said with a smile.

Mike grabbed one of the copper frying pans from the cabinet and smiled. "So, avocado toast and bacon. That's even better."

Shauna walked over to the stove and opened the cabinet. "There is no breakfast without grits. And since mine are world famous, I'll take care of making them."

"That kind of defeats the purpose of me sneaking around your kitchen trying to cook for you."

"I'm just glad you thought enough to do it. But I don't play about my grits," she said with a wink.

They worked side by side cooking breakfast and Mike had to admit, Shauna's grits did look legendary. Once everything was done, he ushered Shauna to the table and filled their plates with grits, bacon and avocado toast.

"Now that you know where everything is, it shouldn't be hard for you to make breakfast in the morning," she said as he crossed over to the table.

He smiled as he set their plates on the table. "So, that means I get to spend the night again."

"Yes, you can spend the night and you can cook and surprise me in bed then you can eat me for breakfast."

"Well damn, I can't wait for tomorrow."

"You're going to have to because today is super important."

"I know you're going to kill it."

"From your mouth to God's ears. There is so much riding on this, Michael. Today could be the end or the beginning of my dream."

"Shauna, I've seen your work, this is only the beginning. Stop doubting your greatness."

"Maybe I need you to stick around and be my hype man."

"How about I'm just going to be your man?"

She leaned across the table and kissed him. "Took you long enough to claim your title."

"And just so you know, I'm not giving it up."

"You better not."

They ate breakfast in a satisfied silence until Shauna's cell phone rang and broke the mood. "Here we go," she said as she rose to her feet and crossed over to the breakfast bar to grab her phone. "Yes, Lily."

"I'm in front of your house with a breakfast of champions, but I see you have company. Tell Mike I said he better make sure you aren't late or I'm kicking his stanking ass."

"That's harsh and you know I'm not going to be late today of all days."

"Walk thru is at noon, so ride that morning wood quick and get ready for the fashion takeover."

"Hey, thank you for believing in me and my dream."

"I'm about to get my money back, it has been my pleasure. We're living our wildest dreams, and you finally got your man. Let's go!"

Shauna looked over at Michael as he finished his breakfast. Yes, she had her man, and it was glorious.

* * *

Mike watched Shauna become a director as she worked with the models who were going to walk the runway. Since she was working with real women and not Insta models, the show felt authentic. The clothes were fitted to every body shape. He loved that, loved that Shauna was a designer every woman could love. Her dreams of fashion success were definitely going to come true.

Her dreams of fashion success were definitely going to come true. But would he get his dream? Would Shauna be a part of his life forever?

Mike was doing the work to make sure he was ready for a real commitment, and he was there. All he could do was hope she was too. He couldn't force her to be ready if she wasn't and he shouldn't have waited so long to tell her how much she meant to him.

But he had and now he wondered if there was going to be more than just words. She had a bright career about to kick into the stratosphere.

"All right, I think we're done. I think we're going to have the best fashion show that Charlotte has ever seen," Shauna said. Everyone on stage clapped and Mike whistled as if he'd just watched the most amazing Broadway show. Shauna turned to him and flashed that amazing smile. If he was a block of ice, he would've melted right there.

"Let's head to make up, ladies," Shauna said when she turned back to her models. Once everyone took off for the stations where the makeup artists were, Shauna crossed over to Mike and wrapped her arms around him. "You're taking that hype man position seriously, I see."

He brushed his lips across hers. "Absolutely. I love what this show is going to look like," he said as he held her. "What can I do to help?"

"Can you make sure the live stream links are working?"

"Of course. I can monitor them during the show too," he said.

She kissed his cheek. "You're the best. I got to go check my models and their makeup looks."

"Go on, Boss Lady," he said then gave her a playful smack on the bottom.

"Don't start nothing," she replied with a wink.

"Oh, best believe I'm going to start and finish *something* later."

Shauna ducked backstage and Mike headed for the computer and cameras that would broadcast the show across social media and Shauna's website.

"Well, well, look who's working," Lily said when she walked in the auditorium.

"You're not in the show?" Mike asked.

She shook her head. "I don't do public spectacles, you know. But I have placed my preorder already."

"You and Shauna are what real friends should be like."

"And what are you bringing to my bestie's life?" Lily asked.

"Wow, no beating around the bush with you, huh?"

"Mike, we're too old to beat around the bush. I just want you to be a spot of joy for my friend. Don't make me have to kick your ass because I'm never too old for that."

"Damn, they always said you were mean as hell, I guess the rumors are true."

Lily shrugged and smiled. "But seriously, I'm glad to see you're here for her and that y'all finally made it. Because y'all got on my damn nerves in undergrad."

"What are you talking about?"

"All of us knew good and damn well that y'all were in love or something."

Mike shook his head. "Was it that obvious?"

"Absolutely," she replied. "Well, until you became the football hoe."

"Lily," Mike said. "Do you think. . .nah, never mind."

"Do I think what? You better just go ahead and tell me, because I'm going to jump to the worst case scenario." She hitched her eyebrow up at him.

"I want to marry your friend, but is that something she would want?"

Lily threw her hands up. "That's not a question I would ever answer. If you want to know, you're going to have to ask her. But don't do it today. Let her have the moment she's been earning it for a long time."

"I don't have a ring, so I wasn't going to do it tonight," he said. "And I'd never take the spotlight from where it needs to be. This night is about Shauna and her line."

"I always knew you were smart. Maybe you should go take her some food or a protein bar." Lily handed him a bar from her purse. "And make sure she eats it."

"Yes ma'am," he said with a mock salute.

"Jackass," Lily laughed.

* * *

Shauna was happy that everything was moving at the right pace, makeup, flawlessly done, touch ups on the gowns were done and fit each model perfectly.

But she kept looking for . . .*No! Not doing this. Today isn't about the other shoe, it's going to be fine and successful.* Shauna closed her eyes and tried to think about the showstopper moment at the end of the show. She visualized the applause and the orders for her elegant gowns. . .

"Shauna," Michael said from behind her. "Are you good?"

"Yes, I'm all right, I just need to calm down."

"And eat." He handed her a protein bar. Shauna laughed.

"I see Lily's been here."

"Yeah and I have instructions to make sure you eat." He handed her the bar.

Shauna shook her head as she tore the bar open. Maybe food would clear her mind and make the negative thoughts disappear.

"Thank you," she said after taking a bite. "I needed this."

"Nervous?"

She nodded as she chewed. "But I shouldn't be. I've been wanting this for so long. My team and I have done everything to make this show a success." Shauna took a deep breath. "But I still keep. . ."

"Think about nothing but success. You're showing everybody your talent and vision."

Shauna sighed and nodded. "You're right, I got this."

"Shauna," the photographer called from behind them. "Where do you want me to set up for the show?"

The woman nodded toward Michael. "If it isn't the grumpy groomsman, I know you're not in the show."

"Nope and don't point that camera in my face all day."

She shook her head and laughed. Shauna bumped her hip against his. "We have to take at least one picture together."

Mike leaned in and kissed Shauna on the cheek and the photographer snapped a picture. Shauna smiled and told him, "This one doesn't count because I'm not dressed yet." She turned to the photographer. "Thank you."

"No problem," she said then headed for the stage. Once the woman was out of ear shot, Shauna shook her head.

"I feel so bad because I can't remember her name."

"Jessica, I think. But how are you hiring people when you don't know their name?"

"Clint was the plug. After I saw those wedding pictures, I knew I wanted to work with her. And she went to Smith too. Got to keep the business in the family. She was in our class too, right?"

"I don't think so."

"Oh, okay. Well, I'm done with my bar, so report that to Lily."

"I'm going to leave that to you. Your friend is a little scary."

Shauna laughed. "She's a big softy. Don't let that hard exterior fool you."

"That's some bull right there. She probably kicks puppies."

"You're being rude, she'd kick you before she'd kick a puppy," Shauna said. "Listen, I got to get dressed and you need to make sure my live stream is streaming."

"Yes ma'am but let me kiss you before you get your makeup done," Michael said as he pulled her into his arms. Shauna held his face between her hands and kissed him slow and deep. Michael pressed his body against hers and Shauna moaned as she felt his erection against her thighs. Maybe they could have a quickie and help her release some . . .

"Shauna," Wallace called out. "Oops, I'm sorry."

She turned around and faced her intern. "It's fine, what's up?"

"The showstopper! A seam split on the dress."

"Shit, shit, shit," she exclaimed as she pushed away from Michael. This was the last thing she needed, Shauna thought as she ran down the hall. When Wallace and Shauna walked into the dressing room, she was happy to see the problem wasn't that bad. "Okay, okay, we can fix this. But you're not going to be able to move for about ten minutes. I'm going to have to glue you in."

"What?" Kayla said. "Shauna, I didn't sign up for this."

"It's Got 2b Glue, not Gorilla Glue. I promise it will come off. Listen, you have to be my showstopper, you are everything that my line needs."

"Just know, Greg is going to kick your ass if you damage this beautiful skin I'm in."

"Girl, I got you. No one will ever know."

"You better be sure. I don't want to get stuck in this dress and have to be surgically removed from it, no matter how beautiful it is."

"You think this dress is beautiful?"

"Hell yes and Greg is going to have to buy this one for sure."

Shauna smiled as she fixed the seam. After spraying the wig glue on the dress, she looked at Kayla and gave her a warning. "Please don't sit down for about twenty minutes or you and that chair will be joined at the hip."

Shauna checked on the other models, looking for loose threads and anything that would make her models pop out of the clothes. The last thing she needed was for one of the ladies to be walking and poof, the outfit would be falling off. Her show would not be known for a wardrobe malfunction. She'd never recover, no one would ever want to work with her and . . .

Stop it. Looking for problems will only make more show up, she thought as she took a deep breath.

Then she spotted Jessica taking pictures and saw how all the models were smiling and so relaxed. Women who were her classmates and friends. This was the salve she needed to calm her doubts and focus on the fact that today was amazing.

And so is Michael. Okay, where did that come from? Maybe it was because he has always been the one and now she was seeing it in action. That man was making her feel so good about her dreams and having him in her life. Shauna closed her eyes, and it struck her hard, she wasn't dressed yet. *Fuck!*

She rushed to her dressing room and pulled on her black and gold jumpsuit. Now she was beginning to understand

why Lily loved these suits so much. Shauna was dressed in less than five minutes.

When she sat down with the makeup artist, she closed her eyes and imagined the end of the show with thundering applause and more orders than she could handle.

"Shauna," Wallace called out. "We're ready to go."

She clasped her hands together as she took one last look in the mirror. "It's showtime." Shauna rose to her feet and headed for the wings of the stage.

When she was sure no one was looking, Shauna did a few Muhammad Ali jabs and waited for her cue to take the stage.

"Ladies and gentlemen, please welcome the queen of couture, the woman of the hour, Shauna Carter," the Emcee exclaimed.

Shauna walked out to a thunderous round of applause. She waved to the crowd as if she was Miss America.

"Thank you all for being here tonight. I want to tell you that it means everything to me to have your support. And trust me when I tell you, my designs are for every shape, every

curve that we have and when you wear them, you will be the star of your show. Ladies and gentlemen, I present the Carter Couture Collection."

The lights went down, and Shauna ducked in the wings, watching intently as the models made their way across the stage in the clothes she created. But it was the crowd response that nearly brought her to tears. The applause, the cheers and the ooh's and aww's. Shauna knew her makeup was going to be ruined by the end of the show if she kept this up. She grabbed a paper towel and blotted her tears away.

"You did it!" Lily said in the loudest whisper ever. "I knew this was going to be a smash hit."

"Pinch me, because I'm not sure that I'm not dreaming."

Lily rolled her eyes. "Please tell me that I don't show up in your dreams, because that would be boring as shit."

"Well, usually when you're in my dreams there are guns involved, so I guess I'm wide awake."

"Anyway! Look at this," Lily said as she held her phone up and showed Shauna the website, "Your clothes are selling out fast. We did it, Joe!"

The women hugged and jumped up and down. Then the showstopper came out. And as nervous as she'd been about the seam and using the glue to fix it so that Kayla could be the star of the show, seeing her standing center stage with John Coltrane as her background music in the crystal gown, Shauna really felt as if the sky was the limit for her success.

"That dress is so beautiful, I almost want to get married again," Lily said. And that was the highest compliment Shauna could ever receive.

Now all of the models were on stage, and it was time for Shauna to take her bow. She turned to Lily. "Do I look like I've been crying?"

"No, but so what if you do? This is your moment. Take it!" Lily started clapping as Shauna walked out on to the stage.

* * *

Mike couldn't take his eyes off Shauna as she thanked everyone for supporting the show, she and the models hugged and posed for pictures and all he could think about was seeing her in the crystal wedding dress on their big day. But did she want to get married? Did she want him like that? Their eyes locked and she blew him a kiss.

"What's that all about?" Greg asked as he seemed to appear out of thin air. "Y'all serious, serious now?"

"I love that woman."

"Oh shit. Does she know?"

"Yep and I want to spend the rest of my life with her."

Greg's jaw dropped. "Seriously?"

"Hell yeah. This is the one. Maybe it took time for me to grow up and grow into the man that she deserves."

"The self-awareness is key for me. Often times, we need to make sure when we come into a woman's life that we're everything she needs."

"Big facts. But how do I do this?" Mike asked.

"Well, your woman loves a good show. You better put one on for her. And the perfect place to do it is homecoming."

Mike's mind started spinning. That would be perfect. "Man, you're a genius," he said then gave Greg a tight hug as if they'd won the CIAA championship. "But I'm going to need some assistance."

"Whatever you need, we got you. Clint and I have been waiting for this shit to go down for a long time. But you better go up there and kiss that lady! I'll watch the equipment," Greg said.

Mike headed for the stage and took a beat while the photographer got a group photo before jumping on stage and drawing Shauna into his arms.

"You did it baby! You had over a million people watching your show across all of your platforms."

"For real?" Shauna asked.

Mike nodded. "I'm so proud of you and what you've done here."

Shauna stroked his cheek. "Thank you, thank you for being here and running the live stream for me. You . . ."

Mike captured her lips and kissed her slow and deep. Shauna wrapped her arms around his neck, and it felt as if they were the only people in the world until they heard the cheers from the models on stage with them.

Shauna laughed as they backed away from each other. "I guess we're doing too much right now," she said.

"Or not enough."

Kayla walked over to them with a huge smile on her face. "Ooh, this JCSU love is bubbling. Y'all are so adorable together."

Mike wrapped his arm around Shauna's waist. "She does make me look good, right?"

Nudging him in his side, Shauna shook her head. "Guys don't forget the after party at Aloft in two hours. I hope to see you all there," she said as everyone headed for the dressing room to change.

"Aloft, huh?" Mike asked.

"And if we leave now, we can spend some time alone in my suite before the party."

Mike scooped Shauna into his arms and carried her off the stage. "Don't have to tell me twice."

Epilogue

Homecoming—

Mike made sure he turned his work phone off Friday morning the week of homecoming. He'd told all of his clients that he wasn't going to be available. Emergencies would be handled by the Raleigh office. He had been talking to Clinton and Greg for the last two weeks to get everything set up for the moment he'd waited damn near twenty years for. Okay, maybe not that long, but Shauna Carter was the woman he needed to spend the rest of his life with. She had taken his heart in college, but he wasn't ready or able to be the man she deserved.

Now, he could be that man.

Tonight, was the alumni ball. And he was going to ask his overworked girlfriend to be his wife.

* * *

Shauna didn't like coffee and clearly didn't realize that drinking it mid-morning would lead to an afternoon crash
and burn.

"Shauna, you good?" Lily asked as she shook her friend's shoulder. Shauna was face down on her design desk with an ink stain on the side of her face.

"No! I'm sleepy. I can't believe how many orders we've gotten over the last month and most of these folk want clothes for homecoming."

"At least you're not doing all these shipping and sewing anymore. And our new operation is on point. But honey, you have to rest. And get ready for the alumni ball."

"I think I'm going to skip it and just see y'all at the game tomorrow." Shauna yawned then wiped the ink from her face. Lily rolled her eyes.

"You know if you used your iPad, this wouldn't be happening."

"It's not the same," Shauna replied.

"Not going to argue with you," Lily said. "And you're not
skipping the ball."

"Why? You said it yourself; I need some rest. The same people who will be at the ball are going to be at the game."

Lily shook her head. "Absolutely not. I scheduled a spa appointment for us and it's time to go because you clearly need it, hun."

"Lily, I. . ."

"No one is working today, and the next line can wait thanks to Corey's brilliant work with Belk. It's time to take a break and celebrate," Lily said. "Now, get your ass up and let's go to the spa."

Shauna narrowed her eyes at Lily. "You're being weird, and Michael has been weird this week too, what's going on?"

"How am I being weird? Self-care days are my jam and there's nothing strange about that. I can't speak for your man, but he's probably just excited to hang out with his old football friends."

Shauna shrugged. "Or seeing some ex who. . ."

"Stop that shit. I'm the one who self-sabotages, you're self-aware, remember."

"But something feels off, there have been too many hushed phone calls lately and . . ."

"Girl, let's get to this spa before we lose our reservation."

Now, Shauna was sure there was something going on. Because when in the hell had she laid out possible cheating clues and Lily just let them go without any commentary?

"What are you and Michael doing?" Shauna blurted out.

"Say what now?"

"Lily, I've known you long enough to know when there is something working in the background, and I want to know what it is. I just told you this man is having secret conversations on the phone, and you're worried about missing a spa appointment? Come on now!"

Lily smiled and shrugged. "It took me two months to get this appointment, I'm not going to feed into your crazy conspiracy theories today. Get your shit, Gladys, and let's go."

Yep, her friend was up to something, and she didn't like it. But she wasn't going to turn down this spa appointment.

Once Lily and Shauna arrived at Noire, a new spa in uptown Charlotte, owned by a JCSU alumna, Shauna was beginning to think that she probably overreacted to why Lily wanted to get here so badly.

The blue and white interior of the spa reminded her of a sunny day and the Raspberry Beret video. Soft jazz filled the air and Shauna instantly felt relaxed.

"Since we're here, let me tell you the best part about our treatment today," Lily said as they were led to a room where they could change into plush robes.

"What?"

"V-steaming!"

"Are you serious? Why?"

"I'm single at homecoming and my goal is a one-night stand with somebody's son," Lily said.

"Oh my God, you're ridiculous."

Lily shrugged as she pulled off her clothes and wrapped up in a robe. "Listen, I need a concept for my next book, and this is strictly research."

"Until you get pregnant."

"I rebuke you in the name of Beyonce."

"Don't bring Bey into this. Why are you out here acting as if..."

Lily held her hand up. "I'm not Luther Vandross, I'm not waiting for love. But there's nothing wrong with being like Jodeci." Lily started singing *Freek N You* all off key.

Shauna shook her head and laughed. "You're a whole mess."

"And you say that as if you just met me."

Before Shauna could reply, the spa attendant took them to their first treatment rooms. After three hours of pampering, Shauna and Lily were relaxed and ready to prepare for the alumni ball. Following a quick Google search, they both opted out of the v-steaming, but Lily went with a Brazilian wax. Shauna told her she could've gone her whole life without knowing she'd done that.

After the appointment, she called Michael.

"Hey, beautiful," he said when he answered the phone.

"Hi, what are you doing?"

"Hanging out with Clint and G. We went on campus for a little bit and relived some memories."

"Do I want to know?"

"Yeah, we ran on the field and just so you know, your man smoked them Negroes like a pack of Newports," he said.

Shauna laughed and made herself keep her thoughts light. He wasn't on campus flirting with that AKA or trying to hook up with somebody's daughter like Lily was planning to do with someone's son. "So, do you want to meet at the ball or are . . ."

"Babe, I'm picking you up and giving you the five-star treatment. What time will you be ready?"

"Well, if you stop by early, we can, well you know."

"If I say I'm on my way now, does that give you enough time to get home because. . ."

"I'm here now and I may or may not be naked."

"Yep, I'm on my way. See you soon."

Shauna giggled as she ended the call. He was going to have to explain his strange actions before anything happened between them today, though.

* * *

Mike turned to Clint and Greg. "I got to go, but everything is set, right?"

Greg groaned, Clint rolled his eyes and their wives smiled. Kayla spoke up. "We got the decorations, the special table and the cake. All you need to do is bring the champagne and the ring."

"I know that part, but I feel like I'm forgetting something."

Kayla shook her head. "Where's the ring?"

Mike tapped his jacket pocket and felt the box. "I got it."

"Then calm down, my boy," Kayla said. "We got you."

"Okay, okay, I'm going home to get dressed."

"And be on time," Greg called out to him as he headed out the door. Mike knew he'd be on time because this was the most important night of his life.

When Mike arrived at his west Charlotte home, he took a deep breath and wondered if she would say yes to his proposal. Shauna was riding a wave of success and maybe she didn't want anyone slowing her down. But he had no plans to stand in her way. However, nagging thoughts of being rejected danced in his brain. *Why are you like this?*

Mike grabbed his suit and overnight bag, then headed for the door. As he walked to the car, his phone rang.

"Lily, what's up?" he said when he answered.

"What have you been doing that has Shauna all suspicious? Hushed phone calls? Have you ever heard of texting?"

"I thought I was being careful. Does she know that I'm . . ."

"Quite the opposite, my dude. She's out here with doubts. You better fix it before tonight. See, you should've listened to me and let me plan this."

"You know, you're bossy as hell."

"I'm not bossy, I'm the boss. All jokes aside, Mike Broussard, I'm super happy for you and Shauna. But if you mess this up, these hands are yours."

"I'm not messing up this time. Did that in undergrad and I've learned from my mistakes."

"And you have the ring?"

Mike checked his pocket again for good measure. "Yes."

"All right. See y'all later and congratulations."

"Lily, wait. Do you think she's really going to say yes?"

She groaned. "You two are so damned annoying. This is going to be a marriage made in heaven. I got to go."

* * *

Shauna shook her head as she saw Lily ending her phone call. "Must be a homecoming trend," she said when she approached her friend.

"Business call and I had to remind people that I'm not doing

any work this weekend. Let me get over to my hotel and see if my outfit is back from the cleaners. I had to get it pressed."

"You're wearing one of my designs, right?"

"Absolutely. That gold jumpsuit with the train because you know I love a good jumpsuit."

"Yep, because you secretly think you're Catwoman," Shauna said with a laugh.

"At this point, I'm going to end up fucking the Joker instead of Batman," Lily said with a shoulder shrug.

"You're too much. Try to be well behaved tonight."

"Why would I do that?" Lily laughed and Shauna was a little scared.

"I don't even know why I try," she said as Lily headed for the door. She smiled when she saw Mike walking up the front steps as Lily left.

She stood at the door and waited for his embrace. Michael dropped his bags and scooped Shauna into his arms. "You smell good," he said.

"Spa day with Lily."

He buried his face in her neck. "Do we really have to leave the house?"

"Yes, Negro it's homecoming."

"You know we can . . ."

She brought her finger to his lips. "Don't because if we get started, we won't make the ball and I have to see all of the people dressed in my designs."

"Have I told you how proud of you I am?"

"Several times, but if you want to tell me again, go ahead."

He took her face in his hands. "You followed your dreams and look at you out here killing it. Shauna, I'm so proud of you."

"Kiss me."

Michael captured her lips in a sweet and hot kiss that made her knees quake. Shauna was tempted to say forget the ball and spend the rest of the evening wrapped up in her man. Pulling back from him, she looked into his eyes and all of the thoughts she'd had about the phone calls and things going on that would break them apart floated from her brain like butterflies. When he looked at her, Shauna felt loved. And she loved him right back.

"What if we skipped the ball and just go to the game tomorrow? I'm sure someone will tag me on Instagram."

"No," he said. "I mean, you worked too hard to clothe the alumni not to see it for yourself."

"Fine," she said and thumped him on his chest. "But I want you to kiss me again and then tell me we have to go to this ball."

Michael pulled her closer to his body. "I have to shower and get dressed, but you're really close to making me think skipping the ball is a good idea."

Shauna smiled. "So. . ."

"No, we're not. I'm going to take a shower." He squeezed her ass then let her go. Shauna groaned as she watched him pick up his bags and head upstairs.

Fine, she'd get ready for the ball too.

While Michael showered, Shauna pulled out her dress, which she'd designed. And as much as she wanted to make it a part of her new line, this dress was special because she made it with Michael in mind. The blue and gold gown had a high low hem, the sweetheart bodice accented her shape and made her feel like a goddess. Then there was the cape. The dress was perfect. And easy to take off. Back zippers were great when you had a partner who enjoyed having you naked.

Michael walked into Shauna's bedroom while she was applying her makeup. "Hey babe," he said. "Do you want to get a car to take us to the ball?"

"That's up to you, because you said you were picking me up."

"I'm only asking because Greg and Clint will be at our table, you know they will be bringing some drinks."

"And Lily too. Yeah, we probably should Uber."

"Or," he said holding his phone out to her. "We can take the limo that will be here in an hour."

"Damn, so we don't have time for a quickie?"

He tilted his head to the side. "Seriously?"

Shauna laughed then applied her lipstick. "I was joking because I want to take my time and make slow love to you after the ball. Like slow and deep."

"Stop talking or we won't be leaving," he said in a low growl. Shauna was wet instantly.

"Would it be so bad if we're a little late?" She tugged at his towel and Michael was powerless to resist her. Shauna stroked his dick until he rose to attention.

"Time means nothing." He pressed her backward on to the bed. Shauna peeled her panties off and smiled at Michael.

"Then go slow," she said as she spread her legs. Michael dove between her thighs, face first, kissing her wetness until she screamed his name. Then he sucked and licked her throbbing pearl, Shauna's thighs quivered.

"Michael, Michael, need you. Inside."

One more lick, a little suck and then he was ready to give her what she needed. "You taste so good," he intoned as she wrapped her legs around his waist.

"And," she breathed, "you feel so good." They ground against each other, filling the air with moans of delight and pleasure. Moments later, the couple exploded together. She held on to him tightly and started to tell him they should stay in bed for the rest of the weekend. But Michael took a deep breath and turned on his side, "We'd better get going," he said.

"There's no law saying we have to go."

He turned to face her and smiled. "You know it would be a crime to let my tux go to waste, though and I know your outfit is amazing. We can kick it for an hour and come back for rounds two through twelve."

"Oh, you got it like that Michael?"

"Just for you, babe," he said as he stroked her hip.

"All right, let's go."

The couple dressed and Shauna reapplied her makeup while Michael zipped her dress. Something about this moment felt so natural and right. Turning to face him, she offered him a bright smile. "Michael, it feels good being with you like this."

"I'm glad you allowed me to be a part of your life, after all these years."

"Don't go there. You know you could've been here a lot sooner if you knew how to act."

He shook his head. "You didn't deserve the mess I used to be. I'm thankful you're not holding the past against me."

"We all had to grow and change," she said. "I was never perfect, and we still have our ways, but this is our time."

"You're right about that. Let's go, the limo is outside waiting."

* * *

Mike tried to keep his excitement tampered. But when they got into the limousine and Shauna laid her head on his shoulder, he was ready to pull out the ring and ask her to marry him right then and there. But he hadn't spent all week planning for this engagement announcement to fumble it in the back of the limo. He brushed a kiss across her cheek. "You look so beautiful."

"And you're looking like a whole snack in that tux. We definitely have to take some pictures tonight. I don't want to hear any arguments, either."

"We can certainly do that," he said envisioning her with the six carat diamond and sapphire engagement ring on her finger. Tonight, he'd be happy to have a camera shoved in his face.

Mike held her hand as they rode to the ball. Shauna brought his hand to her lips. "Michael, I love you."

"I love you more, Shauna."

The limo pulled up to the Westin Hotel where the ball was being held. Mike wished he'd thought of dropping rose petals at her feet like in *Coming To America*. Or maybe he should've gotten fireworks. *You don't even know if she's going to say yes.* Okay, he needed his inner critic to shut the fuck up.

The driver opened the door and the couple emerged from the limo. Mike caught a look from Greg who was tapping his watch.

Shauna looked from Mike to Greg. "What's that all about?"

"I lost a bet. But you're the reason why I'm late, so we're going to count that as a win."

She smirked at him as they headed inside. "And what did you lose?"

"Nothing I'll miss," he said then kissed her on the cheek. "I got us a special table."

"Really?"

He nodded. "It's been a while since I've been here for homecoming, and I wanted to make a splash and show off my baby."

"All right let's see this splash," she said as she linked arms with him. Mike led her to the decorated corner where Clint, Destiny, Lily and Kayla were waiting. They'd done a great job with the decorations, gold and blue balloons, sparklers and a chocolate cake.

"What's this?" Shauna asked as she drank in the scene.

"It's about time you two got here," Lily said. Kayla elbowed her in the side.

"Traffic," Shauna replied.

Lily rolled her eyes, Destiny and Kayla smiled at each other. "That's what y'all are calling sex these days?" Kayla laughed.

"Please, the sex isn't why we were late," Shauna said.

Destiny placed her hand up to her mouth and giggled. "Ooh, girl, y'all nasty."

"We really got stuck in traffic," Shauna said as she noticed, Clint, Greg and Michael heading over to the table. She couldn't take her eyes off her man. That tuxedo hugged his body like she planned to do once the ball was over. Grey was a wonderful color on him, whether it was sweatpants or this designer suit.

He walked over to her and kissed Shauna's cheek. "What do you want to drink?"

"From the looks y'all are exchanging, I'm going to say a cup of you, my boy," Greg said.

Shauna rolled her eyes, even though Greg wasn't wrong.

"How about champagne," Lily said as she walked over to the table with two bottles and somebody's son. Shauna glanced at him and realized he was one of their classmates, she just couldn't remember his name. "And this is an upgrade from that swill we had before that Carter Hall party," Lily said.

"Oh, God, I hope so," Shauna said as she reached for a bottle. Lily handed it to her and turned to her new friend.

"Do you have the glasses?"

"Here you go," he said as he handed everyone a champagne flute.

"Didn't you play football?" Shauna asked.

"Yeah, I made these clowns look good."

"Bullshit," Greg said. "Your non tackling ass is why our QB got a broken collarbone."

"Always trying to do things your way," Clint said.

"And getting it wrong," Michael chimed in.

"So, this is jump on Derek night?" he asked with a laugh.

"Not yet," Lily whispered before popping the cork on one of the bottles of Ace of Spades champagne. Shauna shook her head and said a silent prayer for Derek if her friend got him alone.

"I'm glad we're all here together," Michael said. "It's been a while."

"Yeah, you acted as if you couldn't come back to Smith once you. . .Left for Raleigh," Clint said.

"Funny, but I'm going to be honest, I didn't come back to homecoming because I thought I was going to see Shauna sitting here with some dude she called her husband."

Her eyebrow shot up and she shook her head. Michael sat beside her and took her hands in his. "But it took a wedding to bring us back together."

"You're welcome," Destiny said.

Shauna started to roll her eyes because they'd only been at the wedding because of Clint. "Anyway," Michael continued. "Next homecoming, I really hope to see Shauna's husband right here by her side."

"What are you saying, Michael?" she asked.

"I'm asking you to be my wife and make me the happiest Golden Bull in the world." He reached into his pocket and pulled out a black velvet box.

"Michael," she breathed as he opened the box, revealing a sparkling diamond and sapphire ring. It was beautiful. Just like the ring she'd told Lily about when they were in college. Shauna looked around at her friends and it all clicked. They knew he was going to. . .

"Shauna, will you marry me?" Michael asked. She stroked his cheek.

"Yes, yes," she exclaimed, causing her friends and everyone else in earshot to cheer. Michael stood up and lifted Shauna into his arms as they kissed.

Lily popped another bottle of champagne and smiled at her friends. "This is beautiful, right?" Derek asked as he bumped his hip against hers.

"For them, it sure is." Lily filled his glass. "But I want less." She walked over to the happy couple and refilled their flutes. "Mike Broussard, you did good."

"I finally got it right and I'm going to spend the rest of my life with the love of my life," he said as he stared into her eyes. "Michael, I love you and I can't wait to spend every tomorrow with you," Shauna said.

Applause erupted again as Michael and Shauna kissed.

The End

After Halftime
Story Two

Chapter One

Homecoming –

Autumn Brown-Robinson closed her eyes and took a deep breath. Walking was harder these days, but she knew this was going to happen. Today, though, she needed to push through it because she had some important things to handle.

She had to get her college friends together one more time and she wasn't about to allow shortness of breath to get in her way.

However, her son, Tyler, had a different idea. "Mom," he said. "You know we can sit down."

"I'm fine. I've been walking this campus since before you were born. As a matter of fact," she pointed to Smith Hall, "That's where you were conceived."

"Eww, I could've gone my whole life without knowing that. Can we bring back parents being scared to talk about sex
with their kids?"

Autumn pinched his cheek. "You're a legend, own it, baby boy. Your Dad was. . ."

"One of the best drum majors to ever lead the IIOS," he recited a line he'd heard all his life. Autumn laughed because Johnson C. Smith's marching band, known as the International Institution of Sound, was legendary.

"Whatever," she said then coughed.

They made it to the block and Autumn smiled, remembering the time she and her girls put on an impromptu performance after lunch in the center of the space. Everyone outside had been watching and rocking back and forth to their acapella vocals.

Nicole Clarke had written the hell out of that song based on her cheating Army boyfriend. Vivian Leslie had put her soul into the song, even though she hadn't felt a tiny piece of heartbreak at that time.

That was the beginning . . . of the end.

Fall, 1996—

It had been raining all day and that gave Autumn a chance to stay inside and work on some dance moves. Sure, she could've gone to her psychology class, but she had that class on lock and missing one day wouldn't kill her GPA.

Besides, the girls needed new moves and she had them. Dancing had to be a part of their act because everyone on campus loved the Blue Satin dancers and Destiny's Child. Not to mention the icon Janet Jackson.

Autumn had been a Blue Satin dancer for about six months, but then she decided that she wanted more creativity and more range with her choreography. Something the coach wasn't feeling and since Autumn wasn't on scholarship, she didn't mind quitting.

Too bad Sonia had to stay on the squad and attend every

practice. Autumn was happy she could cut her hair like Halle Berry now.

Sure, her mother was going to hate the new style, but technically, she was grown, and she could do what she wanted.

"Knock, knock," Nicole said as she walked in Autumn's room.

"I really got to start locking my door," she said as she tossed a pillow at her friend.

"I said knock, knock," Nicole replied as she caught the pillow and looked down at it. "Didn't I give you this?"

"Yes, that's why it's my weapon of choice when I see you."

Nicole rolled her eyes and set the pillow on the edge of the bed. "I just wrote a song and got us some studio time."

"For real? How did you do that?" Autumn asked excitedly.

"Well, I took a walk across campus and when I got down by Brayboy. . ."

"Nigga, I'm talking about the studio time." Autumn tossed the pillow at her friend again.

"I went to an open mic session last week—you know the one you losers didn't want to go to—and I met a guy who was impressed with my poetry. So, I said you should hear my words put to music."

"And y'all fucked and he offered you studio time?"

This time Nicole used the pillow as a weapon and threw it at Autumn's head. "No, I'm not falling for the banana in the tail pipe trick, again. I sang the chorus to our new song, and he was impressed."

"We actually have real studio time?"

Nicole nodded. "But there's one little issue."

"I knew there had to be some kind of catch," Autumn sighed.

"We can't get in until like three in the morning, tomorrow."

Autumn threw herself across the bed. "What the hell?"

"I know, I know, but a free demo. We have to take a chance for our music. You saw how everyone went crazy for us on the Block last week. That means something."

"It does and I just can't wait to see you convince Vivian and Sonia to give up their beauty sleep to cut a demo."

Nicole smiled and pointed at Autumn, "It's time for us to be Batman and Robin. We want our group to take off and what's sleep when you're shooting for success? Larry said he would play our song on the radio station if we had a demo, so. . ."

"We're talking about a radio station that no one off campus can hear," Autumn said with an eye roll.

"He also just got an internship at Power 98, the station that everyone and their mama listens to. And you know Nate Quick plays new artists all the time. This could be exactly what we need." Nicole bounced with excitement. "Come on, Autumn, this is what we've been waiting for."

"We're going to do it. But if we're going to convince the other two, there has to be food involved. Let's get some Chicken King and act like this is the biggest news we've ever heard."

"Chicken King? I got my work study check; we can do better than that greasy shit," Nicole said.

"And what do you suggest?"

"Simmons. Some good soul food."

Autumn nodded. "I can totally get with that, and I have twenty dollars to add to the pot. I want macaroni and cheese."

"Then let's go and be ready when they get out of class."

Nicole and Autumn rushed to the parking lot and hopped into Nicole's red Chevy Beretta and headed for the restaurant.

Nicole was the group's taxi driver, when Vivian needed a ride to work, Nicole took her.

When they needed to run to the grocery store or head out to a restaurant, Nicole was the one who drove. Each member of the group had talent and combined; they were a force to be reckoned with. The campus knew it, now they wanted the world to know.

"Guess who had the nerve to call me today," Nicole said as they stopped for a red light.

"If you say Nathan, I'm going to jump out the car," Autumn said.

"Don't jump out the car because it was him. Son of a bitch. He had the nerve to tell me that I don't listen, and I only hear what I want to hear. That's why I can't say he cheated on me because we were never in a relationship."

"The fuck? I mean, I read the letter he wrote you and . . ."

"I quote, 'I was lonely, and I knew you were the only one who would write me back.' So, I was like you fuck dumb bitches, bet, forget you know me."

"Wow."

"And then I wrote the song, *Forget You Know Me*. I haven't figured out if it's a ballad or an up-tempo fuck off anthem."

"Let's do it ala Destiny's Child style, we can do two versions of the song if the studio time allows us to do it," Autumn said. "Look at how big of a hit *No, No, No* is."

"I'm not sure how much time we're going to have, but we can totally make it happen. I'm thinking about getting a job since I can't live off this work study check and prepare for our album. I have to save some money so we can get more studio time and at least cut an LP."

"You don't have to do that alone," Autumn said. "Nicole you spend a lot of your money doing stuff for the group. I think all of us need to chip in. It's not like we have a Matthew Knowles supporting us. My mother said I need to focus on my degree and stop pretending that I can sing. We got to be successful just to prove her evil ass wrong."

"Ahh, Autumn, I'm sorry."

She shrugged. "It's fine. I never expected her or the people back home to support me doing something like this, being successful in college or the singing."

"We should be supported in our dreams. It's not fair when the people you love don't believe in you."

"That's why the four of us need to stick together forever. No one is ever going to know what we've gone through when we get that first Grammy."

"Damn right," Nicole said. "We're going to make it and everyone who didn't believe in us can just suck it."

"And choke!"

When they arrived at the restaurant, Autumn and Nicole were sure of two things, they were going to win a Grammy and they should've called their order in first.

Chapter Two

It took an hour for the food to be prepared and Autumn was sure Vivian and Sonia were probably eating in the cafeteria. Even if they were, she knew her friends wouldn't turn down Simmons. "This food smells delicious," Nicole said as she drove. "Hopefully it does the trick, and we can get the crew to agree to the late-night studio session."

When they arrived on campus, Autumn was happy to see Vivian and Sonia in front of Greenfield Hall. "Good, we don't have to carry all of this on our own," Nicole said then blew the horn at her friends. Autumn rolled the window down.

"We got food," she said.

"And if you want to eat, y'all have to help us get it out of the car," Nicole called out.

Vivian and Sonia crossed over to the car with smiles on their faces.

"Thank goodness you brought food because the café was on some bullshit today."

"I don't even know why y'all continue to fool with Food Done Yesterday. They put chemicals in the food to make sure you don't get horny," Nicole joked.

"Well, we know that isn't true," Vivian said with a laugh. "What were you doing last night?"

"I don't eat in the café," Nicole retorted. "But I'm not the one who was out here doing the Tootsie Roll with the basketball team three nights ago."

"That was simply dancing; besides, those boys would do nothing but derail my career."

"Speaking of a career," Autumn said. "We have a chance to make a demo!"

Sonia nearly dropped the bag she was carrying. "Are you serious? Like in a real studio and not someone's closet in Carter Hall, right?"

"Yes," Nicole said. "We have actual studio time in a real studio, thanks to my connections."

Vivian rolled her eyes. "You're never going to let us live this down when we win our first Grammy, are you?"

"Nope," Nicole said with a smile. "Let's eat so that we can go over the details."

Sonia and Vivian exchanged a look. "What's there to discuss? Just tell us when and where we need to be," Sonia said.

"Who gets the fried chicken or the baked chicken," Autumn said. "Because the mac and cheese belongs to me."

"You mean ours," Vivian said. "I'm not eating meat this week."

Nicole rolled her eyes. "Why are you doing that mess again?"

"Because I can," she said as she ran her hand across her flat belly. "But I do want a drum from one of the fried wings. Where are we eating?"

"We can go to my room," Autumn said.

"How are you so lucky to have a single room with no annoying roommate?" Sonia said then hip checked Vivian.

"You're blessed to have a roommate like me," she replied with a smile.

"Umm, the food is getting cold," Nicole said. "Let's eat."

"So, what are the details about the studio time?" Vivian asked as they walked into Autumn's room. Autumn and Sonia pulled out one of the TV trays Autumn used when she was entertaining, which was something she did a lot. The perks of not having a roommate.

Nicole smiled as they opened the boxes of soul food. "There's this DJ we all know who spins at Club 607 and he's a producer now."

Sonia rolled her eyes. "Are you serious? I know you're not talking about Walter McGee. We're supposed to believe that old square head DJ is giving away studio time? What's the catch?"

"I wasn't convinced at first, but then I met three of his artists, heard their demos and they were top notch. That's when I told him to put his hormones away and played that video we made during our performance on the Block."

"What did he say?" Vivian asked.

Autumn shook her head and laughed internally because Nicole carried the video tape of their performance everywhere she went.

"He said with the right demo we could make some great connections and get a deal."

"With So-So Def, I hope," Autumn said then dug into the mac and cheese.

"That would be great because we can sing way better than Escape," Sonia said.

"It's *Xscape*," Vivian corrected. "And remember, we don't have competition. We're above the rest."

"The absolute best," Nicole exclaimed.

Autumn crinkled her nose. "So, what's our group name again? And we need something that just rolls off the tongue, nothing that folks confuse with a whole other word."

"Right," Sonia said. "We should be Neo-Soul Divas."

The other three rolled their eyes. Sonia really wanted that name. And the last thing the rest of the group wanted to be thought of was as a bunch of divas.

"What if we us our initials, the NASV," Autumn suggested. Silence engulfed the room.

"You know, that's not half bad until someone calls us nasty or something worse," Nicole said.

"The Crystals," Vivian blurted out.

"What year is it, 1960?" Sonia retorted. "We need a name that says on people's lips and makes them water with anticipation."

"I got it, LoveSpell," Nicole said. "I mean that's the most known Victoria's Secrets scent and . . ."

"Wait, we could be Sensual Secrets," Vivian said. "Not that Love Spell isn't a decent name, but then we're stuck to having ballads be our main thing."

Nicole and the others nodded. "I like it," Nicole said. "It gives us sexy, cool and amazing."

Autumn and Sonia slapped high fives. "Can we eat now?" Autumn asked.

"Sure, but with a name like Sensual Secrets, this is going to have to be our last heavy meal," Vivian cautioned. "Our audience is going to expect sexy."

Nicole rolled her eyes. "Fuck that," she said. "We're going to eat good, and they will take the bodies they get. We're not

going to get an eating disorder to have a career."

"Florence Ballard was fine the way she was," Sonia shouted.

"And so was Effie White," Autumn said, now appreciating her parents for taking her to see *Dreamgirls* when she was ten, even if it wasn't anywhere near Broadway.

"Who is Effie White?" Vivian asked.

"*Dreamgirls*," Nicole said. "Jennifer Holliday." Nicole started singing the signature song and the rest of the women joined in. They hadn't realized they had an audience until they hit the final note and heard applause coming from the doorway.

"Y'all got a CD yet?" one of the listeners asked.

"It's coming soon," Nicole said then flashed a look at her band mates. "So, are we going to the studio or not?"

"Yes," everyone exclaimed.

Chapter Three

Despite Autumn's beliefs that Vivian and Sonia wouldn't go to a studio at three in the morning, the four of them pulled up to a white nondescript building on Nations Ford Road at 2:55 a.m.

"This better not be the beginning of a horror movie," Sonia said as she got out of the car.

"Calm down, scary," Nicole said then pointed toward the entrance. "He's waiting for us right there."

"That doesn't make me feel much better," Sonia said as the group headed toward the front door. Autumn gripped her pepper spray just in case things took a turn in the wrong direction. But she was praying that Nicole hadn't led them to their doom.

"Ladies," the man said. "I'm glad you made it here safely and on time. DJ McGee is ready for you all in the studio. I'll take you there."

"Thank you," Vivian said with a smile. Even though she didn't ask to be, Vivian was the public face of the group. She knew when to be flirty, when to be crisp and professional and when to let Nicole cuss everybody out. It was the perfect balance.

The man took them to a state-of-the-art studio, which made them all breathe a sigh of relief. Tonight, wasn't going to be a prelude to a *Dateline* episode after all.

"Good morning, ladies," McGee said. "I'm glad y'all are on time, I wish I could say that for other acts I work with. Y'all got that drive in you."

"We're ready to share this talent with the world," Nicole said then handed him a folder with their sheet music.

McGee tilted his head to the side. "Umm, I don't have studio musicians. I thought y'all had a CD with your background tracks on it."

"We have that too, but I thought..." Nicole stopped short as Autumn handed him the CD.

"I hope you're worth the hours of sleep and studying we're losing," Autumn muttered.

McGee smiled. "I mean, if sleep is all that's keeping you from being the next big girl group, then you need to wake up. And I have some ideas of how I could keep you up all night."

Autumn rolled her eyes, thinking that he was just gross.

"Can we get started?" Sonia snapped.

"All right, no need to be impatient. We're going to get to it," he said. "I have to mix this song and then, you guys go in the booth."

Sonia glared at him, and Vivian placed her hand on her shoulder. "So," Vivian began. "Do you have water or tea for us, since we have to sit here and wait?"

McGee shrugged. "Got some Hennessy and weed."

The women glared at him. "I'm sure one of these shiftless

Negroes can go to the damn Circle K and get four bottles of water," Vivian exclaimed then she grabbed her throat. "Got me in here straining my voice."

"Look," McGee boomed. "Y'all bitches in here for free and you're asking for a lot. I'm just trying to make sure y'all get a fucking demo."

"And we appreciate that," Nicole said. "But we need to make sure our voices are ready. We're not rappers, McGee."

He folded his arms across his narrow chest. "My bad, I forgot this is why I don't work with R&B singers. Y'all be acting like divas for real. Leroy! Yo Leroy, come get these broads some water and tea or whatever the hell they said."

When "Leroy" walked into the room where they were, Autumn couldn't take her eyes off him. Tall, cocoa brown skin with coal black eyes that seemed to pierce her soul.

"McGee, you know my name is not Leroy and you got one more damn time," he snapped.

"Nigga, just because your people own the building, don't mean. . ."

"It means I can shut this bitch down if I feel like it," he growled. Autumn wanted to hop in his arms and let him do anything that he wanted to do to her. She wasn't normally this girl, lusting over a foul mouth stranger, but. . .

"My name is Wilson, and you need to remember that" he said. Wilson turned his angry glare on the women. His face softened and he smiled. Autumn was undone. The dimples got her.

"Wilson, I can go to the store with you and show you exactly what we need," Autumn said.

Vivian, Sonia and Nicole shot Autumn a questioning look. "I got this," she mouthed then turned back to Wilson. "Are you ready?"

"You're sure you want to hop in the car with a stranger?"

"I'm trying to give you a chance to say I knew her when," she quipped.

"You're cute and funny. Do y'all want something to eat from the Waffle House or IHOP?" he asked.

"Oh, my God, IHOP, please," Nicole exclaimed. "I just want a Rooty Tooty Fresh and Fruity with blueberries."

"I want one with strawberries," Vivian said. "But sub the bacon for hash browns."

"I just want one pancake with powdered sugar and butter," Sonia said.

Wilson turned to Autumn. "You got all of that?"

She nodded. "I know what these weirdos like. Let's go."

Wilson headed for the door and held it open for Autumn. "You should really find a better studio if you really want to record a great sounding album."

"We're just doing the demo here and then it's off to Atlanta," Autumn said. "Or Houston."

"Aww, y'all got skills like that for real?"

Autumn nodded. "We're talented. But what's your story? You really don't seem like a rapper or . . ."

"I'm not. I'm a business manager. My father believes in throwing his kids in the deep end of the life pool. He bought this studio and told me to do something with it. So, I rent it to assholes like McGee. But I'm not trying to have police harassing us, so I make sure there are no illegal activities going on. If I'm honest, I thought you ladies were . . ."

"Don't say it, I was trying to decide if I like you or not."

He smiled and Autumn returned the gesture. "I tell you what, let me take you out for coffee tomorrow, that is if you wake up after this session, and you'll have all the evidence you need to confirm you like me."

"No choice but to wake up, I have class in the morning."

"Class? You're in high school? What the hell. . ."

"I'm in college. I attend the Johnson C. Smith University."

"Oh, no wonder y'all not scared. Living on the west side is tough. I thought about going to Smith, but I thought I was going to leave Charlotte."

"Are you a college dropout?" she asked.

"Ha, no," he said. "Look, I was just trying to make sure that I wasn't hanging out this time of night with a minor. You have such a baby face."

"That sounds. . ."

"Fine, you're just beautiful. Better?"

"Much," Autumn said as heat rose to her cheeks.

They hopped into Wilson's Mustang and Autumn watched him as he started the muscle car. "Wilson, if you own the studio, why would you tell us to go somewhere else?"

He shrugged as he shifted the car into first gear. "Because I know the equipment needs to be upgraded, I just haven't figured out how to do that yet with my current budget."

"Sounds like you need to go back to school then."

"Are you going to be my roommate?" he asked as they merged on to the interstate.

Autumn laughed. "Absolutely not. You seem like you don't pick up your socks."

"You're assuming that I wear socks."

"Oh, so you got corn chip feet. Yeah, the roommate thing isn't going to work for us. Maybe you can visit."

He shook his head as he took the Woodlawn Road exit. "I really need IHOP to start taking orders over the phone, because driving over here to get food to go and waiting like I'm sitting at a table is annoying."

"You sound like you need a nap," Autumn said with a yawn.

"I'm not the one who has to sing in a couple of hours."

"Why do producers do this? They don't have to schedule everyone at the same time."

"Welcome to the music business. Don't forget that this is a business and you and your group better protect yourselves. Get a lawyer and an agent as soon as possible."

"You know a lot about this stuff, I see."

He nodded as he turned into the restaurant's parking lot. "A lot of talented people get taken advantage of because they forget about the business part. Friends become enemies and someone always gets screwed."

"You're a ball of sunshine," she said sarcastically.

"Would you prefer that I lie to you? If you and your girls are serious about being entertainers, make sure you know what you're getting into."

"Let's get the food and hope we can eat after we record our demo."

Wilson shrugged and pulled into a spot in front of the restaurant. "Just keep your eyes open, if y'all are as good as you say."

"Baby, we're better than I said. I was being humble."

"Excuse me," he said as he got out of the car, then crossed over to the passenger side to open Autumn's door. "Let me soak up every moment with you since y'all are going to be bigger than the Supremes."

"You got it, dude." She flashed him a thumbs up sign.

After they walked into the restaurant, they waited in line to order their food. Autumn surreptitiously checked Wilson out. He was even finer under the overhead lighting in the restaurant. He had a chipped front tooth that added to his appeal for some reason. His tee shirt seemed to be hiding a six pack and she wondered how he'd feel if she asked him to pull up his shirt. Now she wished she'd taken that photography class a little more seriously and bought a camera. Then she could've made up some bullshit about a photo shoot and see what he was working with.

"Is everything okay? Do I have a booger hanging out of my nose or something?" he asked breaking into her wanton thoughts.

"What?"

He closed the space between them. "You keep staring at me like you want something. Just say it."

Autumn opened her mouth, but the host called Wilson's name. Their food was ready, and she needed to put her hormones back in her pocket.

Chapter Four

Autumn smiled as she watched Wilson treat the hostess with such respect. That made her wonder what kind of man he was. Tortured rich boy? Wanna-be music mogul? A good kisser? He had layers and she liked that. *Bring it down, girl. You need to focus on what's important and that's not him.*

"Autumn, did I forget anything?" he asked breaking into her thoughts.

"Umm, I don't think so. You got the syrup, right?"

"Hot maple, although it will probably be cold by the time we get back," he said as he nodded toward the cup on the counter.

"That's smart," Autumn said with an eyeroll. "I hope there's a microwave in the building."

"There's one there, but I suggest you don't use it. I found hair in it this morning. Great reminder, I have to fire the janitorial staff," he said with a finger snap.

"You're mean."

"Don't judge me because I have standards. The last thing I want is to have my building overrun with crap and get a reputation for that. Charlotte is a big town, not a real city yet."

"I guess since you're from here, you can say that." Autumn shrugged, thinking about the small town she'd grown up in. Charlotte was a big city compared to her one stoplight hometown.

Wilson tilted his head to the side. "Let me guess, you're a small town girl and this is your first stepping stone?"

She nodded. "And for the record, I think Charlotte is a great place."

"Don't get me wrong, I love my city, but I know more is out there. Isn't that why y'all come to college?"

"I'm starting to feel like you have something against college students."

"No, I don't. I mean, I told you that I want to go to Smith, especially if there are more girls around the campus who look like you."

Autumn rolled her eyes. "So, you just want to be a campus playboy. Ooh, do you have a pen? I need to write that title down and see what Nicole can do with it."

He reached into his pocket and handed her a Bic pen. Autumn grabbed one of the cardboard inserts from the menu and wrote *Campus Playboy* on it. As she tucked the insert in her pocket, the hostess brought their order out.

"I put some more hot syrup in here for y'all," she said while focusing on Wilson. "I hope you enjoy your meal."

Autumn hid her disgusted laughter. She had no reason the feel any kind of way about this woman flirting with Wilson, but waitstaff in Charlotte did that a lot.

Ignoring the woman at the table and focusing on the man. Little did most of those people know, if Autumn was at the table, she was the one leaving a tip. Even if the service was bad.

"You're ready?" he asked when he noticed that Autumn had paused.

"Yes, sorry."

They headed out to the car and Wilson opened the door for Autumn then placed the food in the back seat. The ride back was quiet, save Jodeci blasting through the speakers. When *Love U 4 Life* started playing, Autumn sang along as if she was the fifth member of the group.

"Whoa," Wilson said as she sang. "You sound amazing. Do the others have a voice like yours?"

Autumn smiled and thought about her group mates, Vivian was the voice everyone recognized, but everyone could sing,

and their harmonies rivaled En Vogue's and Boyz II Men's. The talent was there and when the right person – not just DJ McGee – heard them, the sky would be the limit.

"Yeah, we can all sing."

"Nah, you were *sanging*. I might stick around to hear y'all's session. Just so I can say, I knew them when they recorded their demo in my studio."

Autumn laughed as he turned into the parking lot of the studio. When they walked in, Autumn saw that her girls were pissed. Vivian was scowling, Sonia's hands were clenched into fists and Nicole was pacing. This was looking bad.

"What's going on?" Autumn asked as Wilson set the food on an empty chair.

Vivian glared at McGee who was dancing to a beat blasting in the studio. "This motherfucker is annoying. He keeps pushing our time back and I'm getting sick of it."

Sonia walked over to the food and grabbed a cup of water. "You get what you pay for," she muttered. "I should've known this was too good to be true."

"Listen," Nicole said. "If I had known this was going to be bullshit, I would've taken out a student loan and paid for studio time from someone else."

Wilson crossed over to McGee. "You know you have to be out of here by five-thirty, right? Stop fucking around with these women and get them in the booth."

"Listen, you. . ."

"Do you think you're going to keep using my facility when you keep screwing people over and wasting my electric? Suppose CMPD shows up. How many people, not including these ladies, are going to jail for outstanding warrants and drug possession?"

McGee rolled his eyes. "Which one of these hoes are you fucking?"

"Are you serious? Get them in the booth and then get your shit and get out of here."

"For the night, right?"

Wilson folded his arms across his chest. "Depends on the quality of the demo. Get moving."

McGee shut the music off then waved for the women to head inside.

"Thank you," Autumn mouthed as they walked into the recording booth.

Two hours later, the demo was done, and Wilson walked the women out to their car. Vivian was ecstatic and bouncing around as if she had engulfed a pot of coffee. "We did it!" she exclaimed. "We're going to be stars. Did you hear that playback. The harmonies, the ad libs and my goodness, Nicole, your changes to the lyrics were amazing. Almost makes the bullshit we went through tonight worth it."

"Pump your breaks," Nicole said. "We don't have a deal and we only got to record three songs. We have to. . ."

"Can we go back to campus? Shit, I'm sleepy," Sonia said.

Wilson laughed and touched Autumn's shoulder. "You were right. All of y'all can sing. Bella."

"What did you say?" Vivian asked.

"All of y'all. . ."

"No, no," she said waving her hands. "Bella. That's what our group name should be."

Everyone nodded in agreement and Sonia wasn't so sleepy anymore. "Oh, shit yes! We need to get some photos taken and send them out with the demo. You know Sid owes me a favor and since he's the main photographer for the yearbook, he has a camera."

"And access to developing the pictures for free," Autumn exclaimed.

"What about Jessica? She takes amazing pictures too. Sid is a point and shoot type of guy," Vivian said.

The women nodded in agreement.

"We can check with both of them," Sonia said.

"We need new outfits," Nicole said. "So that we look like the *beautiful* singers we're claiming we are."

"I'm going to let you ladies get to it," Wilson said. "Just give me a shoutout in the album notes." He turned to Autumn and stroked the back of her hand. "But you have to call me after your photo shoot. I owe you dinner and you should give me a tour of JCSU."

"All right," Autumn said. "I need your number, though."

He handed her a scrap of paper. "Don't lose this."

She smiled demurely. "I won't."

Her friends let out low whistles as Wilson walked away. "Okay, what did y'all do at IHOP?" Nicole asked.

"We just talked. Anyway, let's go shower, take a nap then shop." Autumn yawned. "We got a demo, y'all!"

Homecoming, Present Day –

Autumn took in a deep breath as she finally took her son's advice and sat down on one of the blue benches on the block. "I really don't remember campus being this big," she said with a smile.

Tyler rolled his eyes. "You can stop the act," he said quietly. "The campus is the same size it's always been and you're doing too much to try and. . ."

"Tyler, I don't know who you think you're talking to, but I suggest you watch your tone."

He folded his arms across his chest and Autumn couldn't help laughing. That boy was his daddy's twin. "Ma, can you stop acting like your illness is a joke," he said with tears wailing up in his eyes.

"Baby boy," she said quietly. "I'm not doing that. But I'm not going to let this sickness beat me. I have one thing I want to do and I'm going to do it. Let me have that, all right?"

He sat down beside her and wrapped his arms around her shoulders. "Fine," he said with resignation lifting his voice. "But I'm going to be watching you and when you start looking like you're doing too much, I'm pulling the plug and I'm going to call Dad."

"You're really blackmailing me?" she said with a look of wide eyed wonderment on her face.

"Ain't no fun when the rabbit has the gun, huh?" Tyler laughed.

"How are you using my words against me?"

He shrugged then looked at his watch. "I got to go to band practice. When is auntie Sonia getting here?"

"Did I hear my name?" Sonia's high pitched voice exclaimed from behind them. Autumn leapt to her feet and crossed over to Sonia. The women enveloped each other in a tight hug. Sonia pulled back and looked at Autumn with a huge smile on her face. "You look good, babe," she said.

"So do you," Autumn replied. "And look at your nephew."

Sonia turned to Tyler and grabbed his hand. "You out here looking like your daddy. Oh, my goodness. I just hope you're not acting like him when he was in undergrad."

"Hey, Auntie," he said. "And I'm going to plead the fifth in front of my Mama."

"Smart man," Autumn said.

"How's school going?" Sonia asked as she smiled at him.

"I'm ready to graduate and make sure . . ."

"Slow down, son," Autumn said. "Enjoy the last year of not having grown up responsibilities."

"I got to go, can't be late for practice," Tyler said before leaning in and kissing his mother and Sonia. As he ran toward the band room, Sonia and Autumn took a seat on the bench.

"I can't believe we're back here," Sonia said. "After everything that happened."

"I'm kind of glad to be home again. Smith wasn't all bad, you know. And I have to tell you something," Autumn said.

"What's going on?"

"We need to get Bella back together, one last time."

"Are you high? Or you've become a magician? I know good and damn well . . ."

Autumn gripped Sonia's wrist. "Sonia, I'm dying."

She gasped as she looked at her friend. "Autumn, no. . . You. No."

"Outside of my family, you're the only person who knows and I'm not going into details about what's wrong. But I want my three best friends back and not just because I'm sick. We let all the wrong things pull us apart and we need to fix it because life is too short for petty bullshit. We were always more than just the singing group."

"How are we even going to do this? I haven't heard from Vivian and Nicole since *that night.* How are we even going to make that happen?"

"That was a night from hell." Autumn shook her head.

Sonia rolled her eyes. "Tell me about it. I can't watch *Dreamgirls* because we lived it, but without the success."

"You know that movie wasn't real, right?"

Sonia shrugged. "Maybe not, but that's the path so many female groups take. I was really hoping we'd be more like TLC than. . .Listen, I know you're not trying to record something."

Autumn shook her head. "I want us to love each other again. Are you going to help me or not?"

"Of course, but do you know how to get in touch with them?"

Autumn nodded. "Sure do. We're starting with Vivian tonight."

"How?"

"She's right here in Charlotte. We're going to the club."

Sonia frowned. "Now you know we're too old to be clubbing and your health is . . ."

Autumn held her hand up. "Viv owns the club where the Alumni Association is hosting happy hour. I know she's going to be there to show off her success." She opened the browser on her smartphone and showed it to Sonia.

"Well, damn," Sonia said as she read the article about the success of Vivian's club and the music scholarship she

sponsored at Johnson C. Smith. "Look at Miss Superstar still being a diva with a heart."

"So, we'll go at six?"

"Fine. Where are you staying?"

"The Doubletree."

"Ooh, me too. Let's go get some food and not Chicken King, because I'm not trying to relive my bubble guts from twenty-five years ago," Sonia joked. The women stood up and Autumn sent Tyler a text message letting him know that Sonia was taking her back to the hotel and not to worry about her.

Chapter Five

Fall, 1997—

Bella was a restless group. They'd sent their demo to all their favorite record companies, not really knowing how this thing worked. Of course, DJ McGee wasn't speaking to them anymore and Nicole couldn't get the details from him about what their next steps should've been to get a record deal. Autumn was sure that creep didn't know.

"Mail call," Sonia said as she burst into Autumn's room, the unofficial group headquarters.

"Please let a contract be in one of those envelopes," Vivian said as Sonia dropped the mail on the desk.

"Where's Nicole?"

Vivian shrugged. "Said she was going to write. But I think she's sneaking off with Sid. They've gotten close since he took those pictures for us."

"I know and I'm glad we got all of our negatives because you know how Nicole's relationships go," Sonia laughed.

"Y'all are rude," Autumn interjected. "They seem to be happy. And her songs are more upbeat these days."

"But she writes better when she's angry," Vivian said.

"Black women don't get the option to be Alanis Morrisette," Sonia pointed out.

Before anyone could reply, the door swung open, and Nicole walked in with a huge smile on her face and her brown eyes twinkling. "Great news!"

"We got a record deal?" Vivian asked.

"Better. We might have a manager," she said then plopped down on the bed beside Autumn. "Sid and I were at Eastland Mall, and I was singing to him. This lady walked over to us and started asking about what church I sang with and all of that."

"Oh Lord, not a preacher's wife trying to be our manager," Vivian said with an eyeroll.

"That's what I thought at first," she said. "But she said the magic words, I have connections with major record companies. And she wants to meet us. I told her we would because what we've been doing isn't working." Nicole nodded to the envelopes on the desk. "I bet every piece of mail from a record company just has a form rejection letter and our CD in it."

"What's this woman's name?" Autumn asked. "Maybe Wilson can give us some background on her."

"You and Wilson are like a dynamic duo, huh?" Sonia said.

"He's cool and connected in the Charlotte music scene. He doesn't want us to be taken advantage of. He's nice and a great resource."

"Sure, that's not all he wants," Vivian said. "He's fine, girl. You better lock that down."

She shook her head. "I don't want him to think I'm using him, so we're just keeping it friendly."

"Really?" Vivian asked incredulously. "All the time y'all spend together, you two aren't doing anything but talking business?"

"Anyway, can we get back to what's important. Karina Chapman wants to meet with us for breakfast tomorrow morning at Landmark on Central Avenue," Nicole said. "I think we should show up looking like a polished, poised group ready to take over the world."

"The black suits?" Autumn asked.

Nicole nodded.

"Let's do it, because all we have right now is another mailbox full of no thank yous," Sonia said. "I have to go and finish my chemistry lab. You know if this whole music thing doesn't work out, I'm going to have to do the science thing I came to college for, you know."

Once Sonia left, Autumn was filled with uneasy thoughts. What if they never made it beyond the demo stage? They'd come to college with other plans, and they were neglecting their studies trying to chase a dream. A dream Autumn couldn't say she was one hundred percent in on. The music was one thing, but the business part was giving her reservations. She had been studying groups from back in the day that had been hustled out of their masters, their money and ended up hating each other. That was the last thing she wanted to happen among her friends.

"Why are you so quiet?" Vivian asked Autumn.

"Thinking about this comm test, I probably should study and y'all have class, right?"

Nicole looked at her watch. "Shit. I got to book it."

Vivian stood up and followed Nicole out the door. Once she was alone, Autumn walked over to the window and watched the band start practice.

An idea popped in her head. They needed to perform at the homecoming halftime show. But could they make it happen? She glanced at the drum major, James Robinson. The way that man moved his hips should be illegal. Autumn knew he ran the band and had the biggest hand in the homecoming show.

She tore away from the window and ran outside to plant herself in front of the band room. Maybe she could get to him before his groupies came out. A homecoming performance could be the beginning of something big for Bella. J.R., as everyone called him, just needed to buy in.

Autumn tried to look unaffected as he walked up to the band room with his sweat drenched white tank top clinging to his broad chest and his biceps bulging. *Be cool, don't look at his dick.* She'd heard the rumors that swirled around campus about him. Like any red blooded woman, she was curious. But that wasn't the reason why she was here.

"Hey, J.R. can we talk?" she called out, somehow keeping her eyes on his face.

"Autumn, right?"

"You know my name?"

He smirked. "Everybody knows you and your group. But you are the sexiest one, at least to me."

"You can turn the charm off, I want to talk business with you," she said.

"Give me a second to clean my face and then we can talk," he said then headed inside the band room. Autumn told herself that J.R. was just a big flirt and he would've called any member of Bella who approached him sexy. It didn't mean a thing. Seconds later, a shirtless J.R. walked out of the band room with a gold towel around his neck.

Now he was just being arrogant. Autumn steeled her hormones – which was something she had to do a lot these days.

Wilson was making it clear that he wanted more than a friendship and there was that night that he had almost licked her into submission, but she told him her career and school came first. He wasn't happy and left in a huff.

"All right Autumn, let's go."

"Where are we going?"

"My room and don't give me that look, but the longer we stand out here the more people are going to come around and interrupt this business conversation you want to have," he said with a slick smile.

"Never mind," she said and started toward her dorm.

"Wait," he said. "What do you want to talk about?"

"For Bella to perform with the band at homecoming. Can you make that happen?"

He nodded. "I'm sure I can, but are y'all going to practice with us to get ready for the show?"

"Of course," she replied, silently praying that the rest of the group would be excited about this idea. He folded his arms across his chest and smirked.

"Do y'all have an idea of what songs you want to do?"

"Okay, listen, I didn't expect you to just say yes so quickly, but I can get everything you need in a few. . ."

"Hey, J.R.," a girl who Autumn had a class with said seductively as she passed by them.

"What's up, Shauna?" he replied with a smile.

"I'll let you get back to your fan club. Thanks, though." *He flirts with everybody,* she thought as she turned to walk away.

"Wait a minute," he said then reached for her wrist. "Why don't you get your group together later tonight and come to the band room so we can go over somethings. We're going to have to make a presentation to the band director before we officially have a show."

Autumn nodded. "Thanks, and we'll see you at seven?"

"Seven-thirty. Got to give my fan club a show," he replied with a wink. Autumn watched as he took off down the hill toward Smith Hall.

Autumn knew Sonia would be back in her room in about an hour, so she decided to leave a note on her door. Something about the manager situation didn't sit well with her. She couldn't put her finger on it since she hadn't met her yet. What if she could get them in front of Jermaine Dupri? But what if she was all talk and no action?

When Autumn returned to her room, she started writing down songs that they could perform with the band. They could do a medley of classic songs, a current hit and finish up with one of their original songs.

"Autumn!" Sonia called out as she banged on the door. Autumn crossed over to the door.

"That was quick."

"Your note made it sound like something was seriously wrong. What's up?"

"How would you feel about a homecoming performance with the band?"

"IIOS? And us? Girl, that would be amazing."

"Right. So, we got to do a quick audition tonight for the drum major."

"Robinson? Is this some horny trick of his?" Sonia asked with her arms folded across her chest.

"No. I approached him, and he said if we can impress the band director, we can probably join them at homecoming, when everyone is watching."

"Yes! And with all the alumni here, we might hook a record producer or something."

"Exactly."

"You really be behind the scenes making things happen, huh?"

"I mean, shouldn't we be in control of our destiny? I know if I tell my parents about this before we get a deal or have some success, they will come up here and snatch me out of school so fast. I got to make my life count."

"That got deep really fast," Sonia said. "Autumn, you're one of the smartest people I know. Whether we end up with a record deal or not, you're going to make a difference in this world."

Autumn was about to reply when there was a knock on the door. Sonia opened it and Vivian walked in with Nicole. "What's going on in here?" Nicole asked.

"We have a potential opportunity that could change everything," Autumn said excitedly.

"Okay, what's up?" Vivian asked sharing Autumn's enthusiasm.

"We have an audition tonight to perform with the IIOS for homecoming. Just think about how many people will see and hear us?!"

"Wait, how did you pull this off?" Nicole asked. "You and Wilson just. . ."

"This is all Autumn," Sonia said. "All she had to do was flash a smile on the drum major."

Nicole groaned. "That ni. . .So, which one of us is he trying to fuck?"

Vivian threw her hands up and bit her bottom lip. "I thought it was you last semester," she said after a beat.

"His nasty ass invited me to a threesome. I'm not into that shit," Nicole spat.

"Well, this is different and why didn't you tell all of us?" Autumn asked. "I would've never. . ."

Nicole waved Autumn off. "Because it was irrelevant. And I wrote a song about it. If this homecoming show don't come through we're going to record it and I'm going to dedicated it to his nasty ass. So, what would this show look like and I'm not wearing no damn Blue Satin outfits."

Vivian nodded in agreement.

"Blue Satin outfits are amazing," Sonia said defending her former squad.

"We'll get to that," Autumn said as she grabbed her notebook to show her friends the thoughts she'd written down.

Vivian loved the inclusion of the Motown classic, *You Can't Hurry Love*, Nicole was glad they'd sing one of their up tempo songs and Sonia said En Vogue's *Never Gonna Get It* would be a show stopping moment. But they were not going to let the band director, Dr. Jamieson, choose their outfits.

Of course, they'd be sexy, but no hanging ass cheeks for Bella. They wanted to have a look that set them apart from other girl groups. Unfortunately, they hadn't figured out what that look was.

"What time is our audition?" Vivian asked.

"Seven-thirty," Autumn replied. "So, we better get ready."

At seven-thirty, Bella walked into the band room, dressed in black biker shorts and matching sports bras. Autumn was surprised to see all three drum majors and Dr. Jamieson were there. That made everything feel real and she was happy, but nervous as well.

"Good evening ladies," Dr. Jamieson began. "I was wondering what took so long for our campus songbirds to grace us with a performance."

Vivian smiled at the men. "You could've reached out to us," she said.

"But we're here now," Sonia chimed in.

The band director stood up and nodded. "All right let's see what you ladies got. Now remember, we're not using a CD, my band is going to need sheet music if we decide to allow you all to join us for homecoming."

"That's not a problem," Autumn said. "I can bring you. . ."

"We can go over the sheet music with you later," J.R. said then winked at Autumn. She shook her head, silently reminding herself that he was a freak into threesomes. Hormones were in check, because she had business to handle.

"All right, ladies, the floor is yours," Dr. Jamieson said as he took a seat.

After a quick vocal warm up, Bella was belting out the songs they had on the list to perform. By the time they got to En Vogue's hit, the room was eating out of their hand and J.R. was playing the drums.

Dr. Jamieson held up his hands. "I've heard enough! We

have to do this before y'all blow up and we can't afford you. James, make sure you get the sheet music so we can start practicing tomorrow."

"Yes sir," he said then turned to Autumn. "You look cute in your little shorts."

"Boy shut up," she said more for the benefit of her friends because her cheeks were on fire.

"I'll stop by in a little bit to get the sheet music. You live in Greenfield, right?"

"Yeah, room 308," she said.

He winked at her. "See you soon."

"Make sure you keep your door open," Nicole said.

J.R. smiled at her. "All of y'all can come. That way we can discuss choreography."

"We don't need you for that," Vivian said. "We have our own moves and two of Blue Satin's best dancers ever."

"I beg to differ. You ladies have the voice, but the IIOS has a standard and we need to make sure your moves measure up," J.R. said.

"We're not Blue Satin dancers, nor are we flag girls," Nicole said. "We have a routine and we're sticking to it."

He threw his hands up. "You can work with me or Dr. Jamieson. Trust me, I'm easier."

"So, everyone on campus says," Nicole said then started singing *Campus Playboy*. "Always looking for his next toy, he's nothing but a campus playboy."

"Every day he has to plaaayyyy," Vivian chimed in with her perfect soprano.

"Campus playboy looking for another toy," Sonia and Autumn sang.

"All right, I see y'all out here making up songs about people," he said. "Cute."

"Actually, this song wasn't about you but if the sneaker fits," Autumn said and immediately thought about Wilson.

Maybe she should reach out to him and tell him thank you. But he knew her number and could easily call her. He was the one tripping, not her.

"Anyway, see you in a little bit," J.R. said to Autumn specifically. "I'll bring you something for your celebration."

She narrowed her eyes at him. "What celebration?"

"Becoming the first woman on campus to let me walk out of her room without trying to fu. . ."

"Yeah," Vivian called out. "We wrote that song about you. So, trifling."

Nicole laughed. "Definitely fits him."

Sonia nodded and Autumn dropped her head. She'd been the one who'd come up with the concept for the song and J.R. had been the last person she was thinking about.

J.R. shrugged and took off toward Smith Hall. When he was out of earshot, Sonia sucked her bottom lip in. "He could get it, though. But I wouldn't tell a soul."

"He's probably a walking STD," Nicole said. "But if I wasn't scared to be a freak, I would've joined that threesome, since we're being honest out here."

Vivian shook her head. "Y'all are nasty. I'm waiting for my prince to come, and I don't think he's on this campus."

"So, that's why you be sneaking off campus with Charlotteans? Girl, we know what's up when you claim you're going to take the bus for inspiration," Autumn said.

Vivian laughed and rolled her eyes. "I'm an urban development major, I explore the city, because Charlotte is on the cusp and before our singing career explodes, I'm trying to come up with new investment opportunities. I'm too damn smart to be poor. Hell, we all are!"

"Now that's the truth," Nicole said. "How about we grab some food and bring it back to Autumn's room so we can watch Mr. Drum Major flirt with her some more."

"He's not flirting and y'all are weird," Autumn said. "But where are we eating from?"

Nicole looked at her watch. "We got time for Showmars."

"Well, y'all go get it and I'll meet J.R. with the sheet music," Autumn said.

"Leave the door open," Sonia said. "I guess you want a fish sandwich and onion rings."

"Heavy tartar sauce," Autumn called out as she headed inside the dorm. She dashed into her room and looked through the music notes for the sheet music. The only reason she'd picked those songs was because she'd been sure she had that sheet music. But she couldn't find the Supremes one.

Shit, shit, shit! Autumn had spent good money on that because she thought the group would learn the song and use it for an audition or something. While she was still looking, there was a knock at the door. She knew it wasn't the girls, because they knew she kept her door unlocked when she was awake.

"That was quick," Autumn said when she opened the door.

"I don't like to keep beautiful women waiting," J.R. said as he walked in.

"Do you ever stop flirting? And I don't recall inviting you in."

"Telling the truth is flirting now?" he asked, ignoring the non-invitation. "You can't judge me based on my rep. Half of it is a lie anyway."

"It's what's real that concerns me. Let me get you the sheet music and you can be on your way." Autumn turned to her cluttered desk to retrieve the documents.

J.R. touched her elbow.

"Wait. Can we talk?"

"For a minute, Tevin? My girls are coming back soon with our food, and I don't want anyone getting the wrong idea."

"What if I need more than a minute?"

"Too bad, too sad. Get to it, bud."

"What do you say to me and you having dinner together next week? Off campus at some place nice and far away from people and their gossip."

"Why?"

"Because I want to get to know you."

Autumn folded her arms across her chest. "So, this is how it starts? You get a girl alone and do this sweet and kindhearted thing. Then you transition into that J.R. thing you say is a complete exaggeration of who you are?"

"With some, that would be on the money. But there's something different about you.

I've noticed a long time ago, just wasn't sure how to act on it."

"And dinner just seemed like the right thing to offer? Why not a movie or. . ."

"We can't talk in a dark theatre, unless. . ."

"Don't go there."

"And where might *there* be?" he asked with a toothy grin.

That damned smile, she thought as she turned away from him and those cool brown eyes that sparkled with gold flecks when the light hit them just right. And the light always seemed to know where to hit.

"Nigga, you are so full of shit. Just be honest about what you want," she said.

"For now, I just want to have dinner with you. But in the future, I'd like to give you this. . ."

"Well, well, what's happening here?" Vivian asked as she and the others walked in the room with bags of Showmars.

"We didn't realize we were having an extra guest tonight," Sonia quipped.

Autumn handed J.R. the sheet music. "We don't," she replied then turned to him. "This is all you need, right?"

He slipped the papers underneath his arm. "For now. See you ladies and enjoy your meal." He winked at Autumn then headed out the door. She shut the door and locked it. "All right, let's eat."

Three sets of eyes looked back at her, all telling her that the food was going to have to wait.

"Y'all seem pretty cozy," Sonia said.

Autumn waved her off. "We were talking. Can I help it that everyone loves my personality?"

"Whatever. Be careful with that one," Nicole warned. "That's the kind of man that will drive you to sin, repent and do it again."

"Did something happen with you two that we need to know about?" Sonia asked.

"Because I want details," Vivian exclaimed.

"There are no details to share because all I got was a proposition. But from what I heard; I might have missed out. But that boat has sank like the Titanic."

Vivian turned to Autumn, "So, you are thinking about riding that pony?"

"No, I'm thinking about eating my food before it gets cold," Autumn snapped.

"Yeah, let's eat and forget that this room smells like that man," Sonia laughed.

The group ate, talked about their performance with the band and the meeting with Karina.

"Listen," Nicole said as she held up her cup of tea. "We're about to become the next bestselling female group. Our future is bright, and we have to make a pact right now.

We all must stay together."

They all held up their cups and pressed them together. "Bella for life," they exclaimed.

Chapter Six

Homecoming Present Day –

Autumn walked into her hotel room with Sonia and was thankful for the cool air. The calendar may say October, but it was still hot as summer in Charlotte. Sometimes when it snowed in New England and she'd see pictures of her friends in the south hanging out in shorts, she'd be a little jealous. Today was not one of those days.

"Whew, it is cold in here," Sonia said as the door closed behind them.

"Were we outside in the same heat?" Autumn asked as she kicked off her booties.

Sonia released a sigh as if she was remembering what her friend had told her. "I'm sorry. Do you need me to do anything or. . ."

"First, don't treat me like I'm a zombie. I'm not the walking dead, all right. And no, I don't need anything. Just a few minutes to catch my breath, then shower."

"Have you eaten? Because I haven't and I'll grab us something from the restaurant downstairs."

"Or you can go to Showmars. Fish sandwich and slaw sounds good to me."

"The more things change. I'll be back." Before she left, Autumn handed Sonia a room key.

Alone in the room, Autumn stripped out of her clothes, wrapped in a towel and laid back on the bed. She was about to close her eyes when her cellphone rang. Looking at the screen, she saw it was her husband and she rolled her eyes.

"James, what do you want?"

"Are you taking care of yourself?" he asked.

"I am, but I thought you were coming to Charlotte. Your son would like to see you."

Granted, Tyler didn't say that, but he shouldn't have tried to blackmail her.

"You know I'm teaching, and I wish you would come home and get your treatments. Autumn, please do that. Whatever you're trying to accomplish right now isn't worth your health, babe."

"My health's not improving and as much as you and your son want me to get treatment, it's not your body that feels like a wet dish rag for weeks and weeks. Right now, I feel normal. And I want my friends to fix the bullshit that tore us apart before it's too late."

"Autumn, y'all are grown now, this together forever shit is over."

"Is that how you feel about your friendships? About your connections that got you that amazing job you have right now? J.R."

"Don't do that."

"We let people come between us and guess what, no one's dream came true. It's been 25 years and it's time to wrap this shit up. This is important to me."

"Autumn, you're important to me and you always have. . ."

"You're going a step too far because it wasn't that long ago..."

"Autumn."

"Well, let's not rewrite history. We've had our ups and downs, but we worked it out. Why can't I have that experience with my best friends?"

"Where the hell have they been, Autumn?" he snapped.

"James, I love you, but I have to go. Sonia will be back soon with my food."

He chuckled. "That's a real one, fuck those other two."

"Bye, James and I still have airline miles for you to get here. Why don't you use them?"

"I'll think about it, but not hard."

"You know, if you want to do something to make me happy, coming to homecoming would be that thing," she said as she sat up in the bed, feeling a burst of energy. Something about this man always got her blood flowing in the right direction.

"I'll book the flight after class and see you in the morning."

"Ooh, do me a favor and this is the last thing I'll ask you to do."

"Yeah, right," he chuckled. "What is it, baby?"

"Rent a Mustang."

He agreed then told her his next class was about to start. "Love you," he said before hanging up.

Smiling, Autumn ended the call then rose from the bed and headed for the shower. As the cool water beat down on her body, she remembered when she fell in love with the bad boy drum major everyone warned her to stay away from.

Homecoming, 1997 –

The performance with JCSU's IIOS marching band had been a rousing hit. Vivian stole the show, though. Breaking out moves that they hadn't practiced and when the Blue Satin dancers joined in, making everyone look as if they were Vivian's back up dancers. It looked good, but Nicole and Sonia were pissed. Autumn went with the flow because this was the first time they'd had a huge crowd watching them. And from months of studying Motown acts and watching *The Five Heartbeats*, she knew a fight was coming. When the band did their break down, J.R. grabbed Autumn and she performed the popular moves with him and the other two drum majors causing everyone in Memorial Stadium to jump up and cheer. For the last move, which was a dip and a split, the other group members joined the drum majors and Autumn making everyone scream in delight. As they headed off the field, J.R. grabbed Autumn around the waist and lifted her off her feet.

"That was fucking amazing," he exclaimed.

"Calm down, homie. I told you we were that good."

"I'm talking about you, forget them. Shit, I . . ."

"James, get your band in the stands," Dr. Jamieson called out. J.R. nodded then turned to Autumn.

"Meet me after the game," he said quickly before blowing his whistle and getting the band in line.

That's some power right there, Autumn thought as she watched the band return to the stand and make a show of sitting down. She'd been watching them do this for years, but today, knowing what was behind it made her thighs quiver. Until she heard, "Fuck you, bitch," coming from behind her. There was no doubt that the Five Heartbeats argument had started already. And Autumn knew who the bitch was.

Turning around, she saw Nicole and Vivian standing toe to toe as if they were about to pummel each other. "You better get out of my damn face, Nicole. I told you we . . ."

"Bitch, we are a motherfucking group, it's all or nothing!" Nicole bucked as if she was about to swing on Vivian and Autumn jumped in between then.

"Hey! Stop it. This isn't the place or the time for this. People love what we did, we can't show out like this."

Sonia touched Vivian's shoulder. "Come with me so you can cool off."

Vivian shrugged her off. "I'm fine, but this bi. . ." Sonia pulled her away as a group of alumni walked by.

"Man, this is . . .All she can do is sing. We do everything to make this group successful and she pulls this Diana Ross shit. Did you know about it? Because you sure have the band's moves down."

"First of all, slow your roll. I don't like what Vivian did, but we can't have these blow ups in public. Why did we do halftime at homecoming?"

"Because we wanted attention and maybe catch the ear of someone in the industry."

Autumn nodded. "It wasn't what we thought it should've been, but Viv got all eyes on us."

"On her. Man, fuck this. I'm going for a ride. Are you coming?"

"Umm, I-I, have something else to do."

Nicole fanned her hand and stormed off. Autumn dropped her head. They hadn't even recorded an album yet and this shit was happening already. Nicole was right, she wrote the songs, Autumn did the behind the scenes work to get them in front of people. But Vivian was the draw, it was her voice that had gotten them noticed on the Block that day. They were a group where everyone had a purpose. So, why did it seem like everything was falling apart now? It wasn't as if they were any more successful than they were when they'd decided to become a group in the first place.

Autumn wandered around the stadium, trying to figure out if this pipe dream was too big and they needed to let it go.

She laughed at herself, since Bella got started, Autumn's grades had been slipping, she was in danger of losing her scholarship and if that happened, she was going to be on her way back to the small town she hated proving all the naysayers right. The people who thought college and a city like Charlotte was too much for little Autumn. She gritted her teeth and decided that above everything else, she was going to have to put herself first. Autumn wasn't going to allow this drama to get in her way. She wasn't going to continue to be the peacemaker when she wasn't causing the bullshit.

"Hey, you waited," J.R. said breaking into Autumn's thoughts. She hadn't realized that she'd been walking around Memorial Stadium this long.

"I guess I did," she replied.

"You're going to keep giving me a hard time for no reason, aren't you?" he asked, misreading her response.

Autumn tilted her head to the side and smiled. "Maybe. Don't you have some parties or something to get ready for? Why did you want me to wait for you?"

"Because I want to take you somewhere, unless you and your group are going to do some celebrating for a hell of a show."

"I don't think that's happening. But I have to change and. . ."

"So, do I. I can take you back to campus and we can change then I have a surprise for you."

"I don't like surprises," she said with a smile.

"You'll like this one. I'm mean, campus is going to be packed with people and the Greeks are doing the step show, it's going to be loud."

"And I could use some quiet reflection," she whispered. J.R. took her hand in his and kissed it.

"I got you, if you let me."

She looked into his eyes and saw something different. The lustful glints that she'd always noticed were gone and there was a softness in his eyes. "Okay," she replied. "But I want to make it clear, I'm hungry. So, if you don't plan on feeding me. . ."

"Trust me, I'm going to give you everything you want."

Autumn shivered inwardly knowing that this was a ploy, and she was falling for it hook, line and sinker. "Let's get out of here," she said. He wrapped his arms around her shoulders and led her to his car. When she saw his Mustang GT, her mind went to Wilson. He hadn't taken her call when she'd reached out to him a month ago. It was clear that he thought she should've had sex with him because he wanted her. All she'd wanted from him was a friendship. But he accused her of using him and wanted to take credit for creating Bella.

Just because he knew one word of Italian, he thought he was owed something. Bullshit. The more Autumn saw and learned about the industry, the more she was sure it wasn't going to be her entire future. Not as a performer anyway. She'd already submitted her paperwork to change her major from education to music business and technology. She still needed to figure out how to tell her parents. Or maybe she'd just keep it to herself until graduation. It wasn't as if they were paying attention to what she was doing. All they seemed to do was wait for her downfall. And she wasn't going to give anyone that satisfaction.

"Hey, you okay?" J.R. asked breaking into her thoughts.

"Yeah, nice car. I didn't know you were a pony guy."

"This is where I should break into song, right?"

"No, it's where you should open the door," she retorted with a sarcastic smile.

"You got a mouth on you. It's a good thing it's a pretty one."

"Boy, open the door," she said trying to quell the heat rising between her thighs.

Once J.R. opened the door for her, Autumn slid in the car and smiled at him. "You're so kind," she said.

He winked at her. Autumn shook her head as he crossed over to the driver's side. She ran her hand across the leather seat and sighed. "I'm going to get one of these one day," she said.

"Oh, so you do like to ride the pony?"

"Shut up," she giggled.

"You started it. Do you like seafood and I'm not talking fried fish from Mr. C's or Red Lobster," he said as he started the car.

"What are you talking about, then?"

"I know this little spot near UNC-Charlotte. They have the best grilled fish and shrimp."

"Okay, I'll bite."

"And you'll enjoy it," he said. "It's a local place, so I doubt we'll run into anyone from Smith."

"If we do, that's fine with me. I don't have anyone to hide from." She shrugged. "Is that why you want to take me to some far off place?"

"No. I just want to be alone with you."

Autumn chuckled. "You really want to be Tevin Campbell, don't you?"

"Y'all love him, I'm just trying to get some of that love too, especially from you."

"James, can you talk to me like I'm a human and not just another potential notch on your belt? I'm a great friend, but I don't have time for all that extra shit you're known for."

"And what am I known for? If it's Nicole telling you stories, I can explain."

She turned in her seat and faced him. "What do you have to say for yourself, Mr. Threesome?"

J.R. laughed. "I was drunk and probably a little high. So, what happened was, my boy Dex had a party, and he said the girls who were coming through were from Charlotte and they were down for whatever. I'm single, so I was like, bet. A mini Freaknik."

"Oh lord, I'm about to be sorry I asked." Autumn shook her head.

"Hold up, it wasn't like that. The girls who came in looked like they had escaped from a zoo. Then I saw Nicole. She was out of place, and I vaguely remembered seeing her on the yard. So, I approached her to ask why she was there. And here comes that sorry ass DJ and she started talking to him. So, I was like maybe she wasn't here to be a part of the freak show."

Autumn dropped her head in her hands, wondering if that was the night Nicole had gotten them studio time?

"So," J.R. continued, "she handed him a videotape. And I was like, damn we recording threesomes now? Man, everybody started talking about threesomes and these two broads standing by Nicole were like, yeah we're down for it. Mind you, they looked like they should've been in a cage. But I started talking shit and Nicole looked like she wanted to beat my ass."

That sounded like her friend.

"Did you have a threesome that night?" she asked.

"Nah, I just got some head."

"Nigga."

"It was the weed. But I regret nothing," he laughed.

"Anyway, what time are we leaving?"

"Let's look at six, maybe the traffic on campus will have died down a little bit. And you can check on your girls."

"They will be fine. You know this should've been the best day of our budding career and they got out here and acted a

damn fool. They can figure this shit out on their own," she said with anger peppering her voice.

"You don't mean that. I can tell three things about you just from watching you guys these last few weeks. One, you're the glue that holds Bella together. Two, you're not depending on this group's success to be great and finally, you're the best thing that has ever happened to those women. If you're going to act like you don't care, then your group is done."

"When and how did you come up with all of that?" she asked, surprised by his truthful observation.

"I pay attention to things and people I care about. And I've been paying a lot of attention to you."

She wanted to come back with something smart and sarcastic, but for J.R. to read her like a book made her heart swell. No one had ever seen her that way before.

The ride back to campus was filled with old school R&B and Autumn singing along with New Edition's greatest hits and some of her Motown favorites. J.R. seemed to enjoy it. And when Marvin Gaye and Tammi Terrell started playing, she nudged him to sing along.

"So, you can tell everybody I sound like a dying frog, no ma'am. Besides, I was enjoying the Autumn show. You know you should be singing lead sometimes too."

"Nah, I like my spot in the background. And until Nicole writes a song that inspires a powerhouse performance from me, I'm going to stay right where I am."

"What would inspire a powerhouse performance?"

She shrugged. "Certainly not a love song. Something that is funky like Prince, sexy like Vanity 6, but not too dirty."

"You want to do a Prince song is what you're saying without saying it."

"Or Diana Ross *Love Hangover*." She inched closer to him

and started singing the sensual lyrics in his ear. J.R. slammed on brakes and Autumn jumped back. "What the hell?" she exclaimed.

"You can't do that to me while I'm driving or have my eyes open. Damn, you sound so good. Why are you playing like your talent isn't the linchpin of that group?"

Autumn snorted. "Because I'm not the skinny light skinned girl. Let's not act like that's not the number one factor in why all the female groups look the way they do. Vivian is going to get us a record deal, but it's going to be me and Nicole to make sure we're more than a one hit wonder. Everyone plays a part and for now, we're going to have to play those roles."

"You've really studied the business, huh?"

She nodded. "Studying is everything. Haven't you learned that from being in college?"

"I could learn a lot from you," he said as he reached over and grabbed her hand.

"That's if I want to teach you anything. I don't usually accept students this late in the semester. But if this fish is as good as you claim it is, I might make an exception."

"Oh, you will."

Chapter Seven

Moments later, J.R. pulled up in front of Greenfield Hall. The campus was packed with alumni and more cars than the parking lot could handle. "Maybe you should park in the New Res parking lot," she said as she opened the door.

"Yeah, cause there's no way I'd make it through this traffic. I got a bag in the trunk, I could roll up in Greenfield with you, take a shower and then we can leave."

Autumn rolled her eyes. "You're slick as hell, you know that?"

"Someone called me a can of oil once. Is that what they meant?" he teased.

She pinched him on the arm then told him she'd be waiting in the lobby. When she walked into the dorm, Sonia crossed over to her and winked. "I know I didn't see you and the drum major rolling up together."

"You did. And what about it?"

"Nothing, do your thing and be happy because Vivian and Nicole are still going at it. Nicole is hanging out with the Bruhz on their plot and Vivian locked herself in her room because the Que she likes was getting nasty with Nicole. And Nicole was playing it up big time."

"Why are we being the most stereotypical girl group in America right now? Jesus," Autumn said. "It's homecoming and I'm going to enjoy myself. J.R. and I are going to get some fish, you want to come?"

Sonia arched her right eyebrow. "And be the third wheel on your date?"

"It's not a date," Autumn said as J.R. walked in with his IIOS duffle bag.

"Lie again," Sonia whispered. "Hey J.R., you are moving in?"

"Sonia, you're so cute. You see all that traffic out there. Autumn is being gracious and letting me change here."

"So, where are we eating fish tonight?" she asked.

He shot Autumn a questioning look. Autumn shrugged and hid her laughter.

"Umm, it's a local spot," he said.

"Don't worry, I'm not going to horn in on your date and I don't like fish," Sonia said.

"Well, you're welcome to come if you'd like to hang out," he said in a tone that was far from inviting.

"Anyway, I'm going to make sure Nicole doesn't make a mistake. You might want to make sure you don't make one either," Sonia said, then walked away from them. J.R. tilted his head and grinned at Autumn.

"I'm a mistake now?" he quipped.

"Get upstairs so we can shower." Autumn knew the floor should be empty since everyone was enjoying the homecoming events or getting ready for the step show.

The only person who she knew would be on the floor would be nosy ass Clarissa Clyburn. Maybe this would be the one day that Grimace wouldn't be looking for gossip. As soon as they rounded the corner, Autumn knew her hopes were in vain. Rissa, as everyone called her, was standing by her room door talking on the phone. Her eyes widened when she saw Autumn and J.R. She rushed inside, undoubtably to talk about them.

"Well, there goes our secret," she said as she crossed over to her room and unlocked the door.

"It had to come out at some time that I'm crazy about you," he said.

"Shh, some of those other girls you said that to might be at their doors listening. Then they're going to come out here and whoop your ass," she laughed. "Because I have nothing to do with this."

"You want me to shout it out so your friend can really have something to talk about?" J.R. cleared his throat and Autumn covered his mouth with her hand.

"Don't make me regret bringing you up here. I'm trying to be nice, since I know how much work you put in on the field today."

He licked the palm of her hand and Autumn was nearly melted into a puddle of lust. She dropped her hand as if she'd been burned. "That was just plain nasty," she said, attempting to sound angry. It didn't work because J.R. pulled her into his arms and brushed his lips against hers.

"If my tongue can make your hand feel like that, imagine..."

"Stop it. You're living up to your reputation again," she said then opened the door.

"So, my reputation is wanting to peel your clothes off and lick you up and down until you say stop?"

Autumn inhaled deeply. "Listen, James, we're not doing this, okay. You said we're friends, right?"

"Friends with benefits or just plain old boring friends who join the same study group?" He stroked her arm and smiled. Autumn tried not to be affected, but she was. Thighs quivering. Pussy throbbing.

"Boring old friends who eat fish together," she said. "You better go shower before Rissa goes to wait for you in the bathroom." Autumn took a step back and closed her eyes.

"Why don't you come with me? I mean if we were in Smith Hall, I wouldn't let my friend go shower alone."

"Whatever. I'll go because I might as well take my shower now too," she said hoping she sounded calm, cool and collected. But when J.R. winked at her, she knew she'd failed. Autumn grabbed her shower tote and robe then led her *friend* to the bathroom.

She was glad that he got into his own shower stall, but she was curious to see if the rumors about him hanging like an elephant trunk were true. But she wasn't about to get caught. . .

"If you want to see me naked, all you have to do is ask," he said with a chuckle.

"Man, go to hell." Autumn turned her shower on and damn near screamed when the cold water slapped her in the face.

"If you need a cold shower, I got the remedy for that," he said.

"You know, cold showers only work for men," she said as the water warmed up. "When a woman takes a cold shower, it's because she's not satisfied. The cold water makes her nipples hard, touches the clit and makes her cat purr."

"All right, stop, friends don't talk to each other like that when they're naked. And one of them is brick hard."

"I'm not hard," she joked. Seconds later, a dripping wet J.R. stepped into her shower stall.

"What are you doing?" Autumn gasped. She fought and lost the battle not to drink in his naked body. The legend was true. She forced herself to turn away. Of course, he saw her looking.

"Am I still living up to everything you've heard?"

"Why are you over here?"

"Because you said you were holding something and I needed to see what I was potentially getting into," he said with a smile.

Washboard abs, thighs that looked as if they were sculpted from marble. And then there was that. . .She looked away again. "I'm going to finish my shower, go get back in yours," Autumn snapped.

"Why don't we conserve water?" He stepped closer to her. Autumn forced herself to breathe as she stepped underneath the spray.

"You're an environmentalist now?" she asked then turned the shower off. "How about we just get out of here and you feed me like you said you were going to do." She pushed past him and attempted to grab her robe. J.R. stopped her.

"You know you have a beautiful body, just chocolate all over. And I want to be the first to say that I can't wait to see how beautiful your mind is. All you have to do is stop looking for the worst in me."

Now, Autumn was perplexed because those words were a bigger turn on than his pretty dick. "Umm, okay, you got me," she breathed.

J.R. winked at her. "Autumn, I'm going to have every part of you, when you're ready to give it to me," he said then wrapped his towel around his waist.

Autumn looked out into the hallway to make sure it was still empty. Just as they were about to step out, she saw Vivian storming in their direction. They dashed back into the bathroom, hopping in a shower stall and holding their breath. It was quiet enough for Autumn to hear Vivian banging on the door and calling her name. She placed her finger to J.R.'s lips. The last thing she wanted was to get involved in whatever had Vivian that pissed off. He pulled her against his wet chest and smiled. Autumn wanted to kiss him. She wondered if lips that spoke like that tasted like sugar. *No*, she thought as she turned away from him. J.R. was being a gentleman and keeping his hands to himself even though she would've. . .

"Autumn, are you in here?" Vivian called out from the entrance of the bathroom.

They stood in silence until they heard her walk away.

"How long are you going to keep me in here so that you can avoid your friend?" J.R. asked.

"I'm doing this for your benefit," she whispered. "Just give it another minute."

"All right, but just know, I could do this for hours."

"Shh," she said, not giving him a hint that she could too. Minutes passed by, but for Autumn, it felt like days. Their bodies shifted against the drip drop of the water.

"I think we're safe to get out of here now," he whispered.

"All right." Autumn pressed her hands against his damp chest. "We need to make sure no one sees you."

He nodded and winked. "I know how to sneak around here. I've done it plenty of times before."

"Not surprised," she said as she stepped out of the stall.

Autumn left the bathroom first and dashed down the hall to her room. She could feel, at least in her mind, nosy ass Rissa watching from behind her door.

She opened the door to her room and walked in. Part of her knew the smart thing to do would've been to lock the door and put J.R.'s stuff outside. But she left the door unlocked and tried to dry off and put on her underwear before he walked in the room. He'd already seen her naked, so why was she acting like it was a big deal? Because she'd seen him naked too and she couldn't help but wonder if being naked behind closed doors would change everything. J.R. walked in, his towel draped low on his waist. "We did it," he said. "Operation shower was a success."

"Now, let's get dressed and get out of here before Nicole shows up. Everybody thinks I'm the group counselor. Lock the door for me," she said.

Seconds after he locked it and crossed over to his bag, there was a knock at the door. Just as Autumn had predicted, it was Nicole.

"Autumn are you here?" she asked as she turned the doorknob. Autumn placed her finger to her lips and looked at J.R. He nodded and bowed as if he was auditioning to meet the Queen of Egypt. Two more knocks and some grumbling, then silence. Autumn took a deep breath.

"How about when we leave we don't come back until tomorrow," she said with a sigh.

"You sure about that? I know after the step show there's a party in Brayboy and a pool party."

Autumn shrugged. "If you want to go, that's cool. But I'm over Vivian and Nicole already. It's only going to get worse. I'll figure something out."

"First off, I didn't say I wanted to go. I was just letting you know that there were some things happening on campus that could help you continue to avoid your friends. What I'm not going to do is give up a chance to spend some quality time with you."

Autumn smiled despite herself and started humming the Hi-5 hit, *Quality Time.*

"So melodic," he said then pulled her into his arms. Autumn brought her lips to his ears and started singing softly.

They swayed to the sound of her voice. "Autumn," he intoned as she stopped singing. "We need to stop this right now because if I don't let you go. . ."

"Okay," she said then stepped back. "Thanks for respecting me."

"Always and for the record, I respect all women."

"Even the ones who gave you head at that infamous party?" she teased.

"Especially them," he laughed then dropped his towel. Autumn turned away and focused on putting her clothes on, a little black dress to match her Steve Madden combat boots. She glanced over her shoulder and got caught up in watching J.R. smooth lotion on his amber brown skin.

"You want to grab a camera and take a picture?" he asked.

"Oh, shut up," she said then she turned away.

J.R. dressed quickly then crossed over to Autumn as she adjusted her silver choker. "You look amazing," he said.

She turned around and smiled. He was dressed in a pair of Girbaud jeans and a red Polo shirt. "All you're missing is that annoying cane."

"Don't be like that. You know you love it," he said then threw up his fraternity sign. She slapped him on his shoulder.

"Let's go."

When they stepped out of the room, Autumn saw Clarissa was standing in the hallway, being the nosy neighbor who everyone hated. *That bitch needs a life,* she thought. Autumn didn't like Rissa because she acted as if she had to be the Greenfield reporter and most of the time all she did was lie.

She could only imagine what the story about her and J.R. leaving together was going to be like.

Chapter Eight

When J.R. pulled into the parking lot of the restaurant, Autumn was impressed. It wasn't the hole in the wall she'd been expecting.

"Okay, this is different," she said as they exited the car. "It looks a little fancy."

"Well, I hope you weren't expecting a rundown place with questionable sanitation ratings," he said as he wrapped his arm around her waist. Autumn shivered and fell into his embrace. His touch felt good, and she was beginning to crave it. All because she saw his. . .

"Well, ain't this a bitch," a voice said from in front of them. Autumn looked up and saw Wilson walking out of the restaurant. "You change niggas like you change your drawers, huh? I heard about y'all Smith women; never thought I'd see it in action."

"My man, watch your mouth," J.R. said. "You're not going to talk to or about her with that tone."

"James don't even worry about him," Autumn said.

"Let me guess," Wilson said. "You must have some connections that can help the group, which I created."

"Will you stop with that fairy tale," Autumn exclaimed.

"Why don't you just walk away," J.R. suggested forcefully.

"How about you shut the fuck up and mind your business. This is between me and that bitch," Wilson hissed. J.R. didn't say another word, he just swung on Wilson knocking him to the ground. Autumn yelped and grabbed J.R.'s arm.

"We should go," she said as others began pouring out of the restaurant to survey the scene.

"I'm not running," he snapped. "This disrespectful shit ain't going down. Punk ass motherfucker. How are you going to get mad because she's talented? Who the fuck are you anyway? Nigga, you ain't Berry Gordy."

The crowd surrounding them laughed and Wilson slowly rose to his feet. "You're a sucker, that's why you sucker punched me. Square up, bitch," he spat. Even though Wilson was wobbly, he tried to lunge at J.R., but he fell forward and landed on his face.

"Damn," the crowd muttered. JR stepped over Wilson and reached for Autumn's hand.

"Let's go eat," he said. The people standing in front of the entrance parted to allow the couple to walk inside. Autumn smiled at J.R. before taking his hand in hers. "You're going to have a bruise," she said as she looked at his knuckles.

"Won't be the first time. Don't be fooled by that pretty boy B.S. I don't like dudes like that. How do you even know him?"

Autumn narrowed her eyes at him. "Judgmental much?"

"No, not at all, but he doesn't seem worthy of a hello from you."

"He owns the studio where we recorded our demo. He seemed nice and yeah, he inspired the name of the group, but that's where it ends. He never helped with anything else. Just someone trying to get rich off my – our – hard work. It's always some man trying to take advantage." She slammed her hands against her thighs.

"Babe, all men are not created equal, and he will never be able to take credit for the hard work you and the girls have done to make Bella a success."

"And it might be flying out the window, anyway," Autumn muttered. "You see what's happening with us now. And we're just one performance in."

"What do you mean?"

"I thought once we got a manager that things would change, but she's making things harder and loading Vivian's head about being the group's leader."

Autumn shook her head as they headed to a table in the back where the lights were low and no one else was around.

"What are you guys going to do?" he asked as he pulled a chair out for her.

She shrugged. "One thing I want to do is be on the business side of the music industry. I like performing but we should know more about contracts, ownership of masters and idiots who want to say they own the word beautiful in Italian."

"So, that's what you want to do? Not going to chase stardom?"

"You never have to chase what's yours. Being a star has more to do with luck than talent. I mean, we should be on the radio in the morning and not at 4 a.m. So, forgive me if I'm a little tired of this shit."

"Wow. I didn't know you felt like that."

Autumn nodded. "What does the future look like for James?"

"Believe it or not, I want to teach."

"Like high school?" she asked.

"Umm, no. College level music, not a band director, but I want to teach music theory. So, after graduation, I'm off to get my master's degree."

Autumn smiled broadly. "Where are you going?"

"NYU hopefully."

"That's a switch. I don't know why I expected you to keep it HBCU," she said.

"I want to get out of the south for a while. But I'll be back. Would love to teach at Smith for a decade or so," he said as the waitress approached their table.

"Well, hello," the smiling waitress said to J.R., because she didn't give Autumn a fleeting glance. "It's been a while."

"Band season," he said. "And I had to make sure my girl was available to show my lady the best service ever."

She gave Autumn a terse nod. "Here are the menus. If you have any questions, let me know. What can I start you off with for drinks?"

"I'll have water with lemon," Autumn said fighting the urge to roll her eyes. The waitress nodded then turned to J.R. with the biggest smile on her face.

"Your usual?"

"Yes. And can I get three limes on the side?"

"Of course, be right back to take your order," she said then walked away.

Autumn chuckled and shook her head. "Guess you're a regular she'd like to see outside of the restaurant."

"Can I help being irresistible to everyone except you?" He arched his right eyebrow at her. "I mean, you saw me naked, and she's never seen me shirtless."

"Anyway. Where are you from?"

"Richmond, California."

"Did you know 2Pac?"

"Oh, so you're one of those," he quipped. "Just because I'm from California, it doesn't mean I know everyone in the whole state. And I didn't run in the same circles that Pac did in Oakland. My parents were strict and one of the reasons I came to North Carolina for college."

"Well, you're going to have to forgive me. Everything I learned about California came from *Yo, MTV Raps*," she said with a laugh.

The waitress returned to take their orders and Autumn trusted J.R.'s judgment when he suggested crab gumbo.

As they waited for their dinners, Autumn felt comfortable with James, as she decided that she was going to call him by his given name from now on.

He was funny, sexy and smart. A lot more than the reputation he'd gotten on campus. When their food came out, she was glad she'd listened to him about the gumbo and the grilled flounder. The butternut squash was just her gut being right. James had ordered the surf and turf, which was grilled flounder, lobster tail and a N.Y. strip steak.

"This is a lot of food," Autumn said as she savored her gumbo.

"You definitely get your money's worth here," he said. "This place is a hidden gem. A lot like you."

"You can turn the charm down. We're at the part in the story where you got me."

"Is that so?"

Autumn nodded. A comfortable silence enveloped the table as they enjoyed the meal. When they were done, James placed his hand on top of Autumn's and smiled. "Since you're on the run from your friends, want to take a walk on the lake and get a room at the Hilton? I think my boy Marvin is working and he might be able to hook us up with something nice."

"If I agree to this, I hope you know the only thing that's going to happen in said room is sleep."

"There you go assuming that I want to get in your pants tonight. I know you're going through something, and you'd only be using me to forget about it. I'm not a sex toy ma'am, I have feelings too."

Autumn burst into laughter. "You're nuts, but I like it. Let's take that walk."

It was that moment when Autumn knew she and James were going to have a lifelong connection.

Homecoming, Present Day –

Sonia walked in the room just as Autumn slipped on a black cotton dress. "You good?" Sonia asked as she set the food on the desk.

"Yeah. I think I've talked my husband into joining us for homecoming. He should be flying in tomorrow morning."

"Old J.R. I still can't believe y'all have been married this long. How's he doing?"

Autumn sighed. "Annoyed with me being here trying to get us back together."

"Well, I mean, you could be focused on something way more important, you know."

Autumn shook her head. "If you start, I'll kick you out and pretend I don't know you."

"Can we be serious for a second? Is there a treatment that you. . ."

"Sonia, I don't want to talk about it. All I want to do is make the time I have left count and none of us leave this world with regrets. There was a time when all we had was each other. Why have we so foolishly thrown that away?"

Sonia sighed. "I see your point, but . . ."

"No buts, let's eat."

After finishing their meal, Sonia went to her room to shower, and Autumn pulled out her iPad and typed Nicole's name in the Safari search bar. Pages of links about the Grammy award winning songwriter populated and Autumn was so proud. Though Bella never made it to the bottom of the charts, Nicole scaled to the top with her songs. She was even called a mega superstar's ghostwriter by a highly read gossip blog.

Autumn believed it was true because when that diva sang about heartache and pain, she could hear Nicole's voice in some of the songs. She could understand why Nicole wanted to be behind the scenes at this point in her career.

The Bella experience had been extremely disheartening. But she wasn't going to think about that. She was going to show up at her talk tomorrow morning at Belk Theatre. Did she have a ticket for the sold out event? Nope. But Autumn had her ways of making things happen and she prayed her magic would work tomorrow and tonight at Vivian's club. Looking down at her dress, Autumn decided this wasn't the impression she wanted to make on Vivian. Just because she was . . .well, she didn't have to look like it. Autumn crossed over to her bag and pulled out a leather jumpsuit. A suit she'd packed just to be funny when James asked her where she thought she was going to wear that.

To keep her ruse going, she packed a pair of red thigh high boots to go with the suit. James had laughed at his wife before he'd asked her to try it on and then he peeled it off, making her feel alive for the first time since her diagnosis. Making love to James that night had given things a normal feel. She'd missed normal. And what she was doing at homecoming gave her something else to think about. Not an inoperable tumor in her intestines. Tears welled up in her eyes as she tried to wipe the memory of that doctor's appointment from her mind. She couldn't do anything about that, and she wasn't going to allow it to derail her from the task at hand.

Sonia knocked on the door before she unlocked it. "Look at you being sexy," she said when she spotted Autumn. "I'm glad it has cooled off this evening."

"And you're not too bad yourself," she replied as she took note of Sonia's purple bodycon dress and pink come-fuck-me pumps. "What are we trying to do?"

"Let these motherfuckers know we still got it," Sonia said then did a shimmy.

"At least for now," Autumn said under her breath.

If Sonia heard her, she didn't say anything. After Autumn smoothed some ruby red lipstick on her lips, she and Sonia took a seat on the sofa in the suite. It was fitting that Vivian was hosting Homecoming Happy Hour at her club. Even though she didn't make it as a singer, Vivian was often called on to sing at churches, for Black History events and Juneteenth. Entertainment was her thing and she wanted to do more than be known for the girl from that group, at least that's what she'd said to Autumn the last time they'd had a conversation about fifteen years ago. Autumn just hoped there was a shred of sisterhood left in Vivian that would make it possible to heal the group. Part of Autumn could hear James telling her what she was doing was bullshit and it would never work. Still, she wasn't going to stop.

"Sonia," Autumn began with a chuckle. "Remember what was supposed to be our coming out show?"

Sonia laughed. "Grand opening and grand closing. We ought to walk in Vivian's place singing the song we were supposed to perform that night."

"That totally defeats the purpose as to why we're going over there in the first place. We're trying to make peace, not stir up the drama."

"When has there never not been drama surrounding Vivian? Especially after she let Karina get inside her head."

"We're older and wiser now, maybe things are different."

"Whatever," Sonia said. "Do we need to have a few adult beverages first?"

Autumn stroked her chin. "That's not a bad idea," she said. "Should we go to the liquor store or.."

Sonia pulled a bottle of Ketel One vodka from her purse. "We don't have to be the first ones in the door, and we can always take an Uber over there."

"Sounds like a plan," Autumn said.

"You know I got cups in here, but we do need ice," Sonia said as she spotted the empty ice bucket. "I'll grab some."

"All right," Autumn said as she walked over to the desk and took a deep breath. She needed to get herself together so that she wouldn't be in pain when she walked into the club. But if she took a pain pill, she'd be laid out before Sonia came back with the ice. Autumn sighed and sat down in the desk chair. *Just breathe*, she told herself as she took slow, deep breaths. By the time Sonia returned, Autumn felt better. She just hoped she wouldn't have another attack while she was out.

"All right, let's toast to the class of 2000, powered by knowledge, guided by excellence," she said as she filled their red Solo cups with ice.

"I can't believe you remember that slogan," Autumn laughed.

"Remember when we thought the world was going to end at midnight on December 31st, 1999."

"Y2K was supposed to wipe us out. But here we are, stronger than ever."

"And fine as fuck," Sonia said then poured the vodka into their cups. "To us."

Autumn picked up her cup and clanked it against Sonia's. "To us."

Two drinks and twenty minutes later, they were sitting in the back of an Uber Black, laughing and singing off key.

"I've missed this," Autumn said with a smile.

"I can't remember the last time I've had fun with people who didn't want to analyze key changes in Coltrane classics."

"Are you telling me that you and James are that education couple who only host faculty dinner parties and read books?" Sonia asked.

"We would never be that boring. But we're also not in our twenties anymore. Sometimes, falling asleep on the sofa while binge watching a Netflix show is sexy as hell."

"If you say so," Sonia said. "When you're single, that's *Netflix and Chilling*, all that leads to is some lame head."

"Is that what's happening in the streets these days?"

"Only when you make the bad decisions I continue to make," Sonia laughed. "But it's fun. I get to travel and do what I want to without answering to anyone."

"Marriage isn't all that bad," Autumn said thoughtfully. Even though she and James had a few problems in the past, she wouldn't change anything about being his wife.

"And it was never on my radar. I just couldn't see myself sitting in one spot and calling it life."

"Tell me again what you do?" Autumn asked.

"I'm a travel influencer. It's amazing what you can do with a communications degree these days. People pay me to travel to different cities and talk about the places I've seen, the food I eat and the shops where I spend their money."

Before Autumn could reply, the Uber had arrived at Vivian's club. It was in the South End neighborhood, not too far from Uptown Charlotte, but it wasn't anything like the neighborhood had been when they were college students, a rundown place filled with houses that were in dire need of repair. It was shiny and new now. And Vivian's club was sparkling like a place that belonged in New Orleans.

The line outside the door stretched down the sidewalk and they spotted several of their classmates who were laughing and hugging each other.

"Do we really have to stand in this line?" Sonia asked.

Autumn sighed. Part of her wanted to talk their way to the front, but she decided that they should wait.

"Autumn Brown is that you?" a voice said from behind them.

She turned around and came face to face with Jessica Yost. Jessica had been a photographer for the student newspaper. She was supposed to take Bella's album cover as well. But Sid won the job and Nicole for about five minutes. Autumn always wondered what happened to those pictures.

"Yeah, it's me. How are you?" she asked as the two embraced.

"Great. You look amazing. And Sonia? Wow, I'm surprised to see the two of you together."

"Time heals," Sonia said with an eye roll. "How is it going with you?"

"Great. I'm taking pictures of the event tonight. I've seen you trending on social media with your travel vlogs. That's a cool gig."

Sonia nodded. "It is. You know we should connect and do something together," she said. "One thing I love to do is work with creative Black women."

"Oh yes, I'd be honored. Autumn, your son moves like his dad on the field. I know J.R. must be proud."

"That's one way to put it, but he wants his son to figure out what he's going to do after college that doesn't include going into the music industry, but my son is determined to be a conductor. They get on my nerves arguing about that every time they're alone for about fifteen minutes."

Jessica nodded as if she understood. Then she held up her camera. "May I get a picture?"

"Sure," Sonia and Autumn said then posed. Jessica took a couple of shots, then headed up toward the front of the line to snap more photos.

"We should've followed her," Sonia said. "These shoes aren't made for standing in one spot."

Autumn looked down at Sonia's four inch stilettos. "Girl, what were we thinking when we picked these shoes tonight?"

"That it was 1999 and I still had *Megan* knees," she laughed. Luckily, the line moved quickly, and they were inside the crowded club in less than five minutes. They saw people they hadn't seen in years and a couple of folks they hadn't ever wanted to see again. Wilson and DJ McGee.

"Oh, my fucking goodness," Autumn mumbled as she turned her back to the two men.

"What?" Sonia asked.

"Look to your left."

"Ugh," Sonia replied when she saw them. "Raggedy motherfuckers still hanging out with Smith folk."

"Stop looking before they come over here," Autumn said as she grabbed her friend's arm. It was too late, the men ambled over to them. Time had taken a lot from Wilson and McGee, including their looks and a few teeth, which they had no problem showing off with the wide smiles they'd focused on them.

"Bella," Wilson said.

Autumn hiked her right eyebrow and rolled her eyes. "Interesting to see you here, Wilbert."

"You know my name, don't act like that. You still look good," he said.

"Too bad you don't," Sonia said with a laugh.

"Aww, look at the least talented member of the group trying to pop shit," Wilson said.

Autumn grabbed Sonia's arm when she saw her friend tense up. "Fuck you," Sonia muttered. "All right, we're going to walk away now," Autumn said, placing her hand on Sonia's shoulder. When they turned to leave, Sonia pointed toward the bar. "There she is," she said.

It had been years since Autumn had seen Vivian in person and there she was looking stunning, like time had stood still. Her skin was buttery smooth, her afro looked like the iconic Foxy Brown, and she was dressed in a blue sequin jumpsuit paired with gold heels. She looked like a fancy billboard for JCSU. Autumn and Sonia crossed over to her.

"Guys," Vivian was saying to the bartenders. "We need to keep the crowd down at the bar and make sure that we're getting the drinks out quickly and we must keep the bar stocked. If you plan to make money, you need to keep those smiles on your faces."

"Okay, Boss Lady," Sonia called out. Vivian looked at her former group members and smiled broadly.

"Oh shit. Sonia and Autumn!" She walked over to them and hugged them both. "It is so good to see you two!"

Sonia hitched her eyebrow as if she was wondering if Vivian was acting or really meant it. Autumn smiled. "You have an amazing place here," she said.

"You should see it on a Tuesday night when we have live music. It's an amazing group here when we turn the mic on. Are you still an image consultant?"

Autumn nodded, even though she had scaled back her work because of her illness. She did a lot of work from home since she'd gotten ill. James wanted her to stop working completely and focus on getting treatment. He had tried to sign her up for every medical trial he'd seen, or his colleagues suggested. But he didn't have to deal with the side effects. She'd done one that was supposed to shrink the tumor and it hadn't worked. It only made her feel worse.

"And you," Vivian said turning to Sonia. "World traveling and telling people where to vacation. I love how we were all able to pivot."

Sonia pursed her lips and sighed. "Yet you haven't reached out to any of us."

Autumn dropped her head. This wasn't how she'd wanted things to begin. But why did she think it would be all sunshine and roses? There was a lot of hurt between them and Sonia had never been one to hold her tongue, even if it was warranted.

"Neither did you," Vivian snapped. "It's not like . . ."

"Hey, is there some place we can go and have this conversation in private?" Autumn asked.

"Do we even need to have a conversation that's going to turn into another argument?" Vivian asked. She exhaled slowly as if she was contemplating walking away.

"Trust me, no one is here to argue," Autumn said before flashing Sonia a stern look.

Sonia nodded. "We really do come in peace. I just. . . I'm sorry for the aggression."

"All right, we can go to my office," Vivian said as she led her friends through the back of the bar area. When they walked into Vivian's office, it was like an altar to the career she'd wished she had. Posters of her old performances, a painting of the album cover that was never released and a mannequin wearing a gown.

"Do you perform here sometimes?" Sonia asked as she looked around.

"I sang once, but it didn't feel right, and I just decided to hang it up and focus on the business. Aside from singing at a few churches, I'm no longer a performer."

"Really?" Autumn asked.

"I know it's hard to believe that I gave up singing, but it was different without you guys," she admitted.

Autumn and Sonia exchanged a look. "Without us?" Sonia asked. "All of us?"

Vivian's comely face darkened. "Not that bitch. You know, I missed the two of you, but Nicole, she can fall off a cliff and fucking die and I wouldn't. . ."

"It isn't Nicole who's going to die," Autumn called out. Vivian blinked and her mouth dropped open.

"What do you mean?" she asked.

Sonia's eyes filled with tears. "Is this how you're going to do this?" Autumn nodded.

"Do what?" Vivian asked. "What's going on?"

"Do you remember how things used to be?" Autumn asked. "How we were more than best friends, we were sisters. All we had was each other."

"I'm sorry, what does that have to do with someone dying?" Vivian asked.

"Vivian, give me this moment," Autumn said. "For too long we've been holding on to bitterness and bullshit that doesn't make any sense. Especially now that so much time has passed."

"Yes," Sonia said.

"It's time for this to stop," Autumn continued. "Because life is too short for things that don't matter."

"What are you getting at?" Vivian asked.

"I'm dying," she said flatly. "And all I want is for the four of us to fix what's broken between us."

Tears welled up in Vivian's eyes. "Autumn," she intoned. "This. . .What . . .Autumn, what's happening?"

"That's not important. I want us to go back to the days when we were everything to each other and remember those feelings. Fuck that group and all the shit that happened. We've never been a packaged band like NSYNC. We loved each other fiercely."

"Did we? Because what she did was unforgivable," Vivian said.

Sonia sucked her teeth. "You're going to rewrite history and pretend that you were totally innocent in everything? You and Nicole did a bunch of foul shit and neither one of you have ever been good at taking responsibility for what you do."

Vivian glared at Sonia. "Still sitting on the fence, huh?"

"You know what, this is exactly why it took me so long to reach out to any of you motherfuckers," Autumn bellowed. "You want to know the truth about that record deal? Or do you want to keep living this it's everybody's fault but mine? We all played a role in the fact that we never made it."

Vivian took a deep breath. "Really? That's how you remember things?"

Autumn shook her head. "What do you remember? And is it even that important?"

"What do you want us to do? Hold hands and sing kumbaya?" Vivian asked.

"Why can't we just be adults and admit that we still love and need each other. I know you know Nicole is going to be here tomorrow morning doing a talk at the Belk Theatre and we should go," Autumn said.

"I'm not paying to hear her bloviate," Vivian said. "As a matter of fact, I don't want to see her at all."

"Tell me why," Autumn asked. "Why are you so dead set against seeing Nicole?"

Chapter Nine

Bella Performance, 1998 –

Autumn was beginning to hate Karina. She seemed to thrive on causing drama within that group. Autumn couldn't see if they were any closer to getting a record deal than they had been without her. And she had the unmitigated gall to suggest that they change the name to Bella Vivian, since Vivian did most of the lead singing. Sonia threatened to quit the group daily and Nicole started writing songs in a lower register just to piss everyone off. Of course, Autumn could hit those notes, but she wasn't going to sing lead because she was tired of Karina saying that she didn't have the "look of success." Karina made it clear to everyone that Vivian's light skin made her more marketable and without her in the forefront, Bella wasn't going to be successful like Destiny's Child if anyone else sang lead. Of course, Vivian had the look that Karina could get behind, light skin, curly hair, and now she was rocking those stupid green contacts. "She looks like a broke ass Stacey Dash," Nicole repeated on a regular basis.

But tonight, Nicole was on one. "I know she's not calling herself making an entrance," she bellowed as she paced back and forth backstage.

"We have an hour before showtime, calm down," Autumn said.

Nicole speared her with an icy look. "We also have sound check and being that all Vivian does is pose these days, we need to run through the routine."

Sonia groaned. "This is not how I thought our first show would go. Are we still trying to cut an album? Are we even going to make it on tour?"

Nicole sucked her teeth. "That's up to your fearless leader."

Moments later, Karina and Vivian walked in. "Good, you all are here," Karina said. "We need to do a sound check, chop, chop ladies."

"Hold the fuck up," Nicole bellowed. "You come strolling in here acting like we're the problem when you're the motherfucking problem, Karina. Why are you two joined at the hip and so damn late?"

Karina threw up her hand. "You need to watch how you talk to me."

"You work for *all of us*," Nicole snapped and jumped in Karina's face. "You should remember that shit."

"And you should remember that anyone can write a song and if it wasn't for Vivian, you three would be on campus still dancing with the marching band. She's the look and the talent and the rest of y'all are just bad back up dancers."

Autumn grabbed Nicole when she saw her flinch as if she was about to pounce on Karina. She turned to Vivian, hoping she would say something to defuse the situation, but she stood there like a mannequin.

"Okay, can we call calm down and focus on what's important," Autumn said. "Karina, we're a group and you're supposed to represent all of us. Why does it feel like Vivian is your priority? I mean, have you gotten any response to our demo? Who have you sent it to?"

"Autumn, you seem to understand business more than others," she said giving Nicole a snide look, but taking a step back. "I'm going to get you ladies a record deal, but the focus is going to be on Vivian because she's the lead singer. I know all of you have amazing voices, but in groups, there is always that one stand-out performer. For Bella, it's Vivian."

"And let's face it," Vivian began. "It's always been me. Y'all came to me and ask me to join this group. Don't forget that."

Nicole pulled out of Autumn's grip and grabbed a bottle of water. Before anyone could react, Nicole had tossed the full bottle at Vivian hitting her in the head. Vivian yelped in pain and Autumn noticed a small knot beginning to form of Vivian's face.

"I'm tired of this shit!" Nicole exploded. "I started this shit. I put all of this together and I be damned if anyone is going to push me out of the way."

Karina rushed over to Vivian to assess her injury. "What have you done? She can't perform with a gash and knot on her face. Why would you do this?"

"Bella can still perform. If Vivian can't, then so be it. Autumn, you're singing lead tonight," Nicole said. "Time for soundcheck."

Autumn and Sonia looked from Vivian to Nicole, neither one of them sure what was going to happen next. When Karina let Vivian go, Vivian charged at Nicole and tried to grab her around the neck. Nicole shoved her elbow into Vivian's stomach. She doubled over in pain and Nicole lifted her foot as if she was going to kick her. Autumn stepped in between them to stop a further assault. "This is enough. What the fuck is happening here?"

Autumn exclaimed. "This is our first show, and this is how we're getting ready for it?"

"Thank you for being the voice of reason, Autumn," Karina said as she helped Vivian to her feet. "If you all—all four of you—don't get on the stage, no one is getting paid. I need some ice. Maybe we can stop the swelling and cover it up with some makeup."

"We still have to do a sound check; we don't have time to . . ." Sonia began, then turned to Nicole who was packing her things. "What are you doing?"

"I'm leaving. Fuck this shit. Fuck Karina, Vivian and you two if you stay!"

"Nicole," Autumn exclaimed. "This was supposed to be our moment."

"Our moment has been ruined and I don't give a damn about getting paid. I'm done with this shit." Nicole stormed out of the dressing room. Autumn, Sonia and Vivian looked around in shock. Grand opening, grand closing. It took Karina about twenty minutes to talk to the club owner and let him know that the performance wasn't going to happen.

"That fucking bitch," Vivian swore. "Look at my face."

Autumn tilted her head to the side. "You're really going to act like you played no part in all of this?"

"What are you talking about? I didn't do anything. . ."

"Oh, stop the bullshit," Sonia said. "You have been pulling this diva act since homecoming and we have been letting a lot slide because *Karina* said we were so close to a record deal. I don't see no offers; all I see is you pretending that you've created Bella when you know damn well this was Nicole's dream to highlight her songwriting. If it wasn't for Autumn you wouldn't even be a part of this. You would still be begging the AKAs to let you pledge."

Autumn didn't mean to laugh, but she couldn't help it.

"You know what," Vivian snapped. "Fuck y'all. You wanted me to be a part of this stupid group because you bitches knew without me you wouldn't be shit."

"Clearly, *Eddie Kang, J.r.*, we ain't shit with you either," Sonia bellowed.

"Can we stop," Autumn said. "Can we calm down and. . ."

"Oh, Autumn, take that Oprah shit somewhere and spin on it," Vivian said. "You're always on Nicole's side and she doesn't give a shit about you either."

"And who do you give a shit about, Vivian?" Autumn snapped. "Because from the looks of it, all you care about is you. It wasn't always like that, but you let Karina fool you into thinking you were bigger than the rest of us."

"Karina was supposed to get us a deal and she said I needed to be out front for that to happen. Why is it the one thing that I do to try and get us on the map, I'm turned into the fucking villain?"

"Because you put that costume on and it fit so well," Sonia said.

"Sonia, please, you're just here because no one else wanted to be," Vivian hissed.

"You want another knot on your head? You need to watch your damned mouth when you're talking to me," Sonia said as she closed the space between them.

"I'm out of here," Vivian exclaimed. "Because I don't need you hoes to prop me up. Like Karina says, I'm the fucking voice. You hear that!" She tore out of the room and Sonia shook her head. "What now?"

Autumn shrugged. "I guess we go back to campus?"

Sonia rolled her eyes. "Yeah, so you can go spend the night with J.R. Were we really friends or was this just about the group? I gave up a lot to be a part of this circus. Quit Blue Satin, practiced with y'all, cut a demo in a studio full of thugs. And all for nothing. Just a waste of time and now that it's over, you just want to run to your boyfriend. Vivian and Nicole are off on some we hate the world shit. But have any of you given a thought to how I may be feeling?"

"I guess, I . . ."

"Maybe Vivian was right, I have been just a stand in and none of y'all, you included, ever gave a damn about me." Sonia retreated from the room despite Autumn calling after her. This was probably the worst night of her life. Maybe tomorrow cooler heads would prevail, and they would make up. But tonight, she was going to cry in James's arms. What happened tonight was painful, but if Autumn was honest, she hoped without the group, they could go back to being best friends again.

Chapter Ten

Homecoming Present Day –

Vivian stalked the length of her office as if she, Autumn and Sonia were sharing the same memory. The night of their performance had been the nail in the coffin of their friendship. Autumn had gotten pregnant with Tyler that night. Nicole had moved off campus with the same Que who Vivian had claimed she was in love with, and Sonia went back to the Blue Satin crew and started doing the choreography for the dancers during basketball season. For the next year, they'd walked around campus pretending they didn't even know each other. Autumn spent so much time in Smith Hall with James that the resident hall advisors didn't bat an eye when she was in there after co-ed hours.

Nicole hadn't been on campus long enough for anyone to see her. She'd come for classes and head back to her apartment. Little did they know that Nicole was building a foundation that turned her into one of the industry's most prolific songwriters. But how could they know? She hadn't spoken to any of them since the night of the performance brawl.

"You know, I haven't thought about Bella or our implosion since that night and I guess that means I hadn't thought about y'all either. And you're right, Autumn, we were more than just a singing group, but once business came into play, things changed and that was where we messed up. But none of you reached out until today." Vivian folded her arms across her chest and tilted her head to the side.

"That's not true, but if that makes you feel better, you can act like you never read the messages I sent you on Facebook," Sonia said with an eye roll.

"I thought it was spam," Vivian said with a wave of her hand. "Look, I was hurt, and I've been holding on to it for years. That night at the club, y'all really turned your back on me like I was everything Nicole said that I was. My intentions. . ."

"That's the past and we can't rewrite history," Autumn said. "We all made mistakes."

Vivian looked at Autumn and tears welled up in her eyes. "I wish it didn't take this for us to be here."

Autumn shrugged. "We're not anywhere yet. Not until we try to make peace with everyone."

Vivian pushed her afro back and displayed the scar on her forehead. "There's really no peace to be made with that maniac. She really assaulted me and y'all stood there and watched. Like that was some bullshit."

Autumn's right eyebrow shot up. "Really?"

"So, do you want me to say sorry?" Sonia asked. "I know at that moment; I was in shock."

Autumn nodded. "No one expected that."

"And not one of you checked on me afterwards. I never expected Nicole to act like a human, but you two. I thought we were better than that."

"The way you would turn away from me when we passed each other on campus?" Sonia said, "Why was I going to beg you to talk to me?"

"Because I needed to know that I still had friends. Well, I guess what we thought we had wasn't much after all," she said.

Autumn sighed. "Are we forgetting that we were young and didn't know how to deal with real shit. We were all hurt and trying to work through the bad feelings."

"At least you had J.R. How is the drum major these days?"

"My husband is fine. He'll be here in the morning. Maybe in time for Nicole's talk at the Belk Theatre."

Vivian rolled her eyes. "I'm not going to see her. If you reach out to her and she wants to apologize, then maybe we can have a discussion."

"Maybe? So, what you're saying is – fuck my dying wish?" Autumn said.

Vivian shrugged. "This isn't the make a wish foundation," she muttered.

"You're being such a bitch right now," Sonia snapped. "I guess you haven't changed, you just got older."

"And you're still . . .You know what, I'm going to wish you all the best, Autumn, and keep you in my prayers. But I will not be kissing Nicole's ass tomorrow or anytime during homecoming."

"Well, thank you," Autumn said. "I'm going to head over to campus and check on my son."

Vivian rolled her eyes. "You could've come up with a better excuse to leave than that. You know your child is not on campus and if he is, you probably don't want to know what he's doing right now."

"Especially if he is his daddy's son," Sonia laughed.

"Ha, ha, ha," Autumn deadpanned. "Okay, great, I want to get out of here because I'm disappointed. Better?"

"I'm sorry that I disappointed you," Vivian said. "But she never assaulted you. Listen, you guys are here, at least be my VIP guests. We can get a table and a couple of bottles and have a good time tonight."

Sonia nudged Autumn. "Well, we're already here, let's drink her good liquor and have a little fun."

"Well, I won't turn down drinks and a small plate," Autumn said with a grin.

"I don't have any Showmars, and I know your ass ate there as soon as you got here," Vivian laughed.

"And did. Still hits the same as it did in Greenfield," she laughed.

"Maybe you should pull out some calamari and wine or something?"

"My chef has shrimp and wings tonight. Maybe tomorrow we can have dinner at Sea Level," Vivian said. "We can go right after the game."

"Yes, because I have to watch my son perform his last homecoming show. Oh, but wait, James might want to do a family dinner or something. Let's have breakfast."

Vivian hitched her eyebrow. "You're not slick. I guess we all get together for breakfast and then end up at the Belk Theatre? Autumn, just accept that I don't want to see Nicole and . . ."

"Where's the food and drinks?" Sonia interrupted. "We can work out Autumn being manipulative later."

"Right," Vivian said as she squeezed Sonia's hand. "Always a scammer."

"Real funny," Autumn said. "I hope these small plates are going to be worth the abuse I'm taking from you two."

"It'll be worth it. Marlon is amazing with his chef skills, and he knows he's cooking for some real VIPs and me."

"Then let's get to it," Autumn said as a wave of pain washed over her. She prayed her friends didn't see her grimace. They had.

"Are you okay?" Vivian asked as she grabbed Autumn's elbow. She led Autumn to a chair and Autumn closed her eyes while taking deep breaths.

"Do you have your pain medicine?" Sonia asked, since she knew the signs of what was going on.

Autumn waved her hand. "Give me a second," she said. "And I can't take those pills and drink."

"Then don't drink," Sonia shouted. "You can't sit here and..."

Autumn stood up. "I'm fine," she said with forced bravado. "Let's go."

Sonia and Vivian narrowed their eyes at her. "Whatever," Vivian said. "Do we need to go somewhere else? Back to your hotel or something?"

Autumn's pain began to subside. She knew it was going to be a fleeting moment. "I'm fine. These things happen every now and then. I'm going to need you two to stop acting as if I'm about to drop dead every few minutes."

Vivian folded her arms across her chest. "What the hell am I supposed to think? You walked in here and said you're dying, then you look as if. . ."

"If something serious happens, then I will let you two know, all right?" Autumn said with her eyebrow cocked.

Sonia nudged Vivian. "We're going to have to watch her because you know how Autumn gets."

"I'm guessing that hasn't changed, right? Autumn Brown gets an idea, and nothing is going to stop her from making it happen, right?"

"First of all," Autumn said as she glanced at her friends. "It's Brown-Robinson and you're damn right. And I'm not above using everything I got to get it. Now, can we get to the table?"

Vivian led the women out to the main area of the club. The place was packed with alumni from various classes including the mid-2000s. Vivian smiled like a proud mother. "Oh, I'm going to have to do this every year," she said as she pointed to an empty table that was marked reserved.

"Were you expecting us?" Sonia joked.

"Nope, but this table is a thousand dollars, and no one paid for it. I do that just in case I want to come out and watch how things are going," Vivian said.

"Now, what makes this a thousand dollar table?" Autumn asked as they sat down.

Two seconds later a server was standing in front of them with a chilled bottle of champagne and two small plates of shrimp and sweet potato fries.

"All right, I see it," Autumn said with a head nod.

Sonia pulled out her phone and snapped a picture. "Definitely going to have to put this on my list of places to go," she said. "Cause, that had to be some kind of magic."

"On the occasions that I sell these tables, I have to make sure the service is immaculate. There are sensors on the seats, which alert the bottle servers when someone is sitting here."

"Genius," Sonia said. "You have a great place for real."

Autumn nodded. "Do you sell out every night?"

Vivian shrugged. "We do best during our themed nights. I'm not struggling at all, but you're only Charlotte's favorite place until something new comes around."

"Yeah because whatever happened to Club 607?" Sonia laughed.

"Hell, Uptown doesn't look anything like it did when we first got here. Everything is so bright and shiny," Autumn said. "Except Two-Way."

"Lord, I can't believe developers haven't torn that place down yet," Sonia said. "I wonder if freshmen still get the same warnings we got when we went through orientation?"

"It's not the same neighborhood. Those old run down houses where the Ques used to party are million dollar McMansions now," Vivian said. "The gentrification of The Ford is real and disgusting."

"And why did y'all let your mayor tear down McCrorey's house?" Sonia asked.

"Don't even bring that up," Vivian said. "And then she was the commencement speaker a couple of years ago. Ugh. I can't stand her."

"How does she keep getting reelected?" Autumn asked.

Vivian shrugged. "Name recognition and when you have people named Princess running against her, it's like the lesser of two evils."

"Hey," Sonia said. "Y'all are real boring right now. Let's see who is walking around here and who got beat with the time wasn't kind stick."

"Petty mode activated, I see," Vivian said with a smile. She spun around in her seat and looked out into the crowd. "Have y'all seen anyone you remember yet?"

Sonia and Autumn laughed. "Oh yeah, we saw some people who we could've gone our whole lives without seeing again."

"Who?"

"McGee and Wilson," Sonia said. "They look like life beat the hell out of them."

Vivian shook her head. "I ought to have security kick them out. Those two were the worst, trying to act like they wanted to help us."

Autumn snorted, "Wilson acted as if he hated us because we were in college, then he wanted to take credit for the group name."

"I bet his ass has never even been to Italy," Vivian said.

"Just Roma Pizza in the mall," Sonia said.

"Rome is beautiful, if you haven't gone you should," Autumn said with a soft look in her eyes. "James and I wanted to renew our vows there."

"Why didn't you?" Vivian asked. "I still can't believe y'all are married. It's. . ."

"Y'all keep thinking that the rumors about my man were true," she said. "James was more than just a big dick and a good time. Remember the homecoming when we performed with the band?"

Vivian and Sonia groaned. "The beginning of the end," Sonia said.

"Anyway. Most of y'all came by my room looking for me. But that was the night James and I knew that we were going to be together forever."

Vivian cocked her right eyebrow. "You mean I was knocking on your door and y'all were in there fucking? Eww. I needed you."

"We were in the shower waiting for you hoes to calm the fuck down. I guess that never happened," Autumn said.

"Damn," Sonia exclaimed. "You know, maybe we do need to make an effort to see Nicole."

"Ooh, look, there's Michael Broussard," Vivian said. "Remember him? Umm, he's still fine."

Sonia rolled her eyes. "Don't try and change the subject. Vivian, we need to do this, if not for us then let's do it for Autumn. Just think about everything she's always done for us."

Vivian sighed. "Fine, but Autumn, this is for you and that's it. What time is her little speech tomorrow?"

"Ten and be on time. Is that Derek Gadson? Now that dude doesn't look like what he's been through," Autumn said.

"What do you mean?" Sonia asked.

"Wait, wait, Sonia, didn't you and Derek. . ."

Sonia threw up her hand to cut Vivian off. "Don't bring up bad memories. He's a clown. And he acted like he was so in love with that chick. What was her name?"

"Whitney," Autumn said. "They got married, you know."

"Aww, good for them," Sonia said sarcastically and clapped her hands.

Autumn popped her on the arm. "Don't be like that. She died."

Sonia covered her mouth with her hand. "Oh, my goodness. That's so sad."

Vivian snorted. "Yeah and he remarried like six months later. You can't tell me that he wasn't cheating on that woman while she was sick."

Autumn took a sharp breath as her mind flashed back to a conversation that she and James had when her situation became terminal.

Autumn had heard the words come out of the doctor's mouth. Inoperable. Terminal. She'd made peace with her condition, but the look on James's face made her pause. What was life going to be like for him when she was gone? Would he be able to live his life knowing that so many of their plans never happened? More importantly, would he be able to move on? James had a lot of life to live, and she didn't want him to feel guilty for moving on after she was gone. He took her hand in his as the doctor talked about quality of life and end stage. Weight loss. Tiredness. Loss of sexual desire.

That hit her hard. She and James had an active sex life, and she knew everything the doctor was saying was going to make things. . .He needed a girlfriend. They headed out to the car after shaking hands with the doctor. Autumn smiled because he pulled out the Mustang every time he took her to the doctor.

"James," she said as they got into the car. "We need to talk."

"Yeah, we have to get another opinion and see if someone else can give us a different answer."

"No, that's not what we need to talk about. We need to talk about you."

He shot her a questioning look. "What do you mean? Autumn, I'm not going to accept that there's nothing that can be done and I'm supposed to watch you. . ."

"Die, James. I'm dying and you need to come to grips with that. There's going to be a time when I'm not here and I want you to live. I want you to be open to other things in this life that don't include me. Even another woman."

James gripped the steering wheel and groaned. "Autumn why are you so intent on . . ."

"Do you know how much pain I'm in? These treatments and experiments aren't working. This isn't a life worth living and I don't want to stop you from moving forward," she said with tears forming in her eyes.

He pressed the start button on the car but didn't shift it in gear. "What are you saying, Autumn?"

She sighed and closed her eyes. "I'm saying you need to find someone else to love."

"What the fuck, Autumn?" he bellowed. "Why would you say something like that?"

"You've done it before when the stakes were much lower."

"Seriously? You're sitting here telling me . . .When I slipped up with that woman, it was a one-time thing that you said you forgave me for. Why are you bringing it up now?"

"Because you're not going to die, I am. Don't let your life end when I'm not here and if that means you need to find someone now, then do it."

James angrily shifted the car in to reverse. "Fu. . .Autumn, we've been through a lot together and for you to sit there and say some bullshit like that? Why?"

"Because I know you. You're a person who needs someone. Yes, I thought it was always going to be me, but that's not the case anymore. I want your life to continue, I want you and Tyler to be happy when I'm gone. You don't deserve to . . ."

"Just stop," James said as a tear spilled down his cheek. "Don't tell me how I'm supposed to feel or how I'm going to survive now that you've given up."

"Given up? That's how you feel? Do you think that I don't want to fight to be here and spend the rest of my life with you, loving you and . . .Fuck you, James."

"Right back at you, Autumn."

They rode in silence for a few minutes. He glanced over at her after a while. "You want to get something to eat?"

"Yes. Hot wings," she said, realizing that was his way of saying I'm sorry. And hot wings were the acceptance of that apology.

Autumn looked at her friends as they talked about how trifling Derek was and how there was a special place in hell for him. She wanted to tell them that they didn't understand how hard it is to watch the person you love slowly losing faith and dying in other ways. Maybe that had been why Derek moved on so quickly. Would they judge James if he did the same? Would he do the same thing? Autumn didn't know if he'd met anyone else or if he had taken her advice. Other than right now, he'd been by her side, helping her manage her pain. Staying up at night monitoring her breathing and making sure she made it through the night. Every day she loved him more and more. She wished there was a way she could live so that she could be with her man forever. But that was a fairy tale that didn't exist.

"Why are you so quiet?" Sonia asked Autumn. "Are you okay?"

"Yeah, I'm just thinking about James and what people might say about him when . . ."

"Is he cheating?" Vivian exclaimed. "That is. . ."

"No, he's not. But how am I supposed expect him to end his life when I die? What if he falls in love again? Are y'all going to judge him as harshly?"

Sonia and Vivian looked at each other as if they were thinking about the conversation they'd just had. "I-I didn't think about it like that," Sonia said. "Are there protocols in place for how to move on?"

Autumn shrugged. "No one's ever prepared for death. Even when you see it coming. Honestly, James is still on the search for a miracle that's not going to come. If he finds love again, I think he should have the chance to find happiness. My life is ending, not his."

Vivian cried silently and turned away from her friends. "This is real and I just. Damn, why did I let so much time pass without talking to you? Autumn, I'm sorry."

"You know how you can really make things up to me, right?" Autumn said.

"Anything but that."

"Vivian, stop it. Let's just meet Nicole and see what happens. Maybe we all need this," Sonia said vehemently.

"Fine, I'll do it, but if . . .I'll be mature," Vivian said.

Autumn and Sonia exchanged a *yeah right* look. "What?" Vivian questioned with a shoulder shrug. "Okay, okay, I'll try."

"That's all I'll ask for," Autumn said. "Ooh, look, isn't that Lily Graham. Her books are so good."

"I don't care what anyone says, her first book was about Smith," Vivian said. "I just wonder who she was talking about."

"You, of course," Sonia laughed.

"Keep playing and I'm going to cut you off," Vivian said as she waved for the server to bring them a couple of plates of food.

Autumn felt good being with her friends tonight, but she couldn't stop wondering what tomorrow would hold.

Chapter Eleven

When Autumn's phone rang at five in the morning, she realized that she was old. She, Sonia and Vivian had been out mostly all night. After happy hour, they headed to an after-hours party the alumni band held at an Airbnb in South Charlotte. Autumn answered so many questions about her husband and her son that she and her girls started taking shots every time someone asked her about one of them. By the time they'd been ready to leave, they were drunk as hell. Now, she was paying for it so hard.

She grabbed her phone and saw James's face on the screen. "Hey baby," she said, her voice raspy.

"Sounds like your ass forgot that you're not a college student anymore," he said with a laugh.

"It's your band mates' fault," she replied. "They forgot that all of us are older and not that wise when it comes to tequila."

"Are you doing too much?" James asked, concern peppering his tone. "Autumn, I know you want to feel normal, but you . . ."

"What time does your flight land?"

"Oh, so you're going to do me like that. I'm going to keep asking the question and objecting to this bullshit. But my flight lands at seven-thirty and I reserved a Mustang."

"Aww, you really do love me," she teased.

"Forever and always," he said longingly. "Are you going to leave a key at the front desk for me or will you be waiting in the room for me?"

"Well, I really want to see you so, if you can make it here before nine-thirty, I'll be oiled up and naked."

"By nine-thirty? What's going on this morning?"

"Nicole's doing a talk at the Belk Theatre this morning and we're going to see her."

James groaned. "I hope you get what you want from all of this. But what if Nicole acts like the diva she's always accused Vivian of being? I mean she can do that."

"I have faith in what we meant to each other before things fell apart. James, if it doesn't work out, then I'll be happy to wash my hands of all of this. But at least I tried."

"I love you so much," he said. "And I don't want you to be hurt. So, I'm going to say a little prayer that everything works out for you."

"See, marrying you is still one of the best decisions of my life," Autumn said. "I can't wait to see you."

"Me either. And if I get a ticket speeding to you, know that I'm thinking about you naked in the middle of the bed."

Autumn looked down at herself, still dressed in her outfit from the night before, her hair matted to her head. If only he knew what he'd be seeing right now. "Save travels, darling," she said before hanging up. As much as she wanted to roll over and go back to sleep, Autumn pulled herself from the bed, peeled off her jumpsuit and headed for the shower.

Turning the spray on, a wave of pain attacked her to the point that she screamed out in discomfort. Things were getting worse, and she knew exactly what it meant. She sat down on the toilet and took several deep breaths, but it didn't work to calm the throbbing pain in her abdomen. Today she'd take a pain pill, maybe even three. Steam filled the bathroom and Autumn wished she had the strength to turn the water off.

But she couldn't move without feeling as if her insides were being ripped apart. Forty-five minutes passed before the pain subsided and she was able to walk into the main area of the suite and grab her medicine.

popped two pills then headed back to the shower and got underneath the now lukewarm water.

Her body shivered as the water hit her, not because it was too cold, but because she was afraid. Was her time running out sooner than she thought? The pain was coming more frequently, and the pills weren't helping that much, just giving a temporary relief that she needed to be expanded this weekend. But Autumn was realistic, if the end was near, she was ready. Well, kind of. She hoped Nicole wouldn't be holding on to bitterness like Vivian had been. She'd made it and gotten the Grammys they'd dreamed about.

Autumn closed her eyes as the water washed over her and remembered the day they decided to start the group.

Nicole plopped down on the extra bed in Autumn's room. "How did you get lucky enough to not have a roommate? Because every morning I wake up to snoring and grunting from that damned girl I'm forced to live with," she said as Autumn typed on her laptop.

"Luck is the name of the game," she replied. "You and Ashley aren't enemies, so you'll be fine."

"Until she finds out that her so-called man ate me out while he was waiting for her last week."

Autumn turned around and gasped at her friend. "Nicole!"

"What? He challenged me and I never back down from a challenge. Unfortunately, he keeps trying to make things strange. I can't keep this shit going," she laughed.

"Well, if she finds out, my door is open to you."

Nicole pulled out her notebook and started writing. Autumn arched her eyebrow. "Are you journaling about this?"

She shook her head. "I'm writing a song. You know, your voice is amazing, and we could start a singing group."

"You mean a duo?"

Nicole shook her head again. "I mean we can get two other talented members and be bigger than anyone on the charts right now. Of course, you'd be the lead singer."

"No, ma'am. I don't have that Diana Ross vibe. But I know someone who does," Autumn said with a finger snap. "Do you know Vivian Leslie?"

"No, should I?"

Autumn nodded. "She has an amazing voice and she's pretty."

"So am I and so are you."

Autumn rolled her eyes. "And I know the business. Brown skinned girls with amazing voices are overlooked for mediocre light skin girls with long hair."

"Umm, are you saying this Vivian girl is mediocre?"

"Nope, she's talented and that's what would set us apart from the rest of the girl groups out there. Everyone will be talented. We have our songwriter in house, we can dance. Oh, Sonia Williams is a great choreographer, but our director of Blue Satin won't give her a chance to do her thing."

"You know everybody," Nicole said. "We should really do this."

"Nicole, you have an amazing voice and I'm here for us being successful. Just imagine us at the Grammys in the best gowns and walking on that stage grabbing the record of the year award."

"Okay big dreamer. I see the vision. And I love it. I'm glad you're going to be beside me when all of this comes true. But how do we do this?"

Autumn shrugged. "We can run away to Detroit and hope the new Motown finds us."

"Absolutely not. If we go anywhere it's going to be Atlanta."

"S-O S-O D E F," Autumn sang.

"I'm thinking LaFace Records would be a better home for us. I don't want to be walking around in sweatsuits looking like Jermane's favorite girl group. I want to be taken seriously as a grown woman group."

"But we're not that grown. So-So Def reaches our target audience. Maybe on the second album we can expand on our audience. Right now, we're going to have to meet folks with disposable income to buy our music, you know."

"Look at you getting the business side of music ready for us," Nicole said. "We're going to be a huge success, because we're not going into this blind. I love it."

"The problem with a lot of groups is the fact that they don't know that the business part of the music business is just as important as the talent."

"Every group doesn't have an Autumn Brown. Thank God we will."

"Remember that. You're thanking God for me, that means I'm holy."

"Whatever. Okay, so we need to reach out to the other girls and see if they want to make a band."

Autumn looked down at her watch. "No time like the present. Let's go to the café."

"I'm not trying to eat that shit today."

"I said nothing about eating, but that's where everybody is hanging out right now. Besides, after we talk to them, you're taking me to Showmars."

"Damn it, Autumn, I need you to find a new place to eat," Nicole said as she rose to her feet.

"Whatever, you know you want some shrimp."

Nicole nodded. "You're right." They headed out the front door of Greenfield Hall and headed across the yard seeking a musical connection.

Autumn smiled then realized she was crying. How could they forget the joy and happiness they'd felt that day and most of the ones that followed. She shut the shower off and grabbed a towel. When she walked into the bedroom, she heard knocking at the door. Glancing at the clock, she realized how late it was. Sonia must have been ready to go.

"Give me a second," she said as she secured the towel around her body. Without looking out the peephole, she opened the door and James smiled at her.

"You were waiting on me anxiously, I see," he teased then took her in his arms.

"James, how did you get here so fast? And where are your bags?"

"You know I rented a Mustang, and the traffic gods were pleased because there was hardly anyone on the highway and I couldn't wait to see my wife. My bag, because you know I don't check shit, is in the trunk of the car."

Autumn sighed and smiled at her husband. "I'm so glad you're here."

"How are you feeling? And tell the truth."

"I'm good, J.R."

He snorted. "So, this is how we're doing things today?"

"What do you mean?"

"You call me J.R. when you're lying." He crossed the room and picked up her pill bottle, noting how empty it was. "Autumn, the pain is getting worse, isn't it?"

"Yes, James," she said as she plopped down on the edge of the bed. "And before you start, just know that I'm not going to listen to a lecture while I'm naked and wet."

He faced his wife and smirked. "You know, I would ask is that an invitation, but I don't like the fact that you been crying. Are you hurting that bad?" He held her face in his hands.

"No, I was thinking about the ladies and how everything started. It made me sad to know we gave it up because of outside interference."

"Some people say I was a part of that, being that I knocked you up and what not," he chuckled.

"That's because people don't know what really happened and it's none of their damned business. I'm glad you knocked me up," she said. James sat beside Autumn and started massaging her shoulders.

"You ever think about how you could've made it as a solo artist?"

"That was never my calling," she replied. "Nicole was upset that I turned down the opportunity to do it."

James shook his head. "Again, I'm not a huge fan of your girl. You did her a favor singing that song so that she could write songs for those groups, and she repaid you by. . . Well, you know what she did and what she said."

Autumn leaned into James's chest. "You know you don't have to come today if you still feel some kind of way about her."

"Autumn, I'm here for you, not her, not Sonia, not Vivian. You wanted me here and I'm not going anywhere until we go home together. Actually, I take that back, I'm going to see what Tyler has going on for halftime. That boy better represent."

"Don't put undue pressure on my son," she said. "He's doing *his* thing as drum major and stepping out of his father's shadow."

James kissed Autumn's temple. "I know that, but I still need to see that the legacy is intact."

She laughed and relaxed in his arms. A few minutes passed before there was another knock at the door. "I bet that's Sonia. Will you get the door while I get dressed?"

"I'll be happy to," he said then brushed another kiss across her temple.

Autumn grabbed her outfit and ducked into the bathroom.

"Damn, I didn't expect both of y'all," she heard James say.

"Hello to you to, J.R.," Vivian said.

He grunted in response to her. "Sonia, it is good to see you again, since it hasn't been decades."

Autumn knew she needed to hurry up and get out of the bathroom before things got super ugly. She dried the left over dampness on her legs, then slipped her dress on.

"Hey guys," she said when she walked out of the bathroom. "Sorry I'm not ready, but thanks for being on time."

Vivian cleared her throat, "I guess we don't have to ask what the delay was. Somethings never change."

Autumn rushed over to James and slapped her hand across his mouth. And in true J.R. fashion, he licked her palm. She laughed and dropped her hand.

Sonia shook her head and laughed as well. "After all of these years, y'all are still the cutest thing ever," she said.

"Thank you," James said then rolled his eyes at Vivian. "Let's clear the air really quick." He focused a stare on Vivian and took a breath.

"James, do we have to do this?" Autumn asked softly.

"We do," he replied. "Because I'm not going to be able to be Mr. Supportive Husband if I don't get this off my chest. Vivian, you've been a real bitch to my wife, and she might be able to forgive you for that, but I'm struggling with that because I know how it hurt her when she received your letter five years ago."

Sonia looked from Autumn to Vivian. "What letter?" she asked.

Autumn closed her eyes. "James. . ."

"No," Vivian said. "I'm surprised Autumn didn't say anything about it last night and I'm sorry."

James rolled his eyes. "Yeah, but are you going to take responsibility for your role in ruining the group and your friendship? You've been playing the victim for years and blaming everyone because you failed."

Vivian gasped and blinked away tears. "You're right and I was. . .I almost let time run out and that would've been the biggest mistake of my life. Autumn, you were right to walk away and focus on your family. You had something real and if I'm being honest, I hate that I held on to anger and then added jealousy to the pot."

Sonia narrowed her eyes at Vivian but kept silent. Vivian turned to Sonia and sighed. "I owe you an apology too," she said. "You didn't deserve the way I treated you and I don't know why I thought I should've been the center of attention. Maybe it was because all my life I'd been ignored and the only time I felt as if I mattered was when I was singing with you guys. When I lost that and our friendship, I didn't have anything."

"So, taking it out on the people you shitted on was the way you made yourself feel better?" James interjected.

"James," Autumn said. "Why don't we just put a pin in this?"

"No," Sonia said. "Because we should've heard this years ago. Vivian, just because the group didn't work out, we shouldn't have thrown everything else away. And you made it clear that there was no going back. So much so that

I thought we all hated each other. Look at how much time we lost and how much we can't get back."

"But you reached out to Autumn and . . ."

"I sure did because out of all of us Autumn is the only one who ever had the good sense to know that we were supposed to mean more to each other than a fucking singing group," Sonia snapped. "Was that all we were to you?"

Vivian turned her head to the side and wiped her tears. "It was another let down and I'd had so many in my life that I thought we'd be different and when that didn't happen, I just turned inward."

"That's all you have to say?" James asked. "Because it still sounds like you're the victim here."

"James, stop it, I'm serious," Autumn shouted. "Everyone in this room has made mistakes and we've all hurt each other. Let's try to heal while we have time. And we need to get to the Belk Theatre."

"Fine," he said. "Where are the tickets?"

Autumn and Sonia laughed. "Umm," Autumn said. "About that, see what had happened was. . ."

James furrowed his brows. "You don't have tickets to a sold out event? How in the hell are we supposed to get in?"

Autumn stroked his forearm. "Who's going to tell Dr. James Robinson no?"

Chapter Twelve

Autumn was surprised that Vivian and Sonia agreed to take the light rail down to the event, but there was no way the four of them could've packed into James's rented Mustang. The knees weren't what they used to be in the 1990s when they would pile into his car to grab food or go to the mall to hang out.

"This is nice," James said as they stepped on the train. "Imagine the trouble we could've gotten into if we had this when we were in school."

"Oh, we got into enough trouble with the bus and boys with cars," Sonia quipped.

Autumn smiled and squeezed James's thigh. "Isn't that the truth."

"So, am I the bus or the boy with the car?" he asked.

"It was the Mustang, J.R.," Vivian said. "Because if you had a Honda, you might not be sitting here."

The foursome laughed then Autumn leaned over and whispered in his ear. "You know that's not true, right?" He kissed her on the cheek and replied.

"I know. Because even in a Honda, I still have this big. . ."

"Stop it."

Vivian and Sonia smiled at them. "You know, the Alumni Band does a performance at halftime and J.R., you know you still have pull. What if we recreate our one and only good performance," Vivian said.

"Umm, how about no," Sonia said. "Besides, we haven't practiced, and Autumn might. . ."

"I don't want to take the focus off my son," Autumn said, not telling anyone that even if they could pull it off, she wouldn't be able to perform. Not with the pain she'd been experiencing.

Vivian nodded. "I know that's right, and no offense, J.R., he might be better than you were." "Don't tell me you've been watching my son and comparing us," he laughed.

"No, I just listen to people talking about him at the alumni meetings. You two should be proud," Vivian said. "Because you know how JCSU loves that band."

Autumn grabbed James's hand. "We are, even though somebody wants to tell his kid what to do with his career."

"Let's keep that in house," James said. "I just believe he can do more than be a band director or whatever he said. Just because people expect you to do something, it doesn't mean that you should."

Autumn rolled her eyes, knowing that James and Tyler would end up hashing this out without her. But she knew her son's future was bright, and James was going to have to allow him to make his own way.

She cleared her throat. "A conductor is not a band director. And now I'm done."

When they arrived at the Belk Theater, Autumn felt a pain bubbling in her stomach. She thought it was nerves, but the closer they got to the entrance, she regretted leaving her pain pills at the hotel. James noticed the look on Autumn's face. "You good?"

"Yes, I'm just fine. And can we not do this all day," she gritted.

"I'm not making any promises," James said then kissed her cheek. "But if you tell me that you aren't feeling well, I won't have to ask."

"This line is insane," Vivian said. "Who knew Nicole was this interesting?"

"Your bitchiness is showing, you might want to put it in your pocket," Sonia said. "How are we getting in again?"

James looked at the line and then turned to the women. "Y'all look kind of studious. Hold on a second." He walked up to the box office window and the three women waited with bated breath. Autumn wondered if they had a snowball's chance in hell of getting in. If all the people in line had tickets, would they even have a place to sit?

About fifteen minutes later, James returned to the ladies with three lanyards. "All right, research assistants, we're going backstage."

"What?" Autumn exclaimed. "How?"

"I'm a charming son of a bitch when I want to be. Come on, let's go," he said.

They headed to the front entrance where a security officer escorted them backstage. Autumn held James's hand as she felt a wave of pain wash over her.

James glanced at her face and sighed. "We can leave if this is too much for you," he whispered.

"And let all your charming go to waste? I'm fine, James. Just a little pain and we know that's going to happen."

"Your face is saying something else," he said. "I don't like this, Autumn."

She took a deep breath and forced a smile. "I'm good, babe," she said.

Moments later, they were standing outside of Nicole's dressing room.

Autumn turned to her friends and smiled. "Who's going to knock on the door?" she asked. Sonia and Vivian exchanged a look.

"This was your idea," Vivian said. "Go on and take the lead."

James knocked on the door.

"Come in," a voice called out. Autumn immediately recognized it was Nicole.

James opened the door then stepped aside for the ladies to walk in.

"Hi, Nicole," Autumn said as she crossed into the room.

Nicole looked up at her and smiled. "Well, well, it's a reunion," she said as she stood up and walked over to Autumn. "How are you doing?"

"I'm . . ."

"Nicole," Sonia said. "You're going to act like the rest of us aren't here?"

Nicole glanced at Sonia and Vivian and surprisingly, she smiled as she crossed over to them. "I'm really happy to see all of y'all. It's been way too long."

Vivian tilted her head to the side and glared at Nicole but didn't say a word.

As if she could feel the unspoken tension, Autumn cleared her throat. "Yes, it has been a long time and that's why we wanted to come see you since we're all in Charlotte for the first time in years."

"Oh my God, y'all are ridiculous," James muttered. "I'm going to step outside so y'all can have a real conversation."

"No, James," Nicole said. "You don't have to go, because I know that you have something to say, and I want all you to hear my apology."

"Your apology?" Vivian asked.

Nicole nodded at Vivian. "Yes. I'm going to start with you."

"Do you really want to do this before you go on stage?" Autumn asked. "You need to be on point for the audience."

Nicole sighed. "I know, but lately, I've been thinking about us and that's one of the reasons why I accepted this invitation. Part of me hoped that at least one of you guys would be here for homecoming."

"And which one of us did you hope to see?" Sonia asked.

"I wasn't sure, but everything happens for a reason. And look at this, here we all are."

"Do you know why we're here?" Sonia said.

"I know it's time to apologize for what happened back in the day and I'm genuinely sorry for destroying our chance at our dream."

"You didn't do it alone," Autumn said. "We all played a role in it."

"Did we?" Vivian snapped. "I mean, let's not rewrite history."

"If that's the case, then the truth is Vivian, you're the reason Bella didn't make it off the ground because of your light skin privilege," Nicole said.

"Here we go!" Vivian said. "You've been waiting for a long time to say that haven't you?" "Am I lying?" Nicole asked. "You and Karina thought you would be the next Beyonce and guess what, you were not. Not even close. Autumn should've been the lead singer, and I hate that I allowed you and the worst manager in the world get in my head the way you all did."

Vivian folded her arms across her chest. "Are you forgetting that your ass stalked me in the café and asked me to join your unnamed group? This is bullshit, I knew this was a bad fucking idea because this bitch isn't accepting any responsibility for what happened." Autumn dropped her head. "Stop it! This isn't why we're here at all. Nicole, I wanted us to come together and remember what's important. Not the music business, but our friendship, our sisterhood. The time for placing blame is over. But if that's all we're going to do, then fuck it. I'm out."

James reached out for his wife and led her out the door. "Autumn," he asked once they were in the hallway. "Are you all right?"

She closed her eyes as tears fell. "Nope, because this isn't how I thought this was going to turn out and worst of all." She opened her eyes and smiled through the tears. "You were right."

"I'm not glad that I was, because I know this is important to you." James stroked her cheek. "What's your next move?"

Before she could reply, she heard a bang from Nicole's dressing room. "We're going to get the hell out of here," she said.

James and Autumn took off running, not sure what was happening behind them. Once they got outside, Autumn leaned against James's chest and sighed. "Let's go to campus and take a trip down memory lane."

"And check on our son?"

"No. We're going to leave Tyler alone, at least until after practice."

James nodded. "Sounds like a plan. Are you up to walking or should we go to the hotel and get you a pain pill?"

"That's not a bad idea and a nap would be nice," Autumn admitted.

James kissed her forehead. "Whatever you need," he said as they headed for the light rail stop. When they arrived at the hotel, Autumn was in more pain than she was willing to admit to her husband. As soon as they walked in the room, she plopped down on the bed. "What do you need?" James asked. "And if you say nothing I'm calling 9-1-1."

She glanced at him. "Why are you so dramatic? Just give me some water and two of my pills. And don't read the bottle, just give me what I asked for."

"Autumn, tell me the truth. How bad are you hurting?"

She closed her eyes and thought about how she should answer James. Should she tell him that everything hurt? That breathing felt as if she was sucking glass into her lungs and blowing out dust. "Babe," she said. "Call Tyler and tell him to come over here. I-I'm not sure. . ."

James rushed to her side as she closed her eyes. Seconds passed before he realized that he was losing her. He called 9-1-1. Autumn looked at her husband and tried to lift her hand to touch his handsome face. He was crying and she wanted to wipe his tears away. Just like he'd done for her that night when she'd accepted that her sisterhood with Nicole, Sonia and Vivian had ended. Maybe she should've listened to him then and her last moments wouldn't be filled with regret. Her friends weren't any closer than they were before they saw each other again. Autumn was floating, looking down at her body as spasms made it shake. She focused on James, who sobbed as he talked on the phone to emergency services. "Baby please wake up. Not like this, you can't go like this." He held her hand, but she didn't feel his touch and that was the one thing she'd miss, wherever she was headed, would be feeling James's soft skin. She listened as he talked to Tyler and told him to hurry over to the hotel. He didn't try to hide his emotions from his son as he talked to him. It broke Autumn's heart. Then she felt his finger running across the palm of her hand. She opened her eyes as air rushed through her lungs. She squeezed James's hand and looked at the tears falling from his eyes. "I love you," she whispered.

"Shh," he said as he stroked her cheek.

Autumn's heart rate returned to normal, her breathing became less labored, and her mind was clear. "James," she said, "I'm okay."

"Autumn, you stopped breathing, you're not okay," he said before there was a loud knock at the door. James rushed to open it and stepped aside to allow the EMS workers to come in. Tyler was behind them, his face contorted with fear, concern and a glimmer of hope. "Is she okay?" Tyler whispered as the workers rushed over to Autumn.

James shrugged and hugged his son. "If I hadn't been here I wouldn't believe what just happened," he said quietly.

"What happened, Dad?"

"Give me a second," James said as he crossed over to the paramedics who were checking Autumn's vital signs.

In a soft voice, she told them about her tumor, about passing out and her heart feeling as if it had stopped beating. But when they asked her if she wanted to go to the hospital, she shook her head no.

"Autumn," James exclaimed. "You need to let a doctor look at you."

"No," she said, her voice growing stronger. "James, nothing is going to change and I'm not spending homecoming in the hospital."

"You can't be serious right now," he snapped.

One of the paramedics touched his shoulder. "Sir, her vitals are strong, and we can't take her if she doesn't want to go," she said. "But if we have to come back, we will take her to the hospital. This is wild from what was described on the call."

"Maybe today just isn't my time to go," Autumn said as she attempted to sit up in the bed. "Ma!" Tyler called out as he crossed over to her. "I told you that you were doing the most, now look at you." He sat on the other side of her and held her hand. "Stop being hardheaded and go to the hospital."

"Stop acting like you know what's best for me," she quipped. Other than feeling a little lightheaded when she sat up, Autumn felt . . .good. She hadn't had felt like this in a while, but she knew this was temporary. Still, she wanted to try one last time to see if her friends would come together and focus on what was important. Love. She looked from Tyler to James as the paramedics began to pack up and leave the room. They looked back at her, James glaring and Tyler smirking.

"What?" she said.

"It's time for you to give up the ghost, babe," James said. "And I say this with all the disrespect but fuck your friends. You're chasing a feeling that you guys had over twenty years ago and sacrificing yourself and for what? They were still fighting."

"What happened?" Tyler asked. James rolled his eyes.

"Old bi. . ."

"James!"

He cleared his throat. "Old beef that hasn't been grilled and eaten. You know your mama could've been bigger than Beyonce."

Tyler narrowed his eyes. "Why don't y'all ever talk about the whole group that didn't work out? I mean, sounds like some Temptations, Five Heartbeats sh.. ."

"Boy," Autumn said. "Watch your damn mouth."

"Really, Mom?" he said then kissed her on the cheek.

"Do you want to hear the truth or listen to your father ruin the story?" Autumn asked.

James rolled his eyes. "Your mother is going to pretend that this is some story of sisterhood, and it isn't. Because, if I love someone I wouldn't let all this time pass before I reach out to say something," he said as he rose to his feet. "And let's be honest, Nicole is the real villain and selfish one here."

Autumn tilted her head to the side. "James, what are you talking about?"

Before he could reply, the door flung open and Sonia, Vivian and Nicole walked in, looking as if they'd ran there from the Belk Theatre. Nicole didn't say a word as she stalked over to Autumn. "My God," she whispered. "I'm so sorry."

Autumn looked up at her other two friends as Nicole wrapped her in a bear hug. "Who told?"

Sonia sucked her teeth. "It was me because these two are ridiculous as ever. If I stepped over the line, I'm not sorry."

James shook his head as he watched Nicole hugging Autumn. Clearing his throat, he turned to Tyler. "My boy, step out to the lobby for a minute, okay?"

He looked around the room and pursed his lips as if he was about to say something until Autumn nodded at him. "I'll text you, but don't leave."

Tyler pointed toward the door. "Remember I'm downstairs and if I haven't heard from y'all in an hour, I'm calling the police."

"Oh my, he is his daddy's son," Vivian said. The room erupted in laughter as Tyler walked out. James stared at the four women as if he was trying to gather his thoughts. But Autumn had a huge feeling as to what he was thinking.

Autumn looked at the two pink lines on the home pregnancy test. This couldn't be right. But the last three gave her the same positive result. Closing her eyes, she walked the length of the blue rug in her room that stretched from the door to the window. They had always been careful. She mostly always took her birth control pills. Except she had a cold, and those antibiotics had likely interfered with her birth control. What was she going to do with a baby? "Autumn? Are you in there?" Nicole called out as she knocked on the door. Hearing her voice was rare these days. Nicole hadn't said two words to anyone associated with Bella since their failure to launch. That had been over six months ago.

Autumn opened the door. "Well, hello stranger."

Nicole smiled. "Don't start. You know I needed time to cool off."

"Was six months enough time?"

She nodded and dropped down on Autumn's bed. "Excuse you?" Autumn said. "I don't know where your funky butt has been. I have to sleep there, you know."

"But not alone from what they're saying on the yard. You and J.R. are really serious. I'm glad I was wrong about him."

"That makes both of us. I love him," Autumn admitted.

"Whoa. That's heavy. Things must be going very well. And don't get me wrong, I'm all for it, but I have a proposition for you."

Autumn arched her right eyebrow. "How much jail time are we looking at?"

"Funny. I've been thinking about our music and Autumn, you know you have the talent to be a solo artist. You can sing and dance. You're gorgeous and we can grow together in this industry."

"Nicole, I don't know if being a star is still my dream."

"Autumn, I don't mean to beat a dead Vivian, I mean horse, but you should've always been the lead singer. Your voice is better than hers and you're a better performer than she ever was."

"And I told you from the beginning that I didn't want to be out front. Why don't you focus on your songwriting, because one thing I've learned in the music business major, the performers don't make the most money."

"Unless you're working with the right team and honestly, I don't want anyone singing my songs but you right now," Nicole said with a smile. "I wrote a ballad that is made for your voice."

Autumn sighed when she saw the door was cracked open. Before Nicole had shown up, she was waiting for James so that she could tell him that she was possibly pregnant. She hoped that he wasn't going to flake out on her and tell her to go to hell.

Or try to force her to. . .She couldn't even think about having an abortion. Granted, she always believed every woman should have the right to make the best decision for herself, but in her heart, that was a decision she'd never make. "Nicole, I need a secure future," Autumn said. "It's not just about me anymore."

"Is this about J.R.? Girl, you can't dim your light for a man. You're better than that. After college, y'all probably won't see each other again anyway."

"James and I are going to be in each other's life forever," Autumn said as she turned her back to the door, never noticing that James was standing there.

"Why? Because he said so?" Nicole laughed. "They all make promises that they don't plan to keep. You're too talented to let that boy's sweet words keep you from . . ."

"Nicole, I'm pregnant."

She gasped as she shook her head. "Does he know? You don't have to have a baby if he doesn't know. You can just go to the clinic on Wendover and.. ."

"Is that what you want to do, Autumn," James snapped as he burst through the door. "You just want to make a life changing decision without even talking to me about it?"

Autumn looked from James to Nicole. "This isn't how. . .James, I would never do that to you."

He turned to Nicole. "What kind of fucking friend are you?"

"What kind of man are you to knock her up and destroy her future? You have the option to walk away anytime you feel like it and Autumn is stuck with a baby!"

"Hey!" Autumn exclaimed. "How about both of you shutting the fuck up! This is my life; my choice and I don't need approval from either of you."

"Whatever," Nicole said as she hopped to her feet. "Go ahead and throw away your life over this guy. Autumn, use your head."

"Are you just mad because you can never keep a man?" James retorted.

"James," Autumn yelled. "You need to stop."

"I need to stop? I come over here to see you and your best friend is telling you to kill our baby. For what? Another failed chance at a dream that you said yourself you don't want anymore. What's wrong, Nicole? Can't make it on your own because you sound like a drowning cat when you sing?"

"Fuck you," Nicole said then stormed out of the room.

Autumn turned an angry stare on James. "You're out of line."

"Am I? Why would you tell her you're pregnant before telling me?"

"Pump your breaks," she said. "I told her because she's my friend and I was going to tell you when you got here. This is why I wanted to see you."

"Okay, so when are we getting married?"

Autumn hitched her right eyebrow. "What? Don't just say that because Nicole. . ."

"I don't give a damn about anything Nicole said. Autumn, I love you and have loved you since the moment I saw you. This engagement is just coming a little early."

"What do you mean a little early?"

"This isn't how I planned to propose to you. I wanted to be down on one knee when you walked across the stage with your degree in your hand. The ring is in my room, so you know this isn't about the baby."

Autumn sighed and tried not to cry. She failed. James drew her into his arms and held her close. "Don't cry, unless you're happy and about to say yes," he said as he lifted her chin. "Autumn, do you want to be my wife? Can you spend forever with me?"

"James, J.R., my man, I would love to spend forever with you," she breathed. "But are you sure you want to spend forever with me?"

"Yes, I do," he said then brushed his lips across hers.

Autumn pressed her hand against his chest. "Then where is my ring, man?"

"Come on, let's get it and spend the night at the Hilton."

"That sounds so good," she said. "But I have to finish this paper first."

"Bring it with you," he said. "I'm here for you doing your work first and me second."

She shook her head and rolled her eyes. "This is really going to be the rest of my life?" James smacked her bottom. "Yep, every day that ends in Y."

Nicole locked eyes with James and sighed. "You know, I have a lot of atonement to do with this group and I accept that. Vivian and I have made peace, and I thought that was the end of it, but I was a bitch to you and Autumn."

"Yes, you were and maybe you still are," James said matter-of-factly.

Nicole nodded. "I deserve that."

He was about to say something else until Autumn squeezed his hand.

Nicole sighed. "I wanted to be famous, and I wanted it by any means necessary and I thought that meant the right singer singing my songs. It was a good thing that Autumn made another choice because as it turns out, those early songs were trash."

Sonia tilted her head. "Damn, you have evolved because . . ."

"Let her finish," Autumn interrupted.

"Sorry," Sonia said.

Nicole continued, "Yes, I needed to study my craft more and I did. It took me two years after graduation to get someone to take me seriously. I moved to LA and said if doesn't happen, then I'll go to New York and teach or something. But things started happening quickly and I turned up the petty, thinking that I didn't need any of y'all, even though there were moments when I wanted to call. When I wanted to know how you guys were doing and if we could make up, but I just kept saying, tomorrow. Tomorrow turned into ten years and finally today." Tears zig-zagged down her cheeks. "I'm sorry that I tried to make you live my dream when . . ."

"Nicole, it's too late for regrets, I just want us to remember what's important. We used to love each other," Autumn said as she looked at everyone in the room. "We were important to each other."

"And we still should be," Sonia said. "We all made mistakes about how we handled the implosion of Bella. But Autumn is right, we were more than just members of a group."

"We were sisters," Vivian said quietly.

"And I, all of us, lost sight of that," Nicole said. "I knew Vivian was going to make it. And I wanted Autumn to be her rival, the competition I knew she couldn't stand up to."

Autumn tilted her head to the side. "Are you serious? So, had I been crazy enough to listen to you back then, I would've ruined my life for a battle you'd made up in your head?" Autumn laughed until she coughed. She held up her hand when everyone went silent and peered at her. "I'm fine."

James sat down beside his wife and looked at her friends. Autumn wondered what he was thinking, but she knew if she asked him, there would be no telling what would come out of his mouth. She grabbed his hand and squeezed tight.

"I've been to therapy," Nicole said. "Most of my issues had more to do with me than anyone in this room. And even though I wasn't an alcoholic; I need to make amends with all of you." "My cash app is. . ." Sonia quipped. A smattering of laughter turned into a big guffaw.

James kissed Autumn's cheek and for a few minutes, it felt like 1997 all over again. Back when they were all friends with big dreams. Vivian and Nicole looked at each other, their eyes filled with sincerity. "I've missed this," they said in concert.

Autumn nudged James as she watched her friends embrace.

"This is all I wanted," she said. "Now that you have it, you're going to have to stick around to make sure it lasts," he whispered.

"Stop being selfish, my love," she said then planted a kiss on his cheek.

"Autumn, don't leave me with these crazy broads right now."

"Not until after halftime, babe," she said then kissed him slow and deep.

"Oh, my goodness," Sonia said once she spotted Autumn and James's lip lock. "I guess we need to give them the room."

"Yes," James said. "You've made up, go have some brunch and let's make an entrance at halftime, if my son is okay with that."

"That's a great idea and I can announce the Autumn Brown-Robinson music scholarship," Nicole said. "But we can talk later."

The women left and James held Autumn against his chest. She drifted off to sleep and he sent a text to Tyler. *Hey son, you can come back up. We should be here for your mom right now.*

Epilogue

December 31 –

A cold wind blew across James and Tyler as they stood at Autumn's headstone. It had been less than two months since they lost her, even though she looked as if she was ready to take on the world at homecoming. Tyler had never seen his mother move like that before. But when she and his aunties performed with the Alumni Band after halftime, he had been impressed as hell. Sure, everyone talked about the mighty J.R., but he was seeing that his talent came from both of his parents. He had been shocked to see the truce his mom brokered lasted longer than the homecoming game. Auntie Sonia sent him care packages from all over the world. Ms. Vivian would show up on campus to check on him and Nicole freaking Clarke wanted him to be her intern and do some arrangements for a new artist she'd discovered.

He'd taken his dad's advice seriously. Don't allow anyone to make you feel as if you have to fit in a box someone else had built for you. "Autumn never did that and that's the biggest lesson you can carry with you from your mother. She's the best part of all of us."

Glancing over at his father, Tyler wished he could open the door of memories that he seemed to want to keep locked away. *One day,* he surmised.

James caught Tyler staring at him and noticed how much his son had his mother's eyes and smirk. He worried about him. Tyler and Autumn were close, like best friends with parental boundaries. How was his son going to move forward without his mom? "What's wrong, T?" James asked as Tyler dropped his head.

"Nothing, I was just wondering how you are going to move forward without Ma reminding you to breathe and to remember there's more to life than music theory."

James chuckled. "And here I was thinking what my boy is going to do without his biggest fan?" He wrapped his arm around Tyler's shoulders. "We were blessed and fortunate that Autumn chose to love us and mean it."

Tyler nodded as tears welled up in his eyes. "When does it get easier?"

James sucked in his bottom lip. "I wish I knew."

"You think she's watching over us and guiding us to do the right thing?"

James heard cars coming up the gravel road leading to Autumn's grave. "I think she's watching us, but she has guiding to do with those other women."

"One day, someone is going to tell me about Bella and why it was so important to Mom," Tyler said as he watched Nicole, Vivian and Sonia hop out of their Mustangs.

"Just remember," James said as the women walked over to them, "In all the stories you're going to hear, there is just one truth. Your mama loved everyone with her whole heart, even when they didn't deserve it."

The End

About the Author:

Award winning author CHERIS HODGES was bitten by the writing bug at an early age and always knew she wanted to be a writer. She wrote her first romance novel, *Revelations,* after having a vivid dream about the characters. She hopped out of bed at 2 A.M. and started writing. A graduate of Johnson C. Smith University and a winner of the North Carolina Press Association's community journalism award, Cheris loves hearing from her readers. Follow Cheris on Twitter/X @cherisfhodges, friend her on Facebook at Cheris Hodges, or email her at cheris87@bellsouth.net.

Visit her website at www.thecherishodges.com

Don't miss out!

Visit the website below and you can sign up to receive emails whenever Cheris Hodges publishes a new book. There's no charge and no obligation.

https://books2read.com/r/B-A-HQERB-IAOQD

BOOKS 2 READ

Connecting independent readers to independent writers.

www.ingramcontent.com/pod-product-compliance
Lightning Source LLC
Chambersburg PA
CBHW021156160726
47994CB00001B/241